I know this *** ***, but I got together *** **** Todd I was going to the library at Sweet Valley University to research my history term paper. Instead, I met Sam at the beach and then we drove up the coast to Castillo San Angelo, this beautiful old Spanish mansion with a restaurant and public gardens. It's the most romantic spot, and we had the gardens all to ourselves. Sam said that he felt like Adam and Eve in the Garden of Eden and that inspired us to duck behind some ornamental shrubs and kiss. We shared a lot of kisses—for the rest of my life, the smell of honeysuckle will remind me of kissing Sam.

It was a delicious afternoon, but when I got home, I had a total guilt attack. I listened to the messages on the answering machine, and of course there was one from Todd, asking how my research went. I couldn't bear to call him back.

Secretly seeing Sam makes me feel so good and so bad at the same time. One minute I vow never to see him again, and the next I'm counting the hours until I can run off to the beach . . . our beach. What am I going to do?

ELIZABETH'S SECRET DIARY

VOLUME III

Written by
Kate William

Created by
FRANCINE PASCAL

BANTAM BOOKS
NEW YORK · TORONTO · LONDON · SYDNEY · AUCKLAND

SWEET VALLEY HIGH: ELIZABETH'S
SECRET DIARY – Volume III
A BANTAM BOOK : 0 553 50669 2

Originally published in USA by Bantam Books

First publication in Great Britain

PRINTING HISTORY
Bantam edition published 1998

The trademarks "Sweet Valley" and "Sweet Valley High"
are owned by Francine Pascal and are used under license by
Bantam Books and Transworld Publishers Ltd.

Conceived by Francine Pascal

Produced by Daniel Weiss Associates, Inc,
33 West 17th Street, New York, NY 10011

Bantam Books are published by Transworld Publishers Ltd,
61–63 Uxbridge Road, Ealing, London W5 5SA,
in Australia by Transworld Publishers (Australia) Pty Ltd,
15–25 Helles Avenue, Moorebank, NSW 2170,
and in New Zealand by Transworld Publishers (NZ) Ltd,
3 William Pickering Drive, Albany, Auckland.

Made and printed in Great Britain by
Cox & Wyman Ltd, Reading, Berkshire.

To L. D. Ribner

Prologue

It was a typical Friday night in the Wakefield household. In other words, the place was a madhouse. My parents had both whirled in from their respective offices looking as though they'd been caught up in the eye of a tornado, which is probably how they normally feel after a long, busy week. My dad, Ned Wakefield, is a lawyer, and my mother, Alice, runs her own interior design firm. They're both incredibly successful, and therefore incredibly overworked. They're great parents, though, and on weeknights they always insist that we eat dinner together. You know, family bonding, "How was school today?" and all that stuff. It probably sounds corny, but it really does make a difference. We stay in touch with each other that way.

But on Fridays we don't even try to have family time. As my dad puts it, "Who wants to stick around

1

when two teenage girls are getting ready for dates?" He's absolutely right. It's not a pretty sight when my identical twin sister, Jessica, and I duke it out for time in the bathroom. Hair dryers and stereos blast, and we yell to each other for advice about outfits, hair, makeup, what have you. The phone rings a couple of dozen times as our friends and boyfriends check in. Who can blame Mom and Dad for escaping to a restaurant or the theater?

So, as I said, it was a typical Friday night. That is, I'd finally gotten a turn in the bathroom, which Jessica had steamed up by taking a yearlong hot shower. Every time I wiped the mirror with a hand towel, it fogged up again. Jess had created a rain forest.

I was carefully dabbing mascara on my eyelashes when the door burst open and Jessica bounced in. The mascara brush hit the tip of my nose. "Do you mind?" I asked my sister, grabbing a damp washcloth and rubbing my nose. "A little privacy might be nice."

She jostled against me, trying to get a look at herself in the mirror. "I think I should have bathroom priority," she declared, "since I have a date tonight."

"And I don't?" I rejoined. I've been dating Todd Wilkins for ages, and we always go out on Friday nights, as Jessica well knows.

"You don't," Jessica agreed.

"I don't what?" I said, confused.

"You don't have a date."

"What are you *talking* about?"

2

Jessica gave me a wide-eyed, innocent look. "Didn't I tell you, Liz?"

I folded my arms across my chest with an exasperated groan. "Tell me *what?*"

Jessica reached for my mascara and started doing her eyes. "Todd called."

"When?"

"Oh, a couple hours ago," she replied vaguely.

"And?"

"And he canceled."

I blinked at her. "Just like that? What did he say?"

She shrugged. "Nothing. He just said he couldn't make it. Sorry."

I stared as Jessica continued to put on her makeup. Looking at my sister is sort of like looking in a slightly fogged-up mirror. We're both sixteen, five foot six inches tall, with long blond hair, blue-green eyes, and dimples in our left cheeks. But we're so different personality-wise that sometimes I can't believe we're even related. "No explanation?" I pressed. It wasn't like Todd not to leave a more detailed message, but then again, it *was* like Jessica not to get the story straight.

"I meant to tell you earlier," she said nonchalantly. "It just slipped my mind. Seth called right afterward, and needless to say that caused me to totally forget about Todd."

"Well, thanks a lot," I snapped. I don't know why I was furious all of a sudden. It really wasn't *that* big a deal. But I guess I was disappointed that I

3

wouldn't be seeing Todd after all, and annoyed that I'd been going to so much trouble getting ready to go out when it now looked like I'd be sitting home.

"Hey, cheer up." Jessica flashed me a devilish smile. "Now that you're free for the evening, you can come with me and Seth to Lila's party." She skipped a beat before adding, "Lila's looking for someone to check coats at the door."

"What an offer," I said sarcastically. Lila Fowler is the richest and most obnoxious girl at Sweet Valley High and, not coincidentally, Jessica's best friend. "Like she doesn't have enough servants already?"

"How about passing the hors d'oeuvre tray, then? I bet Li wouldn't even make you wear a uniform."

I turned on my heel and flounced out of the bathroom. "Have a good time," I called back over my shoulder. "And by the way, don't even *think* about asking to borrow my new stack-heeled sandals."

"But they'd go perfectly with my—"

I slammed the connecting door, cutting her off.

Even though we have different interests and friends, Jessica and I usually get along great. Our styles compliment each other—we joke and tease each other a lot, but it's mostly good-natured and fun. She can make me laugh more than anyone else. But tonight for some reason I just wasn't in the mood to have it rubbed in my face that she was going to a formal party at Fowler Crest with Seth

4

Frey while I'd be channel surfing with a bowl of microwave popcorn.

I flopped onto my bed with a discontented sigh. From the other side of our bathroom that adjoins our bedrooms, I could hear Jessica blasting a song from the new Jamie Peters's CD. It's a great song, but it's definitely a getting-ready-for-a-party song, and so instead of it lifting my spirits, it only made me feel grumpier.

I think this is a good time to point out that I'm not usually so cranky! It's true that at Sweet Valley High I'm known as the "serious" Wakefield twin (Who wouldn't seem serious compared to Jessica?), but that doesn't mean I don't like to have fun. In general I have a really upbeat outlook on life. I love my family, I have wonderful friends like Enid Rollins, Olivia Davidson, and Maria Slater, and I know I'm really lucky to grow up in a beautiful town like Sweet Valley and to go to a terrific school like S.V.H. It would be a lie to say I like every single one of my classes, but most of them are good, especially English with Mr. Collins, who's also the adviser for the school newspaper. I love writing my column for *The Oracle*—in fact, I love writing, period. I'm pretty dedicated about keeping my journal up to date, and I also write poetry and short stories. I don't necessarily expect to be another Emily Dickinson or Virgina Woolf, but I do think I have some talent. If hard work counts for anything, I bet someday I'll be able to make a living as a writer. Wouldn't that be totally cool?

I also plan to spend the rest of my life with my boyfriend Todd Wilkins . . . at least I did until he canceled our date this evening! Todd's another reason why I wouldn't trade places with anyone. I'm not bragging or anything, but there's no question that my boyfriend is the best-looking guy in the junior class at Sweet Valley High. He's also the nicest, smartest, sweetest, the best athlete . . . need I go on? He's tall and muscular with gorgeous wavy brown hair and these delicious dark eyes, and half the girls at school have a crush on him. But he's mine and he always will be.

Still slumped on my bed, I scowled at the framed picture of Todd on my night table. Then my mood brightened somewhat and I sat up. I didn't even know why Todd had canceled our date. He probably had a perfectly good reason, and as soon as I knew what it was, I could stop moping.

I reached for the telephone to call him. Just then, the doorbell rang. "Jess!" I shouted. "Must be Seth!"

"I'm not ready!" she yelled back. "Will you let him in?"

The doorbell jingled again. Grumbling, I hopped off the bed and stomped down the hall. On my way downstairs, I smoothed back my tousled hair and tucked in my rumpled T-shirt. I hadn't met Seth yet—all I knew about him was that he was the star of Big Mesa High's football team. According to Jessica, he was drop-dead gorgeous. But since I'd only seen him in a uniform, pads, and a helmet, I hadn't had a chance to judge for myself. I had to admit, I was curious.

I found out right away that Jessica hadn't been exaggerating. When I opened the door and looked up into Seth's ruggedly handsome face, an unexpected jolt of attraction shivered down my spine. My knees even wobbled a bit.

Seth's eyes were deep brown. They locked on mine for one long, supercharged second. "Jess?" he said, sounding a little puzzled. Then he chuckled. "Oh, that's right. I forgot. You must be the twin."

The twin. "Yeah," I mumbled, "that's me. Elizabeth. Nice to meet you."

I put my hand out to shake his. Seth was still smiling at me. Then, as he was about to take my hand, his eyes slid past me, focusing over my shoulder.

I turned around. Jessica was slinking down the staircase at a provocatively slow pace. She looked stunning in a simple, ivory silk dress that showed a lot of tanned, smooth skin. Her shimmering blond hair swirled loose around her shoulders. I didn't blame her for making a grand entrance—I'd have done exactly the same thing.

And she got the response she was hoping for. Seth had forgotten that I existed. He stepped around me as if I were an inanimate object—a coat rack or an umbrella stand. "Wow," he murmured appreciatively. "Jessica, you look amazing."

She tossed her hair and rewarded him with her most dazzling smile. "You're not too shabby yourself," she purred.

Seth was holding one long-stemmed red rose. He gave the rose to Jessica, along with a lingering kiss on her cheek, as they headed outside together. Neither of them said good-bye or even so much as glanced in my direction.

The door clicked shut behind them, leaving me alone in the hall feeling like I was standing under my own personal rain cloud. *I'm not jealous,* I told myself as I wandered into the kitchen to search the cupboards for a snack. *I don't even know Seth Frey, and I probably don't want to. If he's Jessica's type, then he can't be my type!* But even as I thought that, I had to admit to myself that it wasn't precisely true. There *had* been times in the past when Jessica and I had fallen for the same boy. In fact, there was one particular time . . .

I shook my head, banishing the lingering image of Seth's sexy brown eyes. Another pair of brown eyes took their place in my mind. Todd's.

I reached for the wall phone as I hitched myself onto the counter. I punched in Todd's number and waited. The phone rang four times and I was about to hang up—I didn't feel like talking to an answering machine—when someone picked up. "Hello?" my boyfriend said, sounding out of breath.

"It's me," I chirped. For some reason, it made me ridiculously happy to hear his voice. "Jessica just got around to telling me that you called before. So, you can't make it tonight?"

"I'm on my way out the door," Todd said briskly. "Can I call you back later?"

"Is something wrong?" I asked, surprised by his tone.

"No. I just don't have time to talk."

"How come? Where are you—"

"Look, Liz, I'm kind of in a hurry."

"Maybe you are," I said, miffed, "but we were supposed to have a date tonight. Don't you think I at least deserve to know what's—"

He cut me off again. "I've really got to go. I'll call you later."

"Don't bother!" I snapped. But I was talking to myself. Todd had already hung up.

I replaced the receiver, feeling dazed. The conversation with Todd had been brief, but it had shaken me right to the core. Tears stung my eyes. Todd was usually so considerate, and we both always tried to be open with each other. Why had he been so evasive and abrupt? "He didn't want to tell me where he was going," I said out loud, sniffling. "And he didn't even explain why he canceled our date. Maybe there *isn't* an explanation." An icy cold feeling started

9

in the pit of my stomach and slowly spread throughout my body. Maybe Todd just didn't want to see me. Maybe that was all there was to it.

I walked slowly out of the kitchen and back upstairs to my bedroom. The house was depressingly empty and quiet. All of a sudden, I wished that my older brother, Steven, was home from college for the weekend, or that my mom and dad hadn't gone out. I'd even have settled for picking a fight with Jessica. Anything but being alone with this horrible new fear.

Todd's tired of me, I thought, sitting down on my bed and wrapping my arms around my tucked-up knees. I wracked my brain, thinking over the events of the past week or so. Had there been any other signs? Every day before school we'd met at my locker the way we always did. We'd hung out together at lunch and during study hall. We'd had a few study dates and we'd gone to the Dairi Burger and Guido's Pizza Palace—the usual spots—with our friends. We'd taken a bike ride in the hills and seen an old Bette Davis movie at the Plaza Theatre, and one night we'd gone parking up at Miller's Point. On the surface, it had been a pretty ordinary week.

But maybe that's the problem, I thought. Suddenly things appeared in a different—and very disturbing—light. Our relationship was in a rut. For example, take that night at Miller's Point, which was the big parking spot in Sweet Valley. Kissing had been fun, but we weren't exactly carried away by passion. I'd even caught Todd checking his watch at one point. As for our study dates, we'd actually *studied* during them!

My head was spinning—a whirlpool of misery threatened to pull me under. "Whoa, get a grip, Wakefield," I advised myself. One broken date, one crummy phone call—they didn't necessarily mean the end for me and Todd. Talk about overreacting!

But I couldn't shake the feeling that something was really wrong. It didn't help to tell myself to be reasonable. Emotions have a life of their own, and mine were in a tumult.

I stood up and walked across my room to look out the window. Outside, the last rays of the setting sun streaked the purple-blue sky with pink and amber. A breeze stirred the fronds of the palm trees in the yard. Only the lonely sound of a distant dog barking broke the still of the evening.

Suddenly I felt an almost overwhelming impulse to reach for my diary. I've been keeping a journal for years and I've filled almost a dozen cloth-covered volumes with reflections on my day-to-day life. Everything's in there: triumphs, disappointments, hopes, dreams, fears, secrets. I understand things better when I write about them—I always turn to my journal when I'm sad or lonely or confused.

11

This time, though, I didn't intend to write in my diary. I wanted to *read* it. Countless entries in the past were about my relationship with Todd. We'd had a lot of ups and downs in our time together. Maybe my diary would provide a clue for what was happening to us now. Maybe it would help me figure out what to do next. If nothing else, reading it could make me feel less alone.

I took a volume from my bookshelf, unlocking it with a tiny key I kept hidden in my sock drawer. Then I curled up on my bed, the comforter wrapped around my legs, and started to skim the pages through eyes clouded with tears.

Part 1

Monday, 7:00 P.M.

Dear Diary,

I'm in the strangest mood tonight. I can't focus on homework even though I should study for the test in Ms. Dalton's French class tomorrow. I don't feel like talking on the phone or watching TV or listening to music. There must be something I want to do or someplace I want to go, but what? Where? I'm like a bottle of something fizzy that's gotten all shaken up. If I had a cork, I'd pop!

I guess I'm just restless because my life seems totally stale and boring lately. Isn't that a terrible thing to say when you're only sixteen? Maybe it's only in comparison to Jessica's. As usual, her life is full of

13

changes and excitement. She's auditioning to be on Eric Parker's talk show, along with every other student at Sweet Valley High. Have I told you about that yet? There's such a buzz about it at school. Eric Parker is a TV celebrity who graduated from S.V.H. a while back and now has his own nationally syndicated weekly talk show. He's doing a special edition called "Growing Up in America," and he decided to tape it right here, in his hometown. He's holding auditions to find a typical teenager to interview on the program. Guess who thinks she fits the bill? Jessica, naturally. And I have to say, she'd be a million times better than Lila Fowler. Can you believe Lila actually considers herself an average American high school student? As if everybody lives in a mansion staffed by a half dozen servants with a walk-in closet bigger than most people's bedrooms and has their very own sports car. Get real!

But Lila's even more vain and starstruck than Jessica (if that's possible!), so I guess it's no surprise she feels entitled to the TV spot. A lot of other kids are trying out too, including Winston and Olivia, but Jessica and Lila are definitely the most intense about the whole thing.

14

They're going all-out trying to come up with impressive stuff for their applications. Jessica even wrote a column for The Oracle *so she could say that she was on the staff of the school newspaper! That was my brilliant idea, actually. Penny was looking for a new feature writer, so I got the two of them together. In no time flat, Jessica rattled off a piece titled "The Worst Dates of My Life." I thought she'd ask me for help, but she did a fantastic job all by herself. The article is hilarious. Penny liked it too. Scratch that: Penny loved it. As in, doubled over with laughter, praising Jessica to the skies, etc., etc. And you know Penny—she's not the type to go overboard. In fact, I can't remember the last time she responded to an article of* mine *with that kind of enthusiasm. . . .*

"Don't be nervous," I said to Jessica as we walked together to *The Oracle* office during lunch period. "Your story's a riot. Penny will probably only ask you to make a few changes."

Jessica clutched the computer printout of "The Worst Dates of My Life" to her chest. "I'm not so sure, Liz," she replied, chewing her lip. "Maybe she'll think it's completely stupid. Why didn't I write about something serious and boring like *you* usually do? You know, *real* journalism?"

15

"Gee, thanks," I said dryly. "For your information, real journalism doesn't have to be serious, and it should *never* be boring. Secondly, when it comes to writing, you should always follow your instincts. You were more comfortable writing in a humorous style. So just stand up for your work."

"Stand up for my work." Jessica straightened her shoulders. "OK. I can do that."

I pushed open the newspaper office door and ushered Jessica inside. Penny Ayala, the editor in chief and one of my closest friends, was waiting for us. "Jessica!" she greeted my sister briskly. "Just in time. We're typesetting the paper this afternoon. What have you got for me?"

Jessica stretched out one arm, the article pinched between trembling fingers. Penny took it and began to read, her lips set in a straight line. Jessica and I watched her, both holding our breath. A few tense seconds passed. Then the corners of Penny's mouth twitched. A few seconds later, she was smiling. By the last paragraph, Penny was laughing out loud.

"Oh, Jessica," she gasped when she was done reading. She leaned back against a desk and wiped tears of amusement from her hazel eyes. "The part about the computer dating service. It's a scream!"

"You liked that?" Jessica asked, practically melting with relief.

"I liked it all," Penny told her. "It's a strong

16

piece from start to finish. You're a natural, Jessica. Isn't she, Liz?"

I was a little surprised to hear businesslike Penny raving this way. I nodded slowly. "Yeah, I guess she is."

"Here's an idea," exclaimed Penny. "We could print Jessica's article right next to Liz's column, 'Eyes and Ears.' The Wakefield sisters side by side. How does that strike you, Liz?"

Jessica's eyes lit up with pleasure. I forced a smile. "Um, great," I lied.

"It's all set then," Penny declared. "Thanks for the good work, Jessica. If you come up with any other ideas for humor features, or anything for that matter, let me know."

"Will do," Jessica promised.

Jessica was about to waltz out the door. I grabbed her arm, holding her back. "Wait a minute," I said. "Penny, you forgot to explain about revisions. Jess doesn't realize that her work isn't done yet."

"But it is," Penny stated. "Her article is perfect."

"*Perfect?*" I echoed, unable to mask my disbelief.

"How do you like that?" said Jessica with a self-satisfied grin.

"But don't you think there are a few rough spots . . ." I clutched at straws. "Like the names. Kevin Klutz and Reginald Rich and the rest. Don't you think it's obvious who she's really talking about?"

Penny laughed. "Yep. It'll probably take the student body five seconds flat to figure out that Bad Date Number One is Winston Egbert and Bad Date Number Two is Bruce Patman. That's part of the fun."

"You don't think she needs to tone it down?" I pressed.

Penny shook her head firmly. "It's perfect," she repeated. "I wouldn't change a single word."

An image flashed into my head: the first draft of my most recent feature article for *The Oracle*, with Penny's editorial comments scrawled in red pen all over the margins. She'd wanted me to change about a million things. "Well, lucky you," I told Jessica.

"Luck had nothing to do with it," Jessica said breezily as she sailed to the door. "Guess I'm just plain talented. See you!"

Penny was still chuckling as the door clicked shut behind Jessica. "Your sister is something else," she said as she turned back to her computer.

"Tell me about it," I mumbled. I started toward the door, then paused, clearing my throat. "So, Penny. Did you get a chance to look over 'Eyes and Ears' this week?"

"Sure. It's fine," Penny assured me, her fingers flying over the keyboard.

"I was experimenting with a little humor myself," I remarked casually. "The stuff about renovating

18

the boys' and girls' locker rooms. Did you pick up on that?"

"Yeah, it was funny." Penny swiveled around in her chair to face me, her eyes crinkling with amusement. "I keep thinking about the part where Jessica describes Bruce—I mean *Reginald*—kissing like a dead jellyfish." Penny giggled. "Boy, is Patman going to be steamed!"

I drummed my fingers on a nearby tabletop. "I imagine so. But back to my column . . ."

"It's good, as usual," Penny said somewhat absentmindedly. "I never worry about 'Eyes and Ears'—I know I can count on you to turn in something solid. Won't it be a kick, though, to put Jessica's piece right next to yours? I can't get over how sharp her writing is. Witty too. It will really jazz up the page."

I'd heard enough about Jessica's literary genius. "So long, Penny," I said. "Thanks again for letting Jessica write for the paper. It'll definitely boost her application for the talk-show spot."

"Hey, she's the one doing *me* a favor," Penny replied. "See ya."

Lunch wasn't over yet, so, out of habit, I headed toward the cafeteria. But I'd lost my appetite. The conversation with Penny had completely depressed me. According to Penny, Jessica's writing was strong, sharp, witty, and all-around perfect. Meanwhile, mine was "solid." Reliable Liz and her humdrum column, the old standby "Eyes and Ears." And I was the one who wanted to be a professional writer someday! *Who am I kidding?* I thought glumly. *Jessica writes ten times better than I do when she's not even trying!*

I heaved a sigh. Jessica was on target to become a television star *and* a hot new feature writer for *The Oracle*. What was left over for me?

I don't mean to sound like sour grapes, Diary. Jessica is genuinely talented and I'm proud of her. I hope Eric Parker picks her to be on his show. But if he does, she'll be insufferable—she's already convinced she's a superior being destined for greatness. Spare me!

Saturday, 6:00 P.M.

I'm going out to dinner with Todd in a few minutes, so this will be short. Jessica was chosen for the TV interview, with Lila as an alternate if Jess gets sick or something. I'm happy for her, but I'd be lying if I didn't admit I'm also a little jealous. It's probably not good for my mental health, but sometimes I can't help comparing myself to my twin. Jessica has so much confidence and charisma. She's always taking on new challenges, and sometimes she falls flat on her face, but usually she succeeds in high style. Look at "The Worst Dates of My Life," her very first attempt at journalism! Speaking of which, the article was a huge hit with absolutely everybody at school. Everybody but Bruce Patman, that is. He was absolutely livid, and people are teasing him like crazy. I'd feel sorry for him if he weren't a conceited jerk who's always assumed every girl on the planet is lusting after him. He may have a harder time getting a date now that the secret's out about his dead jellyfish kissing technique!

Anyhow, Jessica's definitely the Girl of the Moment at S.V.H. And I could use some passion and variety in my life, that's for sure. But maybe Todd can help me out in that department. . . .

At six-thirty the doorbell rang. I grabbed my purse and my new pink Shaker-knit sweater and ran downstairs. Todd stood on the front steps, his hands in the pockets of his khakis. "Hey there," he drawled, smiling down at me.

Todd looked adorable (as always!). He's tall—a lot taller than me—over six feet. He has broad shoulders, and he's completely toned and muscular from basketball practice. His hair is brown and a little bit curly—I love running my fingers through it. And there's always a twinkle

21

in his eyes, which are a dark coffee color. Yum!

His voice is pretty sexy too. Just two little words—"Hey there"—and my heart was beating faster. "Hey yourself," I replied, tilting my face up for a kiss.

He brushed his lips lightly against mine. We hugged for a moment, and then strolled to the driveway where he'd parked his black BMW, my arm around his waist and his around my shoulders.

We kissed again before buckling our seat belts. "What are you in the mood for?" Todd asked as he shifted into second on Calico Drive. "Pizza or burgers?"

I twisted in the bucket seat to face him. "Let's do something different tonight," I said impulsively.

Todd grinned. "You mean, go to Miller's Point *before* dinner instead of afterward?"

I punched him lightly in the arm. "No, I mean something *different*. Don't you get tired of the Dairi Burger?"

He cocked an eyebrow. "But that's where everyone will be."

"So let's go someplace else," I suggested. I thought hard, trying to conjure up a romantic, adventurous scenario. "I know," I exclaimed. "We could stop at Season's Gourmet Shop and pick up some bread and cheese and sparkling cider. Then we could drive up to Las Palmas Canyon and hike up that cliff path. You know, the one to the waterfall? Wouldn't that be a great place to watch the sunset?"

"Yeah, and a great place to break our legs trying to hike back down after dark," Todd pointed out.

"Don't be such a spoilsport," I chided. "You have a flashlight in the glove compartment, don't you?"

"Sure," said Todd, braking at a stop sign. "But actually, the flashlight's not the problem. The road to the canyon's closed temporarily because of a mudslide."

"Oh." I cupped my chin in my hand, considering other possibilities. "Well, how about trying that new Japanese restaurant in El Carro? It's supposed to be great."

"Do you really feel like driving twenty minutes each way?" Todd asked. His tone made it clear *he* didn't feel like it.

"I guess not," I agreed. "You're right. There are plenty of good restaurants right here in Sweet Valley. What do you say we go to Oggi?"

Oggi was an Italian restaurant on the outskirts of town that had tables in an outdoor courtyard and little white lights strung in the tree branches—really cozy and elegant and romantic.

Todd came up with another objection. "Oggi's kind of expensive. I mean, not that you're not worth it, Liz. But places like that are for special occasions. This is just an ordinary Saturday night."

I couldn't really argue with that. "Yeah," I agreed with a sigh.

"It *is* just an ordinary night, isn't it?" Todd reached over to squeeze my knee. "I'm not forgetting our anniversary or something?"

"No, it's just an ordinary night."

"The Dairi Burger's OK, then?" he asked.

"The Dairi Burger's OK," I told him, even though I was annoyed that Todd didn't want to go somewhere new.

"It'll be fun," Todd promised. "Ken and Terri are planning to show up, and Winston and Maria and some of the guys from the team will probably be there too."

"Great," I said with false enthusiasm.

Todd drove down Main Street humming happily to the song on the radio. Meanwhile, I stared out the car window, choking on my disappointment. As we pulled into the Dairi Burger parking lot, I felt like crying. So much for putting some passion and variety into my life! Todd just didn't have a clue. How could we be on such different wavelengths?

We walked into the restaurant holding hands, looking like Mr. and Ms. Sweet Valley High, as always. But my smile was mechanical rather than heartfelt. I kept thinking about Todd's words: "It's just an ordinary Saturday night." True—it was. But couldn't he see I was tired of ordinary?

A boring weekend all in all. Boring date with Todd last night (boring good-night kiss, even!), then a boring day today spent doing boring things like reading the boring Sunday paper and cleaning the boring swimming pool and then doing boring laps in the same boring swimming pool. I cooked a boring dinner for my boring family and then wrote up a boring biology lab report and conjugated twenty boring French verbs.

To cheer myself up, I reread Jessica's "Worst Dates" story, but it only made me feel more pathetic and misguided. Maybe it hasn't all been wine and roses, but she has tons of dating experience. Meanwhile, I've been with the same guy for ages. Todd and I might as well be married, and marriage equals (yes, you guessed it) BOREDOM! Stop the world, I want to get off!

Saturday, 10:00 A.M.
Dear Diary,

I just reread my last journal entry. What a crab! I can't believe that only last weekend I was complaining about my life being dull. *Right now it seems anything but boring. Guess who had her television debut last night? No, not Jessica. ME!*

Wait till you hear this—what a story! It all started with Lila and Bruce, possibly the two nastiest, most selfish and conniving people in the state of California. They were both royally ticked off at Jessica—Lila, because Jess had been rubbing it in her face that Lila was only the alternate while Jessica was going to be on TV, and Bruce because of the dead jellyfish thing. I guess I understand why Bruce was mad, but it still doesn't excuse what they did. He and Lila got together and conspired to sabotage Jessica's chance to be on Eric Parker's talk show. Lila knew that if she put Jessica out of commission, she'd get to be on the show instead. So she took Jessica shopping way up the coast to some outrageously overpriced boutique in Cold Springs. Meanwhile, Bruce phoned the boutique, pretending to be a local police officer passing on a description of a shoplifting suspect. A shoplifting suspect who looked exactly like Jessica!

Needless to say, when Jessica walked into the store, the clerks watched her like a

*hawk. Then, while Jessica was trying some-
thing on, Lila took off. When Jess came out
of the changing room and saw Lila driving
away, naturally she ran outside wearing
this expensive outfit she hadn't paid for
and, also naturally, the clerks called the police. By the time Jessica convinced them
that she wasn't trying to shoplift, and the
police and the boutique realized they'd been
set up, it was too late for Jessica to make it
back to Sweet Valley in time for the talk
show. Can you believe someone would do
that to the person who's supposedly her
best friend?*

*Poor Jessica called us from the Cold
Springs police station, absolutely in tears.
She'd wanted that TV spot more than anything. But right away, I saw that the situation wasn't completely hopeless. I knew
what I had to do, and even though it was
risky, Mom and Dad and Steven were behind me one hundred percent. . . .*

My parents and Steven dropped me off at the
high school at quarter past seven. As they drove off
to park the car, I ducked in a side entrance so no
one would see me. I felt confident about my physical appearance—the short black skirt, white tank
top, and boxy turquoise jacket were from my sister's closet, and I'd even remembered to take off

my watch (she never wears one)—but I was still trying to prepare myself mentally. And the talk show was scheduled to broadcast live in just fifteen minutes! Hundreds of people were crowding into the auditorium to watch the taping, and I could imagine the frenzy behind the scenes. Eric Parker had to be going nuts wondering what had happened to Jessica. As for Lila . . .

Taking a deep breath, I slipped through a door marked Backstage. Sure enough, there was Lila, chatting earnestly with a befuddled Eric Parker. Eric checked his watch; Lila shook her head, feigning puzzlement. Then he patted her shoulder and nodded. I could read his lips: "You'll have to take her place, Lila." Beaming, Lila waltzed into the dressing room to get ready.

As soon as the door closed behind her, I dashed forward. Grabbing a chair, I jammed it under the doorknob. Lila wasn't going to take Jessica's place. *I* was!

I hurried after Eric. When he saw me, a smile of relief creased his face. "Jessica!" he exclaimed. "I'd given up on you!"

"Sorry. I'm always late," I told him ruefully. "Guess I should have written that on my application, huh?"

Eric laughed. "Well, you're here now. That's what counts. Come on." He gestured toward the stage. "The curtain's going up in just a few minutes."

It was probably just as well that I didn't have more time to think about what I was doing or I might have chickened out. I'd posed as Jessica more than once in the past, and she'd pretended to be me too. We look exactly alike, after all, and every now and then, in emergencies, it's just plain handy to switch identities. But I'd never impersonated my twin in front of television cameras. *My face is going to appear on TV screens all over the country,* I thought as the technical crew bustled around me, adjusting my microphone and touching up my hair and makeup. *I can't make a single slip. I have to be Jessica, inside and out.*

For a split second, I felt dizzy with stage fright. Then Eric Parker caught my eye and flashed me an encouraging grin. "Not nervous, are you, kiddo?" he said.

I grinned back. "No way," I replied, with Jessica-esque bravado. "I've been preparing for this moment all my life!"

Just then, the show's producer pointed a finger at us. The curtain started going up and the cameras began to roll. "We're live in five," the head cameraman announced, "four, three, two, one . . ."

When the standing-room-only audience glimpsed the famous talk-show host, they burst into enthusiastic applause. I sat up straight, my legs crossed at the ankles and my hands folded in my lap, set to dazzle the world with my smile, my charm, and my intelligence. And at that moment, I realized something. I wasn't just doing this as a favor to my sister—I was doing it for myself too. *This is going to be fun*, I anticipated, adrenaline bubbling through my veins. If my life had been dull lately, it was my own fault. Opportunities for excitement and adventure were there, as plentiful as leaves on a tree—I just had to reach up and pluck them.

Eric Parker introduced himself. After a few words about the show's special topic, he gestured to me. "Ladies and gentlemen, meet my special guest, Sweet Valley High junior Jessica Wakefield!"

The audience cheered wildly. I smiled and waved, ready to launch into vintage Jessica mode. No one needed to know the truth, that there was a little bit of Liz in the performance. It would be my secret.

I carried it off in grand style, Diary, if I may say so myself! The interview went incredibly well. Eric and I really clicked and the audience was totally responsive—I got lots of laughs. Jessica made it to the auditorium in time to catch the last few minutes of the show, and afterward she snuck backstage to thank me for saving the day. We swapped outfits fast so she could reemerge as herself and bask in postinterview glory.

In the end, she wasn't even that disappointed that she didn't make it back in time for the interview, because half the fun was getting fussed over by all her friends afterward!

No one from school knows that I subbed for Jess except Todd. I couldn't resist telling him when he called just now to make a date for tonight. He said my performance was inspiring. Naturally! And you know, it doesn't bother me in the least that Jessica's getting all the credit for it. It really was her interview. I'm just glad I could help her. She'd do the same for me in a minute.

Anyhow, when Todd asked me what I wanted to do tonight and said he'd treat me to dinner at the Leeward Isles, I felt guilty because I was so hard to please last weekend. So I told him I was in the mood for pizza and a movie and that, always, whatever we do is fine with me as long as we're together. And that's really the truth. I'm thankful to have a boyfriend as loving and supportive as Todd. Naturally we've established a routine—that's how it is with couples who've been together for a while. You can only have one first date, right?

Friday night

Dear Diary,

Todd just left and it's after midnight, but I can't fall asleep. We planned an evening at home, since my parents are out, but it didn't turn out to be as cozy and romantic as we'd hoped. We rented a movie, but then Jessica barged into the family room and insisted on tuning into the music video channel instead because there was a two-hour Jamie Peters special on. I mean, I like Jamie Peters too, but two hours?

Todd and I protested and threw microwave popcorn at her, but Jessica wouldn't budge from the couch. She is obsessed with Jamie Peters. I think I'll lose my mind if I have to listen to his new CD one more time. She plays the hit single from it, "Doing It All for You," over and over, and I know she's pretending that J.P. is singing to her. It's pathetic!

Anyway, there's nothing like a third wheel to ruin the mood. Sometimes Jessica is totally clueless. I wish she'd get a boyfriend of her own so she wouldn't always be in our way! Actually, she usually has a date on the weekend, but for some reason she didn't tonight, and by the time we finally got rid of her, Todd and I were too tired to even kiss goodnight. I mean, we kissed, but we didn't really kiss, if you get my drift. Todd was yawning all over the place, so even though it wasn't that late, I sent him home. We really need to rekindle the magic in our relationship, Diary. Any suggestions?

Wednesday, 8:00 P.M.

Diary, I've had the strangest day. Or maybe strange is the wrong word. Well, judge for yourself. First of all, Enid and I ate lunch with Andrea Slade, a new girl in our class. Have I told you about her? Andrea moved here from New York City, and I think we're going to become close friends. She's on the quiet side, but once you get past her initial shyness, she's really smart and funny—she's an absolute riot when she talks about the differences between Sweet Valley and Manhattan. She's also really pretty: long, curly blond hair, big blue eyes, and a peaches-and-cream complexion to die for. But she clams up when anyone asks her personal questions. All we know is that she lives alone with her dad, but she won't even tell us where her house is. I don't get it, but I respect her privacy. Enid and I both like her a lot, and we've invited her to do a

33

*bunch of stuff with us—you know, to in-
troduce her around to people and show
her what there is to do in Sweet Valley.
Hopefully she'll learn that she can trust us
and open up.*

*But Andrea's not the only mysterious
person in my life, Diary. I think I have a secret admirer! I was walking on the beach
after school today when I noticed this absolutely gorgeous guy watching me. . . .*

The beach is a big part of life in Sweet Valley
since the town is right on the Pacific. Kids from
S.V.H. hang out there a lot. It's the place to be,
especially on weekends. There's always music
blasting from a boom box, a beach volleyball
game or two, a few people body surfing, Frisbees
flying, some guys in baggy shorts skateboarding in
the parking lot. Something for everyone. And
usually I love the scene. I love hanging out with
Todd and Enid and Jessica and the whole gang.
But every now and then, I feel like peace and
solitude. That's when I head to one of the beaches
that's more out of the way, someplace where I'll
be relatively alone with the waves and the seagulls and my own thoughts.

On this particular day, I drove the Fiat about
ten minutes out of town to one of my favorite
spots on the coast. The beach has a tiny parking
lot, so it's never crowded. I brought along a

notebook in case I felt like working on my news-paper column, but when I saw the sun sparkling on the blue water, I left my book bag in the car along with my shoes and went for a long walk at the surf's edge.

There weren't many other people there, so as I headed up the beach, I noticed these four guys about my age tossing a Frisbee. They kind of checked me out as I passed by, in a friendly way, so even though I didn't know them, when they waved, I waved back. Nothing out of the ordinary. But then I caught this one boy's eye. He was tall with curly blond hair, *really* cute, and I realized that I'd seen him at the beach before. We looked right at each other for a few seconds and a defi-nite weird electric *something* passed between us. He smiled and I smiled, and then he actually kind of blushed. As I walked away I felt this funny prickling along the back of my legs. I knew he was still watching me.

Anyhow, I didn't really think that much about it. I mean, there are always cute guys at the beach, and I happened to be going out with one of the very cutest. But when I headed back to my car half an hour later, the blond guy was still there. His friends were gone, but he'd stuck around, and I couldn't help suspecting it was be-cause of me. He was sitting on a driftwood log, a damp beach towel draped over his shoulder, pre-tending to watch some windsurfers. I say "pretending" because I could tell that he'd really been watching me, but he turned his head away fast when he realized I was looking in his direction.

He wants to meet me, but he's shy, I guessed. He looked like a nice guy, not like a creep or anything. And as I said, he was *extremely* cute. On an impulse, I strolled toward him, figuring I'd just say hi and see what happened next.

When he saw me approaching, he jumped to his feet. For an instant, our eyes locked—I was close enough now to see that his were gray, the same color as the Pacific on a cloudy day. A range of emotions, impossible for me to decipher, flickered across his face. Then, before I had a chance to speak to him, he hurried off.

> *I don't know why I felt so disappointed, Diary. I mean, he's just some random stranger. I'll admit it, though: I wanted to meet him. Is that incredibly disloyal of me? I know Todd doesn't scope out other girls at the beach. At least, he'd better not!*
>
> *It's just as well that the mystery guy ran away from me. When I went back to the parking lot, I saw him riding off on a dirt bike. You know my history with motorcycles—not good. I should definitely take that as a sign that he and I aren't meant to be friends. So how*

come I'm making such a big deal out of this? We didn't even speak—it was a total non-event. Why am I writing about something so trivial and unimportant?

Sunday, 11:00 A.M.

Dear Diary,

Romance is in the air. Andrea Slade and Nicholas Morrow are falling in love! Isn't that great? As you know, I think Nicholas is just the world's nicest guy, and he's been one of Sweet Valley's most eligible bachelors for a while now. He's eighteen, smart, handsome, and a little old-fashioned in a good way— sweet and gentlemanly. Anyhow, Enid, Andrea, and I bumped into him at the mall a few days ago and he and Andrea clicked instantly. They've had a couple of dates already, and when Andrea talks about him, she sounds totally smitten. What girl wouldn't be? But I've talked to Nicholas too, and he's running into the same wall with Andrea that the rest of us have—she's really evasive about her home life. According to Nicholas, she won't let him pick her up at her house and always insists on taking her own car. It bums him out a little because he really *likes her and he wants to meet her dad and all that. I told him to give her time, but I can't help wondering myself. What's Andrea hiding?*

For the record, I am on the verge of stomping into Jessica's bedroom and taking her Jamie Peters's Pride *CD and throwing it out the window. Jess is more out of control than ever because she, Lila, Amy, and Cara have actually seen J.P. in the flesh, right here in Sweet Valley, and not once but twice.* Rock and Roll *magazine had a story about how he was thinking about moving to California to break into the movie business—Jessica's been quoting it all week. Isn't it funny that of all places he'd pick Sweet Valley? Needless to say, Jessica and Company are ecstatic. They're scheming up ways to meet him in hopes that he'll decide to cast them in his next music video or something realistic like that. My sister never gives up!*

Sunday, 8:00 P.M.

Guess what? I saw my mystery guy again! The cute blond guy from the beach. He was at the Dairi Burger this afternoon with some of his friends. They're not S.V.H. students—one of them was wearing a

Bridgewater varsity jacket. Do you think Mr. Mystery goes to Bridgewater High? "Why do you care, Liz?" you ask. Well, here's a safe place to admit it: Ever since that day at the beach, I've been thinking about Mr. Mystery. A LOT.

I don't know if he saw me—he and his friends just came in for takeout. Not that it matters. Todd is all I need in the romance department. Even though I have to confess, to you and you only, Diary, that every now and then I get a little bored with my steady. But no one's exciting to be with all the time. Right?

Thursday, 7:00 P.M.

You won't believe this, Diary. Sit down and strap yourself in. Andrea Slade is Jamie Peters's daughter! Isn't that absolutely wild? I found out last night. Jamie Peters called me because he was worried about Andrea—she never came home from school and he'd found my phone number on her desk and thought I might know where she was. I have to admit, when I heard his voice on the phone, my knees got wobbly. It is an incredibly sexy voice. Was Jessica ever jealous!

The whole thing was partly my sister's

fault anyway. She and her nosy friends had followed Jamie to his house—he bought the old Kitterby estate a few doors down from Fowler Crest. They were spying on him, and they saw Andrea with him and jumped to the absolutely ridiculous conclusion that Andrea was Jamie's girlfriend. Can you believe that? Then, of course, even though they didn't have any definite proof, they spread the story all over school and they told Nicholas that Andrea was two-timing him with a rock star. Naturally Nicholas was confused and hurt. He broke a date with Andrea, and that's when she fell apart and took off for a while to be by herself.

The whole reason Andrea didn't want people to know that Jamie was her father in the first place is because she knows from past experience that as soon as kids find out, they treat her differently. Instead of liking her for herself, they only want to be her friend to get close to her dad. She was really hoping to have a normal life in Sweet Valley, and Jessica and Lila, etc., almost ruined it for her.

Luckily, everything's straightened out now. Nicholas and I tracked Andrea down. Nicholas apologized for not giving her the

benefit of the doubt, and Andrea apolo-
gized for not being straightforward, and
then the three of us went back to her house.
And I've got to tell you something, Diary.
Jamie Peters is even cooler and better-
looking in person than in magazine photos
and concert videos. He has this sexy blond
ponytail, an amazing body, a great smile,
and this really cute cleft in his chin. But
now that I know he's old enough to be my
father . . . !

So, at least one of the mysteries of Sweet
Valley is cleared up. As for Mystery Number
Two, I took a walk on the beach today and
didn't see you-know-who. Will I ever see him
again? Or was he just a mirage?

Friday, late

Todd and I double-dated with Nicholas
and Andrea tonight. It should have been
really fun, but something happened during
dinner that spoiled my mood for the rest of
the evening. . . .

"Wasn't the movie great?" Andrea enthused as
the four of us squeezed into a booth at Guido's
Pizza Palace after catching the early show at the
Valley Cinema. "That twist at the end—it totally
blew me away!"

"Didn't you love the scene where the guy's hanging off the helicopter and it flies under the Golden Gate Bridge and he drops onto a speedboat?" asked Nicholas.

"Awesome," Andrea agreed. "And the earthquake part. Weren't the special effects cool?"

At the cinema, Andrea and Nicholas had discovered that they both loved action films. Todd does too, so that made it three against one. I was the only person who wanted to see a movie that actually contained some dialogue! I hadn't complained, though, and I didn't bother pointing out now that practically every character in the movie ended up blown to smithereens. What was the point? All that really mattered was that Andrea was finally able to relax and enjoy herself.

I opened my menu. "So, what do you guys want to do after we eat?"

"Is there someplace to go dancing?" Andrea asked.

"Sure," Nicholas told her. "The Beach Disco has pretty cool music and an outdoor dance floor. But it probably won't compare to the clubs you're used to in New York."

"I'm sure I'll love it." Andrea gazed up at him, her eyes glowing. "As long as we're together."

Nicholas bent his head to hers. I pretended to study the menu so I wouldn't have to watch them snuggle and kiss. *It's been at least a million years since Todd and I were that infatuated and*

42

couldn't keep our hands off each other, I thought wistfully.

Todd must have read my mind. Sliding closer to me, he wrapped an arm around my shoulders. "What are *you* in the mood for, Liz?" he murmured.

I smiled. "Are we talking pizza?"

"That's one possible topic."

"Well, let's see." I pretended to read the menu while he nuzzled my neck. "Maybe something traditional," I said. Todd's lips were on my cheek. "Or maybe something spicy . . ."

I turned my face so we could kiss. But just as Todd's mouth was about to meet mine, I saw something over his broad shoulder that made me freeze. A group of kids had just entered the pizza parlor and the hostess was leading them to a table. I recognized a few of them—April Dawson and Michael Harris both go to Sweet Valley High. But my attention was captured by a tall boy with curly blond hair and gray eyes.

It's him! I thought, my eyes widening.

I pulled away from Todd abruptly, scooting into the corner of the booth. "What's the matter?" he asked, startled.

"Um . . ." I wasn't sure how to explain myself. "I, uh, I'm about to . . ." I wrinkled my nose, then faked a sneeze. "Achew! Sorry," I added.

Todd reached under the table to squeeze my

knee. "We'll pick up where we left off later," he promised.

"You bet," I replied. Inside, though, I wasn't sure we'd be able to. Todd and the others started discussing what to order, but I hardly heard them. Just knowing that the mystery guy was sitting in the same restaurant had me completely distracted. *It's just a coincidence,* I thought, resisting the urge to glance over at his table. *Seeing him should mean absolutely nothing to me.* My head knew that, but my heart had an entirely different opinion. It *did* mean something. And the fact that I kept running into him felt like a lot more than a coincidence . . . it was starting to feel like fate.

> *I don't know why I pulled away from Todd like that, Diary. I love him! But I can't deny that I'm becoming a little bit obsessed with the cute stranger from the beach. Maybe the fact that I know absolutely nothing about him is what makes him so attractive—it's kind of like Jessica's crush on Jamie Peters. There—I've admitted it. I'm attracted to him. Really attracted. Just thinking about him sends shivers down my spine. And I think about him all the time. My fantasy life has never been this active.*
>
> *OK, that does it. This is too much like*

an overripe romance novel! I've made up my mind. I need to find out the vital stats on this guy: his name, how old he is, where he goes to school, what kind of dog he has, his favorite flavor ice cream. I need to hear his voice. Concrete details, you know? That will bring him down to earth. And when he's not a mystery anymore, I'm bound to stop daydreaming about him. Right?

Tuesday, 8:00 P.M.

Dear Diary,

I have to confess this to somebody before it burns me up inside. I've met a guy—an intelligent, caring, and unbelievably handsome guy. But, Diary, it's not Todd Wilkins, my longtime boyfriend, whom I love more than anybody . . . or so I thought, until I met Sam. Sam Woodruff. Isn't that a sweet name? Mrs. Elizabeth Woodruff. I wouldn't even have to change my initials! Oh, Diary, I've fallen hard.

Here's what happened. I went to the beach this afternoon, and yes, I finally met him, the adorable blond boy who was watching me the other day. But I think my plan may have backfired. Instead of being less attracted to him, I'm even more attracted than before. . . .

Since Jessica didn't need the Fiat after school on Tuesday—Amy was giving her a ride home from cheerleading practice—I was free to go wherever I wanted. And I knew where I wanted to go: the beach. Unfortunately, I was forced to tell a few little white lies first. I bumped into Enid after the final bell. "It's pretty warm today. How about a swim at Secca Lake?" she suggested.

We stopped by my locker. I rummaged inside, pretending to look for a book. "You know, I really need to study for Mr. Jaworski's test," I replied.

"So do I," she said. "We can study together, and get a little sun at the same time."

"I can never concentrate if I'm outside, though, and I have a bunch of chapters to get through. I'm *way* behind on the reading," I exaggerated. "I'd better chain myself to my desk. But I'll call you tonight, OK?"

"Sure, Liz." Enid smiled, clearly not suspecting that her best friend could ever be devious and conniving as I was at that moment. "Talk to you later."

I felt even worse fibbing to Todd. He swung by my locker as he always did on his way to basketball practice. "Want to go to the beach later?" he proposed.

I turned bright red. Was my guilty secret written all over my face? "The beach?" I squeaked.

"Yeah, the beach." Todd chuckled. "You know,

the place where the water meets the land? Sand and surf and fun in the sun?"

I made myself laugh. "I meant, oh, the *beach*." I patted my flaming hot cheeks. "I kind of have this . . . rash. I think I'm, uh, allergic to, er, suntan lotion." I remembered what I'd just told Enid and decided I might as well keep my story straight. "I have to study anyway."

"How about a study break tonight, then? I'll take you out for ice cream."

"Perfect."

"Great." Todd swept me up in his arms, enveloping me in a bear hug. He kissed me, then deposited me back on my feet. "Have a nice afternoon, Liz," he called cheerfully as he jogged off down the hall.

I waved after him. "You too. Have a good practice."

Todd's words stayed with me as I drove to the beach. *Have a nice afternoon . . . if he only knew!* I thought, suddenly filled with remorse. He was so devoted and trusting. How could I go behind his back like this?

As I parked the car, though, I reminded myself that I hadn't done anything wrong. At least, not yet. *The mystery guy might not even be here,* I thought, half hoping now that I wouldn't run into him. *If he is, I might chicken out and not talk to him. And if I do talk to him, it probably won't go any further than that. So what's to feel bad about?*

I crossed the dunes through a sea of shimmering green grass that dipped and waved in the warm breeze. As usual, the beach was mostly deserted. There was only one person swimming, and from a distance, I couldn't distinguish his features. Then he rode a wave into shore and stood up to splash through the shallows. Water ran down his tautly muscled, deeply tanned body—he shook his head and drops flew from his wet hair. I gulped, my mouth suddenly dry. *It's him.*

I stopped in my tracks, not sure what to do next. He was toweling himself off, his back turned to me. *I could take off before he sees me,* I thought. But that would have defeated the whole purpose of going there. My last image of him would have been in a bathing suit, dripping wet . . . hardly conducive to curing my crush!

I sauntered toward him, trying my best to look as if I were just there for a casual stroll, so he wouldn't think that I was some kind of psycho stalker. When he turned around, though, the charged look that passed between us gave us both away. Neither of us was at the beach by accident.

His eyes lit up when he saw me—I could tell he wanted to talk to me as much as I wanted to talk to him. But the hope and pleasure on his face were shadowed by regret. He didn't wait for me to draw nearer. Retrieving his T-shirt and sneakers, he started to jog off barefoot down the beach.

This time I wasn't going to let him get away. I ran after him, my heart hammering with nervous anticipation.

Can you believe I was that bold and shameless, Diary? I don't know what came over me. I'm glad I went for it, though. Sam is incredibly sweet and funny—we had the best conversation! And I found out why he's been watching me and avoiding me at the same time. . . .

"Wait a minute! Excuse me," I called out.

The mystery guy stopped and turned around. He looked a little startled to find me chasing after him, and I suddenly felt unbelievably foolish. Now that I'd gotten his attention and we were face-to-face, what on earth was I going to say to him? "Um, er, hi," I panted, blushing hotly.

"Hi," he said, his own face red under his suntan.

I waved at the placid blue ocean. "Nice day, huh?"

"Sure is," he agreed.

All of a sudden, I burst out laughing. "I'm not very good at this, am I?" I said ruefully. "I just wanted to introduce myself. I mean, I've seen you around."

"I've seen you too," he said, his gray eyes crinkling in a smile.

"I'm Elizabeth Wakefield."

His eyebrows furrowed in puzzlement. "Elizabeth? Hold on. I thought your name was Jessica!"

"Jessica?" I echoed, taken aback.

"I saw you on television," he explained. "The interview with Eric Parker."

"Oh, right." It didn't make sense to go into the whole saga of how I'd subbed for my sister on the talk show. "Believe it or not, I have an identical twin. Jessica did the TV interview. I'm Elizabeth."

"I'm Sam Woodruff." He held out his hand. "And there's only one of me. Luckily!"

We shook hands, both grinning. "Would you like to take a walk?" I asked him.

"You bet," he replied.

We strolled side by side along the water's edge. I glanced at Sam shyly out of the corner of my eye. "So, I hope I'm not bothering you. I mean, you probably came to this beach because it's quiet and you wanted some privacy."

"No, actually . . ." He sidestepped a child's sand castle that was slowly being eroded by the incoming tide. "I came to this beach because I hoped you'd be here. I've wanted to meet you ever since I saw you—or I guess it was your sister—on the talk show. I thought you were the coolest, most beautiful girl I'd ever seen. And then when I noticed you at the beach, well, you were even prettier in real life."

I blushed. "Then why did you run away?"

"Because after I saw you at the beach once or twice, I saw you at the Dairi Burger. And the other night—maybe you didn't notice me—I stopped in at the pizza place when you were there."

"I noticed," I said softly.

"Well, I kind of got the impression—I mean, both times you were with this guy . . ." Sam shrugged his broad shoulders. "I figured you were taken so I should just steer clear of you. Not set myself up for a disappointment." He flashed me an uncertain smile. "Here I am—a glutton for punishment. But, hey, at least I got to talk to you once. And you really are the most gorgeous girl I've ever laid eyes on."

There was a wistful note in his voice, a finality. He thought I was someone else's girlfriend, so in gentlemanly fashion, he wasn't going to pursue me. And he was right—I *was* someone else's girlfriend. But for a brief instant, I didn't want to be. I wanted to be free and unattached.

"That other guy," I burst out. "Todd."

Sam raised his eyebrows. "Yeah?"

"He's not . . ." I caught myself. I didn't want to lie if I didn't have to. "He's . . . we used to go out, but then his family moved to the East Coast and we broke up. When he moved back to Sweet Valley, he wanted to get back together but I was seeing someone else, a guy named Jeffrey."

Sam followed my story intently. "And now?"

51

"Jeffrey and I stopped seeing each other a while ago. Todd and I spend a lot of time together but we're just . . ." Again, I stopped. Up to that point, I'd been telling the truth. But to say Todd and I were "just friends" would be an outright lie. "We're really close friends," I concluded instead.

An ear-to-ear grin brightened Sam's face. "Boy, am I glad to hear that," he declared. "Then maybe this walk on the beach won't be a one-time thing! I'd like to see you again, Elizabeth. Close up like this. Not from a distance."

"I'd like that too," I told him, and I meant it.

Oh, Diary, I know I totally misbehaved today. I got myself into a situation where I didn't belong, and then I handled it all wrong. I didn't lie to Sam, but I didn't tell him the truth about Todd either. And if Todd knew that I snuck off to the beach this afternoon in order to practically throw myself at some handsome stranger!

But Sam isn't a stranger anymore, and that's the serious problem here. I like him so much! We ended up hanging out at the beach and talking for two hours! We have tons of things in common, but we're really different in some ways too, and I think that's why I'm so intrigued by him.

Remember how I mentioned he rode a dirt bike? Well, it turns out he races them, and from the sound of it, he's pretty good. I've been kind of afraid of motorcycles ever since I had that accident when I was riding one .with Todd, but when Sam was telling me about this race he was in recently, it sounded so risky and exciting, I have to confess I got really turned on. The neat thing about Sam, though, is that he's not at all macho or anything like you might expect a dirt biker to be. He's incredibly gentle and sincere and down-to-earth. He wasn't trying to impress me with those racing stories, and that's exactly what did impress me.

One thing's for sure. Nobody can ever know about Sam and me—ever! Not even Jessica. She never could keep a secret as big as this one. And if Todd ever finds out, it'll break his heart. I can't tell Sam about Todd either—he's too nice a guy to cheat with another guy's girl. Cheating. That's what I'm doing, isn't it? I feel horrible. This is only going to lead to disaster, I just know it. . . .

I should nip this in the bud, shouldn't I? I shouldn't see Sam again—it's not fair to Todd. But I want to see him. I want it passionately. Talking with Sam today opened up something inside me, some secret unexplored chamber of my heart. It gave me a glimpse of a whole new world of adventure and laughter and possibility. I don't want to shut that door—I want to walk right through it and discover the magic beyond. Is that so terribly wrong?

Thursday, 6:30 P.M.

An uneventful day. School, Oracle meeting, bike ride with Todd. Todd told me I seemed preoccupied and asked what was on my mind. I couldn't tell him the truth . . . that I'm thinking constantly about Sam Woodruff!

I'm in such suspense, wondering what's going to happen next. Has Sam been looking for me at the beach? Will he call me? If he asks me out, what will I say? I have no idea how to handle this. I don't want to be unfaithful to Todd, but I do want to get to know Sam better. Do you think there's any chance Sam and I could just be friends? That's a laugh! Who am I kidding?

Sunday, 10:30 A.M.

Dear Diary,
    This week I received a gift from someone

54

*very special. Nicholas's mother, Skye
Morrow, gave me a beautiful camera that
once belonged to Nicholas's younger sister and my S.V.H. classmate, Regina. I
was so honored and touched. Every time
I use it, I'll think of Regina. She was a
very special person. I still miss her, and I
always will.*

*Speaking of cherished friends, where
would I be without Enid? She came over
yesterday and we had a long talk. It helped
me sort out my confused feelings in the romance department. . . .*

We were sitting by the pool in my backyard, a
tall pitcher of iced tea on the table between us,
soaking up the midday sunshine. It was nice to
relax—we'd spent the morning biking along some
of the more scenic Sweet Valley back roads, stopping every now and then so I could take a picture
with Regina's camera.

"I don't want to get too fried," Enid said as she
smoothed sunblock on her arms, "since I'll be at the
beach later. You're going, aren't you?"

A bunch of our S.V.H. friends were getting together at the beach that afternoon for a volleyball
tournament and cookout, a typical weekend activity. This weekend, though, somebody had decided it would be fun to try a different beach for
a change. Everyone was congregating at a little

beach just north of town . . . the beach where I'd met Sam.

I couldn't risk running into him there, not when I was with all my friends, including Todd. "I actually think I'm going to skip it," I told Enid.

"Todd'll be there, though, won't he?" she asked.

"Yeah, but we're going out tonight." I adjusted the straps of my bathing suit so I'd tan evenly. "I guess I just want to take it easy, have a quiet day."

Enid considered this while she poured herself some more iced tea. "Tell me to butt out if I'm being too nosy," she said after a moment, "but are things OK between you two?"

I should have known I couldn't fool my best friend. I sighed. "Yeah, they're OK. But just OK. If you know what I mean," I added.

She nodded. "I think I do. I went through something like that with Hugh, remember?"

Enid and her boyfriend Hugh Grayson had recently broken up. She seemed to be bouncing back pretty well, although I knew she still missed him occasionally. "It's nothing serious," I assured Enid. "If you asked Todd, he'd probably say everything's fine. But I'm worried that our relationship's starting to feel stale. Sometimes I just wish . . ." I glanced at her, momentarily tempted to confide in her about Sam. I squashed that urge. "I wish we could go back to when we

56

first met and our relationship was brand-new and exciting."

"That's a great feeling, but it's also nice to know someone really well. To be comfortable with each other, to feel secure."

"Security's dull," I declared. I sat forward, hugging my knees. "Be honest, Enid. Isn't it more fun *not* to have a boyfriend? If you happen to meet an interesting new guy, you can go out with him. You can do whatever you want!"

As soon as the words were out of my mouth, I realized I sounded totally insensitive, but luckily Enid just laughed. "Have you been taking Jessica pills?" she teased. "That sounds like something she'd say."

"Well, it's true, isn't it?"

"I don't know, but one thing's for sure. The grass is always greener on the other side of the fence," Enid said. "Sure, being single has its good sides, but I envy you and Todd. You've built something together. You have a past—you share all these great memories. You really *know* each other. That's real love, and that's what everyone else in the world is after."

I couldn't argue with her when she put it that way. *Real love*, I mused, sipping my iced tea. Todd and I had something special—Enid was right about that. But what she'd said about knowing each other well . . . *It's definitely more exciting* not *to know everything there is to know about another person*, I thought. I pictured Sam's adorably handsome face. I knew his name now, but he was still a mystery to me, and I couldn't deny that that was what I liked about him.

Which means I still have a dilemma, Diary. If it came down to making a choice, would I go for the sure thing or the new thing? Actually, I've already made my choice. Enid didn't tell me what to do (she couldn't, since she doesn't even know about Sam!), but she did help me put things in perspective. The bottom line is, I can't risk losing Todd. No matter how cute and intriguing Sam Woodruff is . . . and he IS . . . Todd is cute too, and more important, he's loving and loyal and kind. He's been beside me through thick and thin. Like when Regina died. I remember Todd holding me close—we were both crying. It was such an awful time, but he gave me strength and kept me going.

So, to make a long story short, Diary, I've decided not to see Sam again. It shouldn't be that hard a sacrifice. After all, just a few weeks ago, I'd never even laid eyes on him. I'll just avoid the beach for a while. It shouldn't take too long to get over this itsy-bitsy infatuation.

A busy day. I went to a meeting of the new S.V.H. Photography Club after school. Now that I have such a neat camera, I figure I should learn how to use it! The club will be a lot of fun. For our first project, we're going to put together a gigantic photo mural about Sweet Valley High. Isn't that a terrific idea? We're planning to keep the mural a secret from people who aren't in the club—that way we'll get better candid pictures.

I stopped at the grocery store on the way home because it was my night to cook (we take turns on weeknights, as you know). I was in a pretty good mood, slicing and dicing up a storm in the kitchen. Then the phone rang and shattered my calm. . . .

I'd lined up all my fresh, colorful vegetables on the counter: red and yellow peppers, ripe tomatoes, some big fat mushrooms, a zucchini, and a bunch of crisp, bright green broccoli. I was chopping them up one by one, trying to do it fast like on the wok cooking demonstrations on TV. My mouth was watering—it was going to be my best stir-fry ever.

When the phone rang, I let it ring a couple of

59

times figuring Jessica would answer it, but when she didn't, I put down my knife and grabbed the receiver just as the answering machine was about to pick up. "Hello?" I said.

"Elizabeth?" a boy's voice responded.

"Oh, hi," I said brightly, cradling the phone between my cheek and shoulder so I could slice mushrooms while I talked to Todd. "I was just thinking about calling you. The Photography Club meeting was really—"

"Elizabeth?" the boy said again. "Do you know who this is?"

I dropped the knife, and I almost dropped the phone too. My face turned pale, then bright red. I was so stunned, I didn't speak.

"It's Sam Woodruff." He laughed wryly. "Guess you weren't expecting a call from me."

"No, I, uh . . ." I stuttered. I drew in a sharp breath, patting my chest as if that might slow my galloping heartbeat. "Hi," I managed finally.

"I've been thinking about you," Sam told me, "and wondering if you'd like to—"

I'd made up my mind not to see Sam again, and I knew I shouldn't be talking to him either. An awful possibility crossed my panicked mind. *What if Jessica is listening on the extension upstairs?* I thought. I wouldn't put it past her to casually mention, next time she ran into Todd, that I'd been getting phone calls from other guys.

I cut Sam off in midsentence. "Sam, I can't talk

right now," I blurted out. "There's someone at the door."

"Will you call me back later?" he asked, his tone friendly and easy. He obviously didn't realize I was lying.

"Sure," I promised, sick with guilt.

"Let me give you my number," he offered.

"I've really got to go," I told him. "Are you listed?"

"Yes—in Bridgewater."

"OK. Bye!" I didn't give him a chance to respond.

I hung up the phone, then leaned back weakly against the kitchen counter, counting silently in my head. *One, two, three, four* . . . When I got to fifteen, and Jessica hadn't pounded down the stairs and burst into the kitchen to demand to know who Sam Woodruff was, I started to relax. My secret was still safe.

My secret. I gulped. Of course, Sam didn't realize he was a secret. To him, the situation probably seemed simple. He'd met a girl at the beach—me—and he wanted to see me again. Naturally, he'd looked me up in the phone book and called me.

But to me, Sam's perfectly innocent phone call was a catastrophe. It was as if a quake had rumbled the earth beneath my feet.

I'd been trying not to think about Sam Woodruff. Now, his voice on the phone had brought the memories of our walk on the beach back in a rush. Clearly, I was on his mind too. What was going to happen next?

It's hard, Diary, but I'm sticking to my resolution not to see Sam. I know I said I'd call him back, but I'm not going to, and if he calls me again, I'll just have to tell him right out that I'm not free. That's all there is to it. The end.

I'll call Todd right this minute. That should chase any leftover thoughts of Sam from my head.

Wednesday evening

You're going to be so mad at me, Diary. I didn't live up to my word. I went to the beach this afternoon to look for Sam. Some force greater than my own will was pulling me, like a magnet. I just couldn't help myself.

He wasn't there, and I was unbelievably disappointed, but I guess it's just as well. I want to see him, but I can't. I CAN'T. I trust him, but I don't trust myself.

Even though I didn't see Sam at the beach, though, something did happen there—something disturbing. I had Prince Albert, my golden retriever, with me, and I'd brought along Regina's camera too. That was my excuse to myself for going there, that I was going to shoot a roll of black-and-white film so I'd have something to develop at the next Photography Club meeting. I hung out at the beach for a long time—I was really hoping Sam would show up—snapping pictures of some pieces of driftwood that looked like cool sculptures, a little girl doing cartwheels at the surf's edge, an old man with a metal detector hunting for buried treasures, that sort of thing.

Then, when Prince Albert and I were heading back to the parking lot, I noticed these three men running along the dune path. I'm not really sure why I decided to take their picture. Maybe because they looked odd—they were dressed in street clothes, not exercise gear, and they were running very close together. Not your run-of-the-mill joggers. And the first lesson of photography is that the best pictures spring from moments that are unusual, candid, spontaneous. So I lifted up my camera—CLICK.

The next thing I knew, one of the men charged over to me and actually tried to steal my camera! Prince Albert protected me—he barked and growled at the man while I ran off and started the Fiat. Thank goodness it's a convertible! Prince Albert leapt in the backseat—the man was still chasing us—and we sped off.

It was really weird and scary. Why do you suppose someone would react so violently to having his picture taken? I mean, he didn't even try to talk to me first—he just attacked me. I still have the creeps. The worst part is that I shouldn't have been at the beach in the first place. I have to renew my vow to myself: I'm not pursuing Sam Woodruff. Instead, I'm concentrating on improving my relationship with Todd.

Saturday, 2:00 P.M.

I want my life to get back to normal so I can stop thinking about Sam, but crazy things keep happening. Someone broke into the darkroom at school yesterday and completely trashed it! A bunch of equipment was destroyed, and a lot of the pictures people have taken for the photo mural were ruined. The police don't have any leads on the vandals, but I have this sinking feeling it has something to do with the men from the beach.

Remember the three men I saw running, and how upset the one guy was that I'd taken their picture? Well, you're not going to believe this. The very same night, on the news on TV, there was a story about a major drug inquiry going on in the U.S. Senate. The government's main witness, somebody named Ron Hunter, was scheduled to testify about a huge drug ring. But at the last minute, he changed his mind and wouldn't name any names. This is the unbelievable part: they showed a picture of Ron Hunter on TV . . . and he looked exactly like one of the men running on the beach, the one in the middle. The more I think about it, the more convinced I am that I saw Ron Hunter, right here in Sweet Valley, and that he's being held against his will by the other two men—they don't want him to testify against them! If they're drug dealers, that would explain why they want to destroy the photograph I took of them. But guess what: If the man who tried to steal my camera was the same one who vandalized the S.V.H. darkroom, he didn't find what he was looking for, because I had the prints and negatives with me at home. I could be sitting on dynamite, Diary!

Tuesday, 5:00 P.M.

I showed Todd the photo of the three men, and he agreed that there's a

65

resemblance between the one guy and Ron Hunter. (Todd saw the newscast too—in fact, we watched it together.) He pointed out, though, that Ron Hunter couldn't be in two places at once—in California and also in Washington, D.C., testifying to the Senate. But I know it's the same person—I just have a hunch. And I feel responsible now, because of what happened to the darkroom at school. Whether I like it or not, I'm involved. So, I told Todd that if he wanted to help me, great, but if not, I'd sleuth around on my own. One way or another, I have to get to the bottom of all this. . . .

Todd and I met at my locker after school. I was clutching a folder to my chest. I'd been carrying it around with me all day, afraid to let it out of my sight. Todd nodded at the folder. "Is that what I think it is?" he asked.

"Yep," I confirmed.

"What are you going to do now?" he wondered.

I glanced over my shoulder. I didn't want to talk about it in the crowded hallway. "Walk me to the parking lot," I suggested.

When we were safely outside the school building, I slipped a five-by-seven photograph from the folder: the one of the three men running near the beach. "I want to fiddle around with this a little bit," I told Todd, showing him the print. "See the younger guy on the left? There's lettering on his T-shirt. I can't quite make it out, but maybe if I enlarge it . . ."

Todd peered at the picture. "It probably says something totally unhelpful and generic. Hard Rock Cafe or Life's a Beach or something like that."

I slipped the print back in the folder. "Then again, it might be a clue," I reasoned. "I won't know until I try. That's why I asked Amy Sutton's dad if I could use the darkroom at his photography studio, since the one at school is still out of commission."

We continued walking. "If it *is* a clue, and if those men really are drug dealers," Todd said slowly, "and if they're the vandals . . . this could be dangerous, Liz."

"You're right," I agreed calmly.

He stopped and put a hand on my arm, turning me to face him. "You shouldn't do this alone," he stated.

I had a fleeting image of myself racing down the coast highway on the trail of a carful of criminals. Except the person by my side was Sam, not Todd.

I blinked a couple of times, focusing on my boyfriend's earnest face. *Don't you dare think*

67

about Sam Woodruff, I lectured myself silently. I never would have gotten into this mess in the first place if I hadn't been chasing after Sam!

"Are you saying you believe me?" I asked Todd. "That there's a connection between my photo and Ron Hunter and the drug investigation?"

"I'm saying I'll help you find out," Todd replied.

I smiled. "I guess that'll have to be good enough. Come on, then. Let's go!"

We spent an entire hour at Mr. Sutton's studio trying to get an enlargement clear enough to read the elusive lettering. Finally, as Todd and I bent over a basin watching a black-and-white print develop, the words on the T-shirt sprang into focus. "Rick's Place," we both said out loud at the same moment.

I moved the print immediately to the stop bath. Without prompting, Todd slipped from the darkroom and returned with the phone book. My heart thumping with expectation, I watched him flip through the white pages, then turn to the yellow pages. "Yep, it's in here," he announced, his deep voice resonant with excitement. "It's a restaurant in Big Mesa."

"I knew the T-shirt might be a good lead!" I exclaimed triumphantly. "Maybe the guy in the photograph works at Rick's Place."

"What do you say we go there for dinner and find out?" Todd invited.

"You've got a date," I said.

Todd is picking me up in fifteen minutes. I'm excited, but I have to confess I'm also a little bit nervous. Todd thinks it's unlikely we'll run into any of the men from the picture, but he has to admit there's a chance. What will we do if we see them? They're bound to recognize me. I guess we'll just cross that bridge when we come to it.

Jessica's getting ready for a date too. When I tried to ask her about it, she said she was too busy to talk to me. She's just mad because earlier in the week she was trying to tell me about the funny way she met this great new guy (Chad, I think, or Chuck), but I was all caught up in what was going on at the darkroom at school and didn't have time to listen to her. I swear, sometimes my sister acts like she's six instead of sixteen. I suppose if she still likes this guy after tonight, I'll hear about it eventually. Although knowing how fickle Jessica can be, the romance will fizzle fast. With her, it almost always does.

Time to go—Todd's here!

Tuesday, late

Diary, this ended up being just about the most terrifying and exciting night of my

69

life. I'm too hyped up to sleep, so I might as well write about it. Todd and I caught the drug dealers!

It was definitely one of those truth-is-stranger-than-fiction experiences. We went to dinner at Rick's Place, the way we'd planned. When we arrived at the restaurant, I showed the photo of the three men on the beach to the hostess and the bartender. When they both recognized the younger blond man as someone who'd been in the restaurant a couple of times, I knew we were on the right track. So we settled down at a table and ordered appetizers. Then dinner. Then dessert. We were about to give up on the guy showing up, when he walked into the restaurant. And this is the shocking part. He wasn't alone. . . . He was with my sister, Jessica!

I can't tell you how I felt at that moment, Diary, when I realized that my sister's date was possibly a very dangerous criminal. I could see by her body language that she was tense, even afraid— she wasn't enjoying herself, that was for sure. And even though she drives me crazy sometimes—all the time!—she's my twin sister and I love her more than anyone in the world. I remembered how she'd tried to tell me a funny story about how she and Chad got together. Why hadn't I listened? It couldn't be a coincidence that they'd met—obviously, he'd approached her, thinking she was me. That was the only explanation. Which meant he and the other men were still after the photograph I'd taken at the beach. The only question was, how far were they willing to go to get it?

We found out soon enough. From where Todd and I were sitting, we could watch Jessica and Chad in a mirror on the restaurant wall, although the two of them hadn't spotted us. We thought we'd be able to get to Jessica fast, if she should need us, but we almost blew it. She and Chad started to argue, and then all of a sudden, Chad stood up and practically dragged Jessica out of the restaurant. We ran after them, but they were in Chad's car by the time we got outside. We got into Toss's car, and he floored the gas pedal on the BMW. We'd almost caught up to them on the highway when, wouldn't you know it, we got pulled over by a state trooper for speeding!

It turned out to be a blessing in disguise. We told the police officers what was going on, and then we all set off after Chad and Jessica. We caught up to them at the high school—Chad had taken Jess there to look for the photograph. It was really dramatic, Diary, just like some television cop show: All these other squad cars had been radioed to the scene and a whole bunch of officers charged into Sweet Valley High. Todd was the one who actually caught Chad, though! I have to say, even though I'm still fantasizing about Sam, Todd was incredibly heroic. Chad and Jessica were at my locker (she was pretending to look for the picture even though she had absolutely no idea why Chad wanted it), and when Chad tried to run, Todd tackled him. It was awesome!

What a relief to see Chad in handcuffs, being led away by the police. Jessica and I hugged each other as if we'd never let go. Neither of us wanted to think how close she came to serious harm! At the police station later, we learned the whole sordid, complicated story. It turns out the man in the photograph I took was in fact Ron Hunter, who was supposedly testifying before the Senate drug committee. Ron had been involved with a big nationwide drug ring, but he decided to go clean and he was going to blow the whistle on the whole operation. The reason Chad and the third man wanted to destroy the picture is because they'd kidnapped Ron . . . so that Ron's twin brother, Rich, could take Ron's place in Washington, D.C., and change the testimony so as not to incriminate all the other people involved in the drug ring!

The day I took the picture at the beach, Ron had momentarily broken away from his kidnappers—I spotted them just as Chad and his accomplice were hustling Ron back to their car. The photo I took was proof that the real Ron Hunter wasn't in D.C. and therefore it was potentially really dangerous to the bad guys. Understandably, they were desperate to get their hands on it. And when Chad bumped into Jessica and assumed she was me—they flirted a little and she seemed interested in him—Chad thought he'd found an easy way out: He'd go out with her and then force her to give him the photograph. Meanwhile, my crazy sister let him go on thinking she was me because she thought Chad was hot! Talk about a poor judge of character. Jess was really, really shaken up by all this, though. I don't think she'll ever be quite that reckless again.

When Todd dropped me off tonight, he

gave me a big hug and a long goodnight kiss. It was the most passionate moment we've shared in ages. I think if I try I can forget about Sam Woodruff.

Wednesday, 7:30 P.M.

Dear Diary,

You will absolutely not believe what happened today. Todd came over after basketball practice and we were hanging out by the pool. I was feeling pretty cheerful because all sorts of good things had happened at school today. First of all, the Photography Club unveiled the photo mural and everybody loved it. Secondly, Mr. and Mrs. Morrow dropped by to see the mural, and while they were at S.V.H., pledged to donate funds to rebuild the school darkroom in Regina's memory. Isn't that incredibly generous of them?

Speaking of Regina, she's really been on my mind. It occurred to me that it was sort of like fate that I used her camera to take the photograph that helped bust a big drug ring. You remember that Regina died from a brain seizure—she got in with a bad crowd of kids in Sweet Valley and they pressured her into experimenting with drugs, and she had a fatal reaction. See what I'm getting at? It's as if justice has been done. Regina lost her life to drugs and nothing can bring her back, but a lot of other lives may be saved because Chad and Company are behind bars now.

Anyhow, Todd and I were taking a swim and talking about Regina when the doorbell rang. When I saw who was at the door, I nearly fainted. . . .

Todd and I were in the shallow end of the pool, waist-deep in water, hitting a volleyball back and forth. "Didn't you think the Photography Club mural turned out great?" I asked him.

"Could've used more pictures of handsome basketball forwards who shall remain nameless," he teased.

I skidded the heel of my hand across the surface of the water, splashing him. "Conceited."

Todd laughed, serving the ball over to me. "The mural's terrific. And your pictures were the best."

I hit the ball back to him. "You don't have to say that," I protested, but the praise pleased me. "Do you really think so?"

"I really think so," he confirmed.

"I wonder what kind of project the club will do next," I said, swimming over to retrieve the ball that Todd had lobbed over my head.

"You mean you'll keep going to meetings?" he asked.

"Sure." I lobbed the volleyball to him. "Why wouldn't I?"

Todd spiked the ball back. "I just thought, now that the mural's done, and you solved the Ron Hunter mystery, you'd have other things to do with your time. Like, stick to writing."

"I don't plan to drop writing for photography, but why can't I do both?" I asked him.

"I just meant, writing's what you're really good at, and there are only so many hours in the day, right?"

"But I want to develop different aspects of my creativity," I exclaimed, diving for a shot. The ball landed in the water and I scooped it up, droplets flying. "I want to try new things. I don't want to go through life playing it safe, just doing stuff I'm already good at."

Todd wore a bemused expression, as if he weren't sure where I was coming from. *Sam would understand,* I found myself thinking. That day on the beach, I'd told him a little about my love of writing and he'd gotten me to admit I'd like to write a documentary screenplay someday, maybe even direct my own movie. *Sam would encourage me to stretch, to dream.*

The distant sound of the doorbell drifted out through the sliding glass door. "Want me to get that?" Todd offered.

I pulled myself out of the swimming pool and began toweling myself off. "No. I'll just run

76

around the side of the house," I told him. "Be right back."

I strode across the grass, knotting the damp towel around my waist as I went. As I rounded the corner of the house into the front yard, I automatically checked the street, looking for a delivery truck or one of Jessica's or my friends' cars. Instead, I saw a dirt bike parked alongside the curb.

The next moment, I recognized the tall, blond boy standing in front of my house. It was as if my thoughts had conjured him into existence!

Sam Woodruff flashed an easy smile as I approached. I felt my cheeks turn hot pink. It was hard to say which feeling was uppermost in my heart at that moment, pleasure or panic. I couldn't deny that it was fantastic to see him. That smile made me melt like chocolate. But while Sam stood on my front step, Todd was just a few feet away in the backyard!

"Uh, hi," I croaked.

"Sorry to catch you off guard like this," Sam said. "I hope I'm not totally out of line, stopping by without an invitation."

"No, um, it's OK," I said weakly. "But I'm kind of—I mean, there's someone—I can't really . . ."

"I won't stick around if it's not convenient," Sam hurried to assure me. "I just thought . . . well, you never called me back the other day. So I thought, well, maybe she's not interested. Or maybe she's just busy. Anyway, I was in the neighborhood. Sort of." He grinned. "I figured I didn't have anything to lose. You might tell me to get lost, but then again, you might agree to go out with me."

He couldn't have been sweeter or more polite. *Here's my chance,* I thought. *I'd better tell him the truth, that I'm not available. Then I've got to get him out of here before Todd sees him!*

I gazed up into Sam's blue eyes. They were bright with hope . . . and utterly irresistible. Words poured out of my mouth, but they weren't the words I'd intended to speak. "I can meet you Sunday night, around six-thirty, at the beach," I said in a rush. "Will that work for you?"

"Sure." Sam smiled broadly. "I mean, I'd prefer tomorrow night, but I can wait."

"Good." I glanced nervously over my shoulder. "I've got to go, Sam, OK? I'm . . ." I said the first thing that came into my mind. "Babysitting. For my neighbor's kids. By the pool."

"Yeah, you'd better go," he agreed. "See you Sunday, Elizabeth."

"See you."

I darted around the side of the house, then watched from behind a palm tree until he'd started up his dirt bike and was safely out of sight. Walking back to the swimming pool, I breathed deeply, struggling to compose my features. My heart was still palpitating. I felt flushed and a little shaky and a lot guilty.

Todd was lying on his back on a towel spread

out on the pavement next to the pool. Drops of water sparkled on his suntanned skin. "Who was it?" he asked casually.

He didn't even bother opening his eyes . . . thank goodness. "It was, uh, this guy looking for Jessica," I replied, draping my own towel on the back of a chair and hurrying to the edge of the pool. "I told him she was at cheerleading practice."

"Not another Chad type, I hope!" Todd chuckled.

"No," I said quickly. "I don't think so."

I dove into the cool, blue water before Todd could ask anymore innocent questions. That way I wouldn't be forced to give him any more not-so-innocent answers.

Do you think I'm totally weak and spineless, Diary? I should have told Sam I already have a boyfriend. Instead, I told him I'd see him this weekend! And then I lied to Todd. I really thought I'd disentangled myself from this situation, but now I'm in deeper than ever. I'm going to see Sam again—only this time, it won't be a casual, "accidental" encounter at the beach. It's a bona fide date. Help!

Friday, 8:00 P.M.

I went for a hike with Todd and Robin Wilson at Secca Lake this afternoon. It was

79

*a beautiful day, but Robin seemed kind of
depressed. I think she misses her boyfriend,
George Warren. Since he's a freshman at
UCLA, they've always had a semi–long-
distance relationship, but apparently now
they're spending even less time together because he signed up for a really intensive flying class. (He wants to be a pilot.) Anyway,
Robin kept apologizing for being a third
wheel, which made me feel totally secretly
guilty because, of course, while Todd and I
still look like the perfect couple on the outside, I'm constantly thinking about another
guy on the inside!*

*Todd and I were supposed to get to-
gether again tonight for dinner and a
movie, but he canceled because there's a
five-page paper due in Mr. Collins's
English class on Monday and he hasn't
even read the book yet. I can't lie, Diary.
Instead of feeling disappointed, I was relieved. . . .*

"You really didn't have to do that," I scolded Todd.

It was six o'clock, and he'd driven over to my
house with a big bunch of daisies and tea roses
bundled in florist's paper. We were sitting side by
side on the family room sofa.

"I can't help it," he said. "We had plans tonight,
and I bagged out on you at the last minute." He

shrugged, smiling. "I could pretend it's just be-cause I love you, but it's mostly a guilt offering."

I buried my nose in the bouquet to breathe in the sweetness of the roses so that Todd couldn't see my expression. *I should be the one making a guilt offering,* I thought. In exactly forty-eight hours, I'd be getting ready for my rendezvous with Sam Woodruff! "Anytime you have an impulse to buy me flowers, go for it," I said lightly.

Todd brushed my hair with a kiss. "I will. I just don't want you to think I take you for granted. I really do wish we could be together tonight."

"Me too," I told him.

"You know, if you want you could come over to my house and help me with my English paper," he teased, stroking my cheek with the back of his hand.

"No way," I replied in the same lighthearted tone. "I've already written a first draft of *my* paper. I'm taking it easy tonight."

Todd pretended to sulk. "What's the point of having a journalist for a girlfriend if she won't help you with your English assignments?" he grumbled.

"I'll look over your paper *when* you finish a first draft," I relented.

"Thanks." Todd engulfed me in a big hug.

I pushed him away from me. "Watch out. You're crushing the flowers."

"Sorry." He took the bouquet and placed it carefully on the couch. Brushing a strand of hair from my forehead with his index finger, he lowered his mouth to mine. "Love you, Liz," he murmured.

I tried to respond warmly to the kiss, but I couldn't. "Love you too," I said, again wriggling away from him. "Good luck with your paper," I added pointedly.

He got the hint and stood up with a sigh of resignation. "Yeah. I'll call you tomorrow."

I walked him to the door. "'Night, Todd."

"'Night, Liz."

I put the flowers in a pitcher of water and left them downstairs in the kitchen. I don't want them in my room, reminding me of what a devoted boyfriend Todd is. I don't deserve him, Diary. I mean, I haven't actually been unfaithful to him yet. I only just met Sam Woodruff—I haven't kissed him, or even held his hand. But I'm cheating on Todd in my heart just by thinking about Sam so much.

Friday, a few hours later

I think it was really good for me to have this night to myself. After I wrote in here earlier, I took a long hot bubble bath. Then I bundled myself up in a warm fuzzy terry-cloth robe and slippers, made a big mug of hot chocolate, and watched an old Katherine Hepburn–Spencer Tracy movie on cable. Back in my room, I read in bed for a while—Jane Austen's Sense and Sensibility. I would love to be able to write a novel as good as that someday! And now I'm feeling a whole lot better than I did when Todd came by before with the flowers. I feel more in control. I don't have to let myself get carried away by reckless impulses. I can choose to be loyal to Todd, and that's what I'm going to do. I was actually on the verge of picking up the phone and calling Sam Woodruff to cancel our date, but then I decided that was cowardly. He's a sweet guy—I owe him an explanation for how I've been behaving, and that will be easier to do in person.

I'm going to turn out the light now. I hope I dream about Todd.

Sunday, 11:00 A.M.

My stomach is in knots. Dad made the usual big Sunday breakfast, but I couldn't eat a bite. I didn't sleep at all last night. Every time I drifted off, I started dreaming about Sam! I'm so mixed up, Diary. I thought I could be clearheaded about this, about meeting Sam at the beach tonight. I thought I'd made up my mind to be true to Todd. But I have no faith in myself.

Even though I've rehearsed the lines in my head ("Sam, I haven't been entirely honest. I'm sorry, but I can't see you again because I'm involved with another boy"), I have no idea what I'll actually do or say when I'm face-to-face with him. I should just call him up and cancel.

I will. No, I won't. I should. But I can't!

Sunday night, late

Once again, I can't sleep, but for a different reason this time. Diary, I had the most magical evening with Sam! I went to the beach at six-thirty, like we'd arranged, and I was fully intending to give a short little speech, ask his forgiveness, and then speed home in the Fiat. Instead, he and I spent four hours together. Four hours! Time just flew by . . . except when he was kissing me. Then it was like the world stopped spinning on its axis. I was so aware of him and he was so aware of me and the moment was so intense and perfect and eternal. . . . Yes, we kissed, Diary. Are you ready to hear all about it?

After meeting at our beach (I was already thinking of it as "our beach"), Sam suggested heading up to Bridgewater, where he lived, to get something to eat. Wimp that I am, I'd put off telling Sam about Todd. As soon as I saw him, I realized I didn't want to say good-bye quite so soon. *I'll tell him at dinner,* I promised myself.

But we were so busy talking and laughing at Bob's BBQ that I just didn't get around to it. The restaurant was funky—just a shack, really, with picnic tables and rolls of paper towels instead of napkins. There was country music on the jukebox and lots of bikers in black leather. The food was great, and the atmosphere was so offbeat and casual, I couldn't help loosening up and enjoying myself.

"Having fun?" Sam asked, in between bites of sauce-covered ribs.

I was in the process of gnawing on a chicken drumstick, so all I could do was nod emphatically. A minute later, I wiped my mouth with a paper towel and glanced over my shoulder at another couple sitting a few picnic tables away. Their motorcycle helmets rested on the benches beside them; they were both dressed in dusty leather. Out of the blue, I surprised myself by telling Sam, "I've always had this secret fantasy about dressing in skintight black leather and riding a Harley."

He grinned broadly. "Sounds good to me!"

I laughed. "I can imagine what my friends at S.V.H. would think."

"What would they think?" he asked.

Todd wasn't the only thing I hadn't told Sam about. I hadn't talked much about school, *The*

Oracle and my other interests, the S.V.H. social scene, my family. And all of a sudden, I realized that I didn't want to. I didn't want to be limited by an old definition of who Liz Wakefield was. It was way more fun to reinvent myself, minute by minute.

"Let's just say it would be a radical departure," I told Sam. "They wouldn't recognize me! But what about you? What's your fantasy?"

"You on a Harley in skintight black leather doesn't count?" he kidded.

I laughed again. "No. About yourself. If you could do something wild, be someone different. Or is dirt-bike racing all the excitement you need?"

Having polished off the ribs, he started in on a mountain of coleslaw. "Hmm," he mumbled thoughtfully in between bites. "I guess maybe I'd be an actor."

"That's not so radical," I pointed out. "Every other person in southern California wants to be a movie star."

"Yeah, but it's worlds away from who I am," Sam said. "Think about it. It starts out with just words on paper. You read a script. Then you have to absorb a totally new and foreign personality, take it inside yourself, then pour it out again, bring it to life, for the camera or on stage." He shook his head. "It just seems so cool. To be a chameleon." He smiled wryly. "I'm the kind of guy who can't fake anything, you know? Give me a costume, a mask, it doesn't matter. I'm just plain me, all the time."

We were looking straight into each other's eyes. Sam's legs were long—under the table, our knees touched slightly. My face felt warm—my whole body felt warm and alive. "I think that's a fine way to be," I said softly.

After dinner, we had to drive back to the parking lot at the beach because Sam had left his dirt bike there. "Will you let me take you for a ride?" he offered as I parked the Fiat. "It's not a Harley, but I brought a spare helmet. I'd really love to make at least part of your fantasy come true."

I shook my head. "Thanks, but not tonight." I didn't want to get into the whole story about the time Todd bought a motorcycle. My parents had forbidden me to ride on it with him, but I went anyway and we ended up having a pretty serious accident. One day maybe I'd get over my fear— that was what my fantasy was about, I guess. Getting over fears. Putting the past behind me. But right now I didn't want to talk about the past. I didn't want it to exist. I wanted there to be only this moment, here and now, Sam and me. "Some other time," I promised. "Let's take a walk on the beach instead."

The sun had set and the night sky was a deep velvety blue. Without speaking, Sam and I kicked off our shoes and ran barefoot toward the ocean. "Like it?" he asked, gesturing to the glowing crescent moon hanging over the water. "I ordered it just for you."

"I *love* it," I exclaimed.

Dark waves fizzed up on the sand, leaving behind a silvery trail of sea foam. As we strolled up the beach, it seemed completely natural for Sam to take my hand and twine my fingers in his. The chemistry between us was undeniable, just a fact, a reality like the sand under our feet and the night breeze in our hair.

My pulse was racing with expectation. When Sam slipped an arm around me, I shivered.

"Are you cold?" he asked, stopping. "Here." He shrugged off his nubby cotton crewneck and wrapped it around my shoulders, knotting the sleeves. "Is that better?"

We were standing very close to each other. His hands gently gripped my bare arms. I looked up into his face, his eyes wide in the darkness. "Elizabeth," I heard him whisper.

Before I could step back, his lips found mine. At first the kiss was soft, tentative. There was a question in it: Is this OK? In response, I clasped my arms around his neck, pressing my body against his.

The kiss grew deeper, hungrier. Explosive. It rocked me like an ocean wave, sweeping away my inhibitions.

Then, at the same moment, we both paused for breath, and it was as if the wave deposited me back on the shore. My head stopped whirling, and I was standing on the earth again. *I can't believe I'm doing this*, I thought, overcome with remorse.

Sam's arms were still around me. I twisted sharply, breaking free of his embrace. "I—it's getting late," I choked out. "I have to get home."

"Stay a few minutes longer," Sam pleaded.

I was already hurrying off into the darkness. "I can't. I'm sorry. Thanks for a wonderful evening."

"When will I see you again?" he called after me.

I knew how I should answer. Never. Instead, I called back to him, "Soon."

Monday morning, dawn

I know I should feel horrible, Diary. I did something pretty bad last night. But I'm actually kind of happy. Make that delirious! I'm still floating from that kiss. Am I a monster?

I'm sure when I see Todd in school today, it will hit me. I haven't been thinking about what the consequences of my actions might be. But for a few more precious minutes, before the day gets started, while I sit here writing in my journal and the sun rises, I don't have to.

Wednesday, 10:00 P.M.

Dear Diary,
I know this was totally wrong of me, but I got together again with Sam today. I

told Todd I was going to the library at Sweet Valley University to research my history term paper. Instead, I met Sam at the beach and then we drove an hour up the coast to Castillo San Angelo, this beautiful old Spanish mansion with a restaurant and public gardens. It's the most romantic spot, and on weekdays it's practically deserted—we had the gardens all to ourselves. We talked about what California must have been like a few hundred years ago when the Spaniards first arrived—how pristine and wild and unspoiled it must have been. At that point Sam said that he felt like Adam and Eve in the Garden of Eden and that inspired us to duck behind some ornamental shrubs and kiss. We shared a lot of kisses—for the rest of my life, the smell of honeysuckle will remind me of kissing Sam.

It was a delicious afternoon, Diary, but needless to say, when I got home, I had a total guilt attack. I'd forgotten to give Sam back the sweater I borrowed the other night at the beach—there it was, draped over the back of my desk chair. I hid the sweater in the back of my closet and then listened to the messages on the answering machine, and of course there was one from

Todd, asking how my research went. I couldn't bear to call him back.

What is it about Sam, you're wondering? Part of the attraction is definitely the mystery. We still don't know each other that well. I haven't told him a thing about my life or my past. Instead, we talk about our dreams and fantasies. He's so open—he brings out a playful, daring side in me I didn't even realize I had. Todd and my friends, and my family too, think they know me inside and out. They assume my personality's set in stone. They expect me always to be good old reliable Liz, and that label doesn't leave a whole lot of room to change and grow. But with Sam, I can be whoever I want to be. You don't know how good that feels!

Which is my whole problem right now, Diary. Secretly seeing Sam makes me feel so good and so bad at the same time. One minute I vow never to see him again, and the next I'm counting the hours until I can run off to the beach. . . our beach. What am I going to do?

Thursday after school

This was a gray, gloomy day. Definitely not beach weather, if you get my drift.

Although I almost drove over there despite the drizzle. Isn't that pathetic? I wonder if Sam is thinking about me as much as I'm thinking about him. I keep lapsing into these very steamy daydreams. . . . I'm with Sam on the moonlit beach or in the Castillo San Angelo gardens. . . . I've just never been kissed that way before. It's intense. Mind-blowing.

I was a mess at school. I was so tired and distracted, I couldn't pay attention in any of my classes. Even Mr. Collins gave me a hard time for not participating in our English class discussion about Mark Twain. And seeing Todd is absolute agony, Diary. He has zero clue that anything's wrong with me, and here I am, going behind his back in the worst way. I feel torn right down the middle—literally. I have a killer stomachache. An ulcer, probably!

Robin Wilson looked as bad as I felt. I'm worried about her, Diary. She's completely gaunt and she has huge circles under her eyes. I asked Jessica's opinion. As you know, she and Robin aren't exactly best friends, but they spend a lot of time together because they're cheerleading co-captains. In her typically sensitive fashion, Jess waved off my concerns. "Robin's dieting," she told me. When I pointed out that

Robin's already really slim and doesn't need to lose any more weight, Jessica said it's a "maintenance" thing, and did I want Robin to get fat again? Robin did used to be pretty heavy, it's true. Her life really changed when she went on a diet and got in shape—she's a happier, healthier person. Or rather, she was happier and healthier. Up to a point, dieting can be a good thing, but not when you take it too far. . . .

I was sitting with Jessica and her friends from the S.V.H. varsity cheerleading squad at lunch because I'd volunteered to help them with publicity for the fund-raiser they were organizing for a new gym floor. They'd named the fund-raiser Super Sundae. The plan was to get local ice cream shops to donate tons of ice cream, then dump it all in plastic kiddie pools and top it with whipped cream and fudge sauce. Then they would sell tickets to people, with which they could get spoons to dig in to the enormous ice cream sundaes.

"I sketched out an idea for a poster," Sandy Bacon announced, holding up a spiral notebook. "What do you guys think?"

Maria, Annie, Cara, Jean, Amy, Robin, Jessica, and I all peered at Sandy's drawing of little cheerleaders standing on top of a giant sundae. The slogan was "Three Cheers for Super Sundae!"

"It's perfect," Annie enthused.

"It is," agreed Robin. Taking out a small notebook and a pen, she made a careful checkmark. "When you've drawn the final version, Sandy, give it to Liz and she'll handle the printing. You're also writing up a piece for *The Oracle*, right, Liz?"

"Right," I said.

Robin made another checkmark. "OK," she continued, her tone brisk and businesslike. "Annie, did you call the Party Warehouse about donating spoons, bowls, and paper napkins?"

"I was going to yesterday, but then—" Annie began.

"Super Sundae won't get off the ground if we don't all do our parts," Robin interjected testily.

Annie's green eyes widened. "Sorry, Robin."

"Maybe I should do it," Robin said, tapping her pen on the table.

"I can manage," Annie assured her.

I caught Amy and Jessica rolling their eyes at each other. I really couldn't blame them. Why was Robin being so bossy?

Robin ran through the rest of the to-do list in her notebook, grilling the other cheerleaders about their assigned tasks: ticket sales, soliciting ice cream donations, that type of thing. Her expression remained tense and unsmiling, even when Maria announced that her father, the town's mayor, had agreed to serve as honorary chairman of the event.

I watched Robin discreetly, a puzzled frown on my face. Since when was she such a control freak?

Then I noticed something else. She wasn't eating. Everyone else at the table had a normal lunch: a hamburger and fries, or a tuna sandwich, or yogurt with granola, or a big chef's salad. Robin had purchased a small salad—no dressing—but it was sitting in front of her untouched. Well, not exactly untouched. With her fork, she'd pushed the cherry tomatoes and cucumber slices to one side of the plate and the lettuce to the other. She kept picking up her fork, but then she'd put it down again and reach for her can of diet soda.

I took another look at Robin herself and wondered why I hadn't noticed before that, in just a few weeks, she'd gone from attractively slender to painfully skinny. *Maybe because she's wearing a loose sweatshirt and baggy jeans,* I mused. One thing was for certain. Robin hadn't needed to lose weight, but she'd dieted anyway and clearly she was still dieting.

I was just about to offer her half of my turkey and sprouts sandwich when Jessica piped up. "By the way, Robin," she said sweetly, "how is George's flying class going?"

At Jessica's question, the color drained from Robin's face. "Um, fine," she mumbled.

"Is that gorgeous girl Vicky still his flying partner?" Jessica wanted to know.

"Uh, yeah, I think so." Robin shoved back her chair abruptly. "I have to go. See you guys at practice."

As Robin bolted from the cafeteria, I shot an

accusing glance at my twin. Jessica arched her eyebrows, all innocence. "What did I say?"

I didn't bother pointing out the obvious—that the topic of George's flying class had upset Robin, and that Jessica could have guessed that Robin might be insecure about George spending so much time with another pretty girl. Instead, I grabbed my book bag and scurried after Robin.

I caught up to her just outside the cafeteria door. "Robin, are you all right?" I asked, falling into step beside her.

She didn't even look at me. "I'm fine," she replied, her eyes fixed on the floor.

"What do you say we stop by the vending machines and get a snack, then sit outside for the rest of lunch period," I suggested.

"I'm not hungry," Robin said.

"But you didn't finish your lunch," I pointed out.

"I'm not hungry," she repeated stubbornly. "And I'm busy. I need to make some phone calls about this fund-raiser. I'll see you later."

As she started to walk away, I put my hand on her arm impulsively. "Robin, wait," I begged. She turned to look at me with reluctance. "Robin, I hope you won't think I'm being nosy, but . . ." I faltered. I didn't want to lecture her—I wasn't her mother, after all. "I know you want to keep slim," I attempted. "We all do. But if you overdo it, you'll end up—"

"Thanks, Liz, but I can take care of myself,"

she snapped, pulling away from me. "I've really got to run."

I bit my lip, chagrined. "Sorry," I said. "I was only trying to . . ." The sentence trailed off, unfinished. Robin had hurried away down the hall. And I knew that even if she could hear me, she wasn't listening.

Robin says she can take care of herself, but as far as I can tell, she's not doing a very good job of it. I'm really afraid that she's on the verge of being anorexic, or maybe even already is. I think she's having problems with George, but she won't talk about it. How bad will things have to get before she lets someone help her?

Speaking of help, I wish someone had some answers for me. I'm not used to being in a situation like this, where I feel so divided. Usually my sense of right and wrong is really solid, and as you know I pride myself on being an honest person. I'm avoiding Todd as much as I can because I'm sure that if he looks deeply into my eyes he'll see the truth there, that I've betrayed him. But I can't run from him, from THIS, forever. If I never saw Sam again, maybe I'd be able to face Todd. . . . I just don't know if I have the willpower, Diary.

I talked briefly on the phone with Sam today. He wanted to get together, but I had other plans, which is just as well. Jess walked in the room when we were on the phone and I made an excuse to hang up fast and then lied to her and told her it was Olivia. Help!

Super Sundae tomorrow. Hope the cheerleaders bought some mint chocolate chip!

Super Sundae was a big success yesterday. The cheerleaders raised almost seven hundred dollars to contribute toward the school's gym renovation fund. But it wasn't all fun and games. A really scary thing happened, just as we were making the giant sundaes. Robin fainted! Luckily Todd was standing right there and caught her before she hit the ground. She had to be rushed to the hospital—I rode with her in the amubulance. The doctors say she has pneumonia, which she caught because she's malnourished. She's been literally starving herself! Isn't that awful?

Poor Robin. We all knew there was a problem, but we had no idea it was that bad. Anorexia nervosa . . . it makes me shake just thinking about it. I visited her after school today and it wrung my heart to see how weak and small she looked in that big, white hospital bed. Getting better is going to be a long, hard road. . . .

When I got to the hospital, I found Robin's boyfriend, George, reading a magazine in the visitors' lounge. I sat down next to him. "How are you?" I asked.

He looked as if he hadn't slept in days, but he cracked a smile. "Better," he told me. "Because *she's* better. She actually ate some breakfast."

I squeezed George's hand. I understood that even a few bites of toast represented a huge victory. "Is she asleep?"

He shook his head. "She's resting, but she'll be happy to see you."

I walked to Robin's room. The door was ajar and I knocked lightly. "Come in," a small voice invited.

When she saw it was me, Robin's eyes lit up. I greeted her with a warm smile, careful not to let my emotions show, but it was hard not to look shocked. Could this pale, emaciated girl with the IV dripping into her toothpick arm really be athletic, vibrant Robin Wilson, varsity cheerleader and champion diver?

I pulled a chair close to the side of her bed. "How are they treating you?" I asked, my tone light.

"Pretty good," Robin said. Two spots of pink color brightened her white cheeks. "Liz, does everybody think I'm incredibly stupid?"

I took her hand and held it tightly. "Of course not, Robin," I assured her. "People are worried about you, but no one thinks you're stupid."

"I just don't know how this happened." She looked away from me, her gaze growing fuzzy. "Or maybe I do. I was so worried that George was going to dump me for Vicky. He didn't really give me any reason to be jealous, but I started to get obsessed about my weight. You don't know how afraid I am of getting fat again!"

"George doesn't love you because you're thin," I told her. "He loves you because you're Robin."

"I understand that now. I think. I only meant to lose a few extra pounds, Liz. But the less I ate, the less I wanted to eat." She shuddered. "It got to a point where it made me sick just to *look* at food. I know I should have talked to someone about how I was feeling, but I just couldn't."

"It's OK," I said gently. "The important thing is that you're getting help now. You're not alone."

Robin's brown eyes brimmed with tears. "Thanks for being there for me, Liz."

"You bet," I said.

"And tell Todd thanks too. For catching me when I fainted."

"I will," I promised.

"We're lucky to have such great boyfriends, aren't we?"

I looked at Robin, my own eyes suddenly damp. "Yeah," I whispered.

Visiting Robin in the hospital really made me think. Teenage girls today are so worried about their appearance. It's not only the effect of the images on TV and in advertising, but that's part of it. We set this impossible standard for ourselves and then feel terrible when we don't live up to it. I mean, how many people really look like supermodels? And why would we want to, anyhow? Sometimes you see models who have some flesh on their bones, but most of them are way too thin. I know girls at school who are dieting all the time—Robin isn't the only one. And supposedly eating disorders are a lot more common than you'd think. People just keep them secret. It makes me wonder: Who's next?

I can't forget about my conversation with Robin for another reason. It's ironic, isn't it, Diary? Robin started dieting obsessively because she thought her boyfriend was cheating on her. In fact, George was as loyal as could be. Meanwhile, Todd is completely trusting. He'd never in a million

101

years suspect me of cheating. But I did cheat. I went out with another boy. I kissed another boy.

Todd just called to ask about Robin and I passed on her thank-you message. I'm glad I didn't have to tell him in person—I'm sure I'd have burst into tears. I've never felt so guilty in my entire life, Diary. Todd is so kind and loving and generous and I'm so fickle and selfish and dishonest!

My secret is tearing me apart. I can't sleep, I can't eat, I bombed my last French quiz, and I submitted "Eyes and Ears" late, so the newspaper went to press without it. Todd doesn't know it, but I've put the two of us on a course to self-destruct because I'm diving into a new relationship without dealing with the old. How much longer can I go on leading a double life?

Part 2

Saturday, 3:00 P.M.

Dear Diary,

I played doubles this morning with Todd and Enid and Enid's cousin Jake Farrell, who's visiting for the weekend from San Francisco. Tom McKay and Penny and her boyfriend Neil Freemount, and a few others were there too— Enid organized a round robin because Jake's a serious tennis player. I didn't want to go at first because I wasn't in the mood to socialize, but I made the effort for Enid's sake, and I'm glad I did. In addition to being an awesome tennis player, Jake's a sweet guy with a great sense of humor. I ended up having a pretty good time. But I just can't be myself around

103

Todd. I can't believe he doesn't see right through me. . . .

"Good set," Enid said to Todd and me as we all headed for the water fountain.

She and Jake had just beaten Todd and me six games to one. "It wasn't even close," I pointed out wryly as I pushed my sweaty hair off of my forehead. "I'm afraid we weren't much competition for you, Jake."

Jake took a swig from a bottle of neon green sports drink. "You were terrific," he assured me with an easy smile. "Wilkins has a killer serve."

At that moment, Tom McKay arrived at the courts with his S.V.H. tennis teammate Barry Rork. As Enid introduced the two boys to her cousin, Todd put an arm around my waist and steered me over to a bench that was out of earshot of our friends.

"Liz, are you feeling OK?" he asked once we were sitting down.

A feeling of panic fluttered in my stomach. I darted a fast glance at him, trying to guess what had prompted the question. I was planning to meet Sam at the beach later—it would be the first time I'd seen him since our romantic day at Castillo San Angelo ten days earlier. Could Todd tell? "I know I didn't play my best," I mumbled.

"It's not that," said Todd. "You played fine. You

just seem . . . I don't know. Distracted or something."

That was the understatement of the decade, but I couldn't own up to it. I took a deep breath, then stretched my mouth in a bright smile, hoping I looked cheerful and untroubled. "I was just a little nervous, I think, because Enid's talked so much about what a good player Jake is, and I didn't want to double fault all over the place and look like an idiot in front of him," I improvised.

It was a feeble explanation. I'm not usually insecure and self-conscious when it comes to sports, or anything else for that matter.

To my boundless relief, though, my fake smile seemed to satisfy him. "Jake's in a different league, but he was pretty gracious," Todd said. "I think he had fun. Come on. Let's get revenge by trouncing Neil and Penny."

Grabbing my hand, Todd led me over to the far tennis court where Neil and Penny were hitting balls. When they saw us, they waved. I waved back with genuine enthusiasm. I hadn't been much in the mood for tennis before, but all of a sudden I was dying to get back behind the baseline. Once we were playing, Todd wouldn't be able to ask me any more personal questions!

"So," you say, "if two-timing makes you feel so crummy, why did you just

105

spritz some of Jessica's new Romantique
perfume behind your ears?" I'm heading
out now to meet Sam at our usual spot
on the beach. I can't stay long because
I'm going out tonight with Todd, Enid,
Jake, and a bunch of other people. I
hope Sam doesn't ask too many ques-
tions about my plans. Todd isn't the only
one I'm deceiving.

Later the same day

Todd will be here in a few minutes to
pick me up to go to the Beach Disco. I just
have to write down quickly what happened
at the beach with Sam. . . .

As I drove the Fiat toward the coast, I was
already having second thoughts about meeting
Sam. Not only because of the usual conflict,
that I was two-timing Todd, although that continued to gnaw at me, of course. I was also
being unfair to Sam, since I only had about an
hour before I'd need to head home again . . . to
start getting ready for my date with Todd. I'd
neglected to mention that to Sam, who was
probably assuming we'd spend the whole
evening together.

He was waiting for me in the parking lot,
leaning back against the weather-beaten rail

fence that separated the pavement from the sand dunes. When he saw me, a happy smile creased his tanned face. I strolled over to him, trying to look casual, but when he wrapped an arm around my shoulders and pulled me close for a hello kiss, my reserve melted instantly. The warmth between us was intense—my whole body sizzled.

We were both wearing swimsuits, and we plunged right into the waves to cool off. After a few minutes of playful splashing, we collapsed on Sam's oversized beach towel. "I like the beach as much as the next guy," Sam said. Propping himself up on one arm, he reached over to brush a damp tendril of hair out of my eyes. "But you should really let me pick you up at your house next time."

I lay on my back, gazing up at him and hoping he wasn't a mind reader. "This is so much easier, though," I reasoned. "Kind of a halfway point, you know? My house is really out of the way for you."

"It's no problem," he insisted. "Plus, if you don't want to ride the dirt bike, I can borrow my mom's station wagon. It would feel more like a real date." He sat up and placed a hand on the towel on either side of my body. Then he bent over and kissed me straight on the mouth. A shock of pleasure radiated through me. Even my toes tingled. "Besides," he murmured, his lips still close to mine, "I'm ready to meet Mom and Dad and that identical twin sister of yours."

Of course it wasn't strange for Sam to want to pick me up at home and meet my family, but I couldn't help reacting somewhat violently to the suggestion. "No," I blurted out before I'd had time to think.

He pulled back, lifting his eyebrows. "No what?"

I sat up, hugging my knees to my chest. "What I meant was no, not today. My parents and Jessica . . . they're, um, not around."

"Next time, then?"

"Maybe."

Sam frowned slightly. "Why 'maybe'?" he asked, sounding a little bit hurt.

I bit my lip. "Look, Sam," I said. "It's not you. I mean, I'm not trying to hide you or anything." My face turned bright red, because of course that was *exactly* what I was trying to do. "It's just that . . . I'm not ready. I haven't even told my family that I'm dating someone new." That much at least was true. "I just don't want to deal with the questions, the pressure. Do you know what I mean?"

He gazed into my eyes, his expression somber. I could tell he was trying hard to understand where I was coming from . . . which had to be a challenge, since I didn't even know myself. "I guess," he said cautiously.

"There's plenty of time for all that," I assured

him. I put a hand on his arm. "Right now, isn't it fun to just be *us*?"

The sun had crept behind the clouds for a minute, but now it was shining again and Sam was smiling again too. "You bet," he said as I pulled him back down on the towel for another kiss. "I can't argue with that."

I still had to break the news that I couldn't stay long, but for a few minutes, I let myself forget about Todd, Jake, Enid, and the Beach Disco. Sam and I lay in each other's arms talking about whatever popped into our heads: our favorite rock bands, movies we'd seen recently, books we'd read, places we wanted to travel to. "My friend Nathan just got back from the coolest vacation," Sam told me. "Scuba diving at the Great Barrier Reef off Australia. Wouldn't that be amazing?"

"I'd love to go there," I agreed. "I just read this really great novel that takes place 'down under.'"

"Speaking of Nathan, he's having a party tonight," Sam went on. "After we get a bite to eat, we can swing by his house. We don't have to stay long, but I've been telling my buddies about you, and they're dying to meet you."

I was glad I had an excuse not to go with Sam to the party. How could I explain that I didn't want to meet his friends, or rather, simply couldn't? I couldn't be his girlfriend in public . . . not yet, and maybe not ever. *What if he's friends with somebody from the Bridgewater High basketball team?* I thought. *Someone who might know Todd?*

"I actually have other plans for tonight," I said. "I was just about to tell you."

"Oh?"

"See, my best friend Enid's cousin is in town, so a bunch of us are going out dancing. You know, just to show him a good time while he's in town."

"That sounds fun," Sam said. "Sure, let's do that instead."

I blanched. The only thing that was more unthinkable than going with Sam to his friend Nathan's party was taking him with me to the Beach Disco! "No, what I mean is . . . Don't take this the wrong way, Sam," I said softly. "I'd like you to meet my friends . . . at some point. But tonight just wouldn't be good. I sort of need to help Enid entertain Jake. He doesn't know anybody in Sweet Valley. It just might be a little . . . distracting . . . to have you there too. Next time, OK?"

Sam looked disappointed, but he nodded. "Sure, Elizabeth. I understand. But you know, I'm ready to go public. I'd like you to meet my parents and my friends."

"I'd like that too," I said. "One of these days."

We kissed again. Then I got to my feet, wrapping my beach towel around my bare shoulders. "I have to run," I told Sam reluctantly.

"I'll call you."

"No, I'll call you," I promised as I waved goodbye and hurried off across the sand.

It was definitely awkward fending off Sam's questions. Naturally, he's starting to wonder why we always have to meet at the beach and why I make such sudden exits. I think I can put off the introduction-to-family-and-friends thing for a little bit longer, but he won't be satisfied with my lame excuses forever. But then, this situation can't go on forever. At some point either I'll stop seeing Sam on the sly or I'll be able to be his girlfriend openly, like he wants. Which would mean breaking up with Todd. Oh, gosh, I can't believe I even wrote those words down! Breaking up with Todd. No, that's not at all what I want to do . . . is it?

Sunday, noon

Dear Diary,

I slept in this morning because I was up really, really late last night. The Beach Disco ended up being much more interesting than I thought it would be. I expected a run-of-the-mill evening. Todd and I have

111

*had some very special dates there, but as
you know, my mind is sort of elsewhere
these days. There must have been something in the air, though! The Beach Disco
was like the enchanted forest in* A
Midsummer's Night Dream. *Girls chasing
boys, boys chasing girls, people falling in
and out of love. . . .*

*Not surprisingly, my sister managed
to be in the middle of all the romantic
mischief. She and Lila were vying to see
who could dance the most with Enid's
cousin.* Jake is remarkably good-
looking—dark curly hair, hazel eyes, styl-
ish clothes—and has turned a lot of
heads. I myself planned to stay on the
fringes of all the flirting, but I ended up
falling in love. . . .

True to its name, the Beach Disco is right near
the water, with an open-air dance floor adjacent
to a sandy beach. When the music isn't blasting,
you can hear the pounding of the surf, and with
the moon and stars overhead, it's hard to imagine
a more romantic spot for slow dancing with the
one you love. Which meant it was kind of hard to
explain to Todd why I wasn't really in the mood to
dance. "I think I'll sit this one out," I told him
when a slow song came on. "I'm really thirsty. Do
you want something to drink?"

"I'll get us both some juice," he offered.

As Todd disappeared into the crowd, I headed for a quiet corner where I wouldn't have to talk to anybody. Before I could escape, though, I was ambushed by my twin sister. "Liz!" Jessica said, grabbing my arm. "Have you seen Jake?"

"On the dance floor," I told her.

"He'd better not be slow dancing with Lila!" Jessica declared, tossing her long blond hair.

I laughed. "Why, what are you going to do to him if he is?"

"It's what I'll do to *her*," Jessica said. "I want Jake to fall in love with *me!*"

"Who says he's going to fall in love with anyone?" I asked. "He's only here for a weekend, after all. Maybe he's not looking for a romantic encounter."

"Who's *not* looking for romance?" Jessica countered. "Especially when it's with me?"

I couldn't argue with that. I watched as my sister whipped a makeup tube from her purse, then began touching up her lip gloss, which was the same bright red as her swirly miniskirt. A close-fitting, scooped-neck black top and black bangle bracelets finished off her outfit, which was definitely eye-catching. Any boy would take a second look.

"Well, good luck with Jake," I said.

"Don't wait up for me when you get home," she replied with a playful wink.

At that moment, she spotted her prey and

charged off with the fearless determination of a big-game hunter. I was about to wander inside to the bar to look for Todd when I noticed a tall blond guy standing in the shadows of a palm tree just outside the circle of sparkling lights that illuminated the dance floor. He was watching me, and when our eyes met, my heart stood still.

It was Sam.

I was immediately seized by conflicting impulses. I wanted to run *to* him and *away* from him at the same time. I considered pretending I didn't see him, but it was too late. He tossed me a half smile and a sheepish wave—I had no choice.

After glancing over my shoulder to make sure Todd was nowhere in sight, I hurried over to Sam. "What are you doing here?" I asked, taking his arm to draw him deeper into the shadows.

"I hope you're not mad," he said. "I know you're here with some other people, but I just really wanted to see you tonight."

"How did you know where to find me?"

"You said you and your friends were going dancing," he answered. "This was a lucky guess. So, how about it?" He smiled down at me, his eyes glowing. "Would you like to dance?"

Somehow, his arms had slipped around me. The embrace was so tender, I never wanted it to end. *But if anyone sees us!* . . . I thought, my heart hammering at the risk I was about to take.

114

"I'd like to dance with you," I said somewhat breathlessly. "Very much."

When he started to pull me toward the outdoor dance area, I gestured toward a side door that led back into the club. "It's more private inside," I told him, knowing that the Sweet Valley High crowd preferred to dance under the stars. "More romantic."

I took Sam's hand and he followed me inside. The slow song was still playing. We melted into each other's arms, our bodies swaying as one. "You're a great dancer," Sam murmured.

"This isn't really dancing," I pointed out. "It's something a lot more basic."

He kissed the smile that was teasing the corners of my mouth. "It's fun, though, isn't it?"

I nodded. It certainly was!

His mouth lingered on mine, sending the usual shiver of pleasure down my spine. I was savoring our closeness, but I didn't let myself get completely carried away. I knew this magic moment could be only that: a moment. I'd have to go back to Todd. Soon.

"I saw you with your sister," Sam remarked.

"Did you have trouble telling us apart?" I asked. In contrast to Jessica, I'd dressed casually, in khakis and a striped tank top.

"No way," Sam said. "She's beautiful, of course, since she looks almost exactly like you. But you . . . there's just something special about

115

you that sets you apart from all the other girls here. You're . . . you're *Elizabeth.*" He laughed wryly. "I must sound like a lovesick idiot."

"No." The sweetness of his words brought tears to my eyes. "Sam, I have to tell you something," I blurted out.

"What is it?" he asked.

I looked up into his eyes. They were so trusting, so full of love. *I have to tell him,* I thought. Then, a split second later, *I can't tell him.* "Oh, Sam," I cried, my throat constricting. "You're such a wonderful person. But I'm . . . I'm not the girl you think I am."

"What do you mean?"

"There's something you don't know about me. I—" I stopped. I couldn't bring myself to spell it out.

"There are plenty of things I don't know about you," Sam said.

"But this one . . ." I dropped my eyes, ashamed. "If you knew," I continued in a tortured whisper, "you'd never want to see me again."

I expected him to let me go, to step away and take another look at me. Instead his arms tightened around me. "I don't believe that, Elizabeth," he said. "Nothing could make me feel that way."

"But, Sam, I—"

"Ssh." He placed a finger gently across my lips. "Don't tell me, then. I was being nosy this

116

afternoon at the beach, asking you a lot of personal questions. I don't need to know any more than I know now. I know enough about you to be sure that you're the most wonderful girl I've ever met and that I'm crazy in love with you."

It was the first time either of us had spoken of love. I stared up at him, amazed that such strong feelings could have grown between us in such a short time. "I—I—" I stuttered, not certain I was ready to say the words back to him.

Sam didn't pressure me. Instead he pulled me to him, cradling me against his chest. We didn't talk further, but just held each other close, swaying to the music. I knew it was time to get back to Todd, but I clung to Sam for just a minute longer. *Is this love?* I wondered, my head spinning. And if it was, what did it say about my feelings for Todd? Could I truly love two boys at the same time?

I can't tell you how weird it was to go from the arms of one boy straight to another. Luckily, Sam didn't stay long at the Beach Disco after our conversation, so he didn't see me slow dancing later on with Todd. As for Todd, when he asked where I'd disappeared to, I said I'd been to the girls' room. Needless to say, he didn't press me for details. If there's one thing guys don't want to know about, it's what goes on in girls' rooms!

Back to Sam. I can't believe this has gone so far, so fast. It's not just a casual fling anymore. He told me he loved me! And I was on the verge of saying, "I love you too."

Sam promised he wouldn't ask me any more personal questions, but my nerves are still on edge. I'm juggling two boys at once, and neither knows about the other. At least tonight, I'm pretty sure I'll only have to deal with Todd. Enid's giving a party for Jake's last night in Sweet Valley, and I have to put in an appearance. Jessica's planning to go too. Ordinarily she wouldn't be caught dead at a party of Enid's, but she's still hoping to snag Jake Farrell. I wish Jessica would meet someone nice and settle down. It's kind of ironic that when Sam and I first met, he assumed I was the Wakefield twin he'd seen on TV. It probably would've been better if he'd hooked up with Jessica! She's the one who's looking for a boyfriend. No, I don't mean that. Sam's not Jessica's type at all. He's adventurous and funny, but he's also smart and sensitive. He's perfect for me . . . but then again, so is Todd. That's the problem!

I called Sam from a pay phone in town this afternoon. It felt so clandestine and wrong, but I just wanted to hear his voice. I told him I had a really busy week and wouldn't be able to see him until the weekend. It will be hard to stay away from our beach, but that buys me some time to figure out what I'm going to do.

Enid's been acting kind of upset and preoccupied this week, and yesterday I finally persuaded her to tell me what's on her mind. It turns out that she found out this past weekend that her cousin Jake is gay. She was so surprised when he told her that she's worried she wasn't as supportive as she should have been. It must have been a really difficult conversation for them both. Jake must know from experience that a lot of people are shocked at first when he tells them. But as far as I can tell, Enid did and said all the right things. After she got back her composure, she let Jake know that of course she still loves and supports him. Their relationship won't change because of this. I told her I

119

was really proud of her. I think she's incredibly caring and empathetic. I don't know how I'd react if a cousin or close friend of mine made a confession like that. I think I'm pretty open-minded and tolerant, but you never know how deep your convictions are until they're put to the test.

I promised Enid that Jake's secret would be safe with me, but I almost wish I could tell Jessica. Jess still thinks that if Jake had only spent another day or two in Sweet Valley, he would have fallen madly in love with her. Talk about barking up the wrong tree!

Thursday, 7:30 P.M.

I had an interesting encounter at Project Youth today. Have I mentioned Project Youth in here before? It's a teen center in town where kids can go for support groups and counseling about all sorts of stuff like drug and alcohol abuse, sexuality, and dealing with family and school problems. They have a hotline too, that's staffed by volunteers from S.V.H.

Anyway, I'm writing an article about the clinic for The Oracle, so I dropped by to talk with the director and interview some of the volunteers. While I was there, I bumped into Tom McKay in the waiting room, and he was reading a pamphlet called "Teens and Homosexuality." It was an awkward moment, to put it mildly—Tom turned as red as a beet. But we ended up having a really good talk. He's trying to make up his mind whether to tell the people he's close to what's going on with him, and it's especially hard because he's not even sure yet that he is gay. He's sort of just questioning his sexuality. I really hope that, if and when word does get out that Tom's gay, kids at school will be accepting. It's wild, though, isn't it, Diary? This explains why his relationship with Jean didn't work out. I wonder how Jean will react? How would I feel if it were my boyfriend or ex-boyfriend?

I learned something else at Project Youth. Amy Sutton's one of their hotline volunteers! I interviewed her for my article, and talk about a revelation. I hate to admit it, being a blond myself, but I've always privately labeled her a dumb blond. Apparently, though, although she is flaky and boy crazy (she's been chasing the wrong guy lately, though . . . Tom McKay!), she's not as self-centered as I thought. She started volunteering at Project Youth to get some background for a sociology paper she had to write for school, but she found out that she really enjoyed it, so she told me she's going to stick with it. You should hear the other staffers rave about how good she is on the phone lines!

It just goes to show you can't judge a person by what's on the outside. Personality and character are really complicated things. I discovered that today about Amy and Tom. I guess we all have secrets, Diary. It takes courage and honesty to examine yourself and uncover what your secrets really mean about you, though. I'm falling in love with Sam, but I still love Todd. I wish I knew what that secret means about me. Maybe I should call the hotline!

Sunday, 5:30 P.M.

All's well that ends well (at least, according to Shakespeare!). Enid called Jake in San Francisco the other day and made it clear that she loves him for who he is. He promised that he'd visit Sweet Valley again before too long. I'm really glad for both of them. Enid's a true *friend, and even though her cousin seems like a strong, self-confident guy, I bet there will be times when he'll need to lean on her.*

I have some news about Amy Sutton too. It looks like after dating every other boy at S.V.H., she's found true love at last —Barry Rork! I've never seen her so happy. I think this relationship will do wonders for her.

Sigh. I remember a time when my love life felt as if it were wrapped up just as neatly. Now I'm so confused, I can't think straight about anything. Last night, I went over to Todd's and we rented Casablanca. It seemed like a good choice, because it's my favorite and his too. I really wanted us to feel connected while we watched it—I was trying so hard to get that magic back. But instead, even though I was in Todd's arms, all I could think about was Sam. . . .

Todd and I have both seen *Casablanca* a zillion times. It's such a great, great movie.

On the surface, everything about this particular evening should have been perfect. Todd's parents were at the symphony, so we had the house to ourselves. Todd had dimmed the lights in the family room, and we were cuddled as close as we could get on the overstuffed leather sofa, our arms and legs comfortably intertwined. He was stroking my hair, his body keeping me warm, while on the television screen Humphrey Bogart and Ingrid Bergman were generating some heat of their own.

Everything was perfect, but the movie wasn't having the effect I'd desired. It was getting to me, but in all the wrong ways.

"I can't stand to watch," I moaned, when it got to the part where Ilse was going to have to choose between her husband, Victor, and her lover, Rick.

"What do you mean?" Todd slid a hand under my shirt and tickled my ribs. "She picks the right guy."

I shook my head. "She doesn't love him, though."

"Sure she does," Todd said.

"Well, OK, but she loves Rick more."

"Ssh," said Todd. "This is the best scene."

It's just a movie, I reminded myself as the suspenseful story played itself out. And it wasn't as if I didn't know how it would end. Ilse and Rick had fallen in love in Paris during World War II. She'd thought her husband, the famous resistance hero Victor Laslo, had been killed by the Nazis. But then Ilse and Rick were separated. He retreated to Casablanca, where she eventually turned up . . . with Victor, who wasn't dead after all.

As the movie neared the end, I had to fight

back the tears. "Why doesn't Rick take the two border passes and escape to America with Ilse?" I said with a sniffle, fumbling for the box of tissues on the end table.

"Because underneath his cynicism, he's a gentleman," said Todd. "He's honorable. And no matter how much he loves her, he can't forget that she's another man's wife."

I stared at the TV, my eyes swimming with tears. It was the final scene, on the misty airport tarmac. "The problems of three little people don't amount to a hill of beans in this crazy world," Humphrey Bogart said to Ingrid Bergman. "If you don't go with him, you'll never forgive yourself."

"She should stay with Rick," I whispered. "He's the one she really loves."

"What?" said Todd.

I shook my head, a tear rolling down my cheek. One step ahead of the pursuing Nazis, Ilse got on the plane with Victor. The plane's engine roared as it disappeared into the mist, leaving Rick standing alone on the airstrip. Bogie spoke the movie's great last line, to Claude Rains as the constable: "I think this is the beginning of a beautiful friendship."

Todd clicked the remote, rewinding the tape. I was still sniffling. "Liz," he said, laughing. "It's supposed to be a happy ending."

I hiccuped. "How can you call that happy?"

125

"OK, not happy, but inevitable," he amended. "It couldn't have ended any other way." He wrapped his arms tightly around me, nuzzling my neck. "What a great love story, huh?"

I nodded mutely. What Todd couldn't know was how much *our* love story resembled the one in *Casablanca*. Ilse, Rick, and Victor were caught in a triangle, and so were Todd, Sam, and I. Just like Victor, Todd had no idea there was another man in the equation. Just like Ilse, I was bound to one man, while pining for another.

I lay limp in Todd's arms as he kissed me. *Sam*, I thought, the ache in my heart almost unbearable.

I can't go on like this, Diary. I have to make a choice, just like Ilse did. And once I make it, I'll have to live with it forever, just like her. There will be no going back. If I break up with Todd to go out with another boy, he'll never forgive me, and if I end things with Sam, I'll never see him again. I'm trying to understand my heart, but it's just so hard. Whom do I love more, Todd or Sam? Are my feelings for Sam genuine, or is it just the thrill of a new romance? Do Todd and I have the potential to rekindle the fire that used to burn between us? If I choose one boy over the

126

other, will I always be haunted by the ghost of the love I let die?

Sunday afternoon

I haven't written in here for weeks and weeks. I've been too depressed to pick up a pen. But I think my broken heart is finally beginning to mend.

I made the choice, Diary. Two days after my last journal entry, I stopped seeing Sam. As much as I cared for him, I had no alternative. Todd just means too much to me. But it was the hardest thing I've ever had to do. . . .

It was a gray, damp day at the beach. The wind had a sharp edge that cut through the thin fabric of my cotton sweater. But I knew that, even if it had been sunny, I still would have felt chilled to the bone.

Because of the weather, only a few die-hard surfers were out on the waves. Sam and I were alone on the shore. He'd arrived first, and as I walked toward him, I could almost believe for a moment that we were the only two people in the world. But I knew better. These stolen hours at the beach with Sam weren't my real life. Sam loved me, but someone else loved me even more, because he'd loved me longer.

When I reached Sam, he put his hands on my shoulders, rubbing them briskly. "Elizabeth, you're shivering," he observed.

"I—it's cold," I stammered.

"I rode over as fast as I could." Still gripping my shoulders, he looked into my face, his forehead creased. "You sounded upset on the phone. What's up?"

I didn't want to say what I'd come to the beach to say, but I had to. Prolonging the scene would only make it more painful. "Sam, I can't see you anymore," I said bluntly.

His hands dropped from my shoulders. "Elizabeth, what's happened?" he asked.

"Nothing's happened," I told him. I reached in my pocket for a tissue. "I just . . . can't. I'm sorry. We've had a lot of fun together."

Sam's face turned pale. "I don't understand," he said gruffly. He too, appeared to be struggling with his emotions. "If it's because of what we talked about the other night at the Beach Disco, I swear, Elizabeth, I won't pry into your life. I just want to be part of it. I'll take whatever you'll give me."

I shook my head, the tears starting in earnest. Why did he have to make this so hard? "It wouldn't work, Sam. Take my word for it." I thought about how I'd been shortchanging Todd lately. "A relationship can't be a halfway, part-time thing. I care about you, but I can't commit myself fully to you."

128

"Why?"

The question shouldn't have come as a surprise. I'd have asked the same thing, if our positions had been reversed. Nevertheless, it stunned me momentarily. The answer was simple, but for some reason, I choked on the words. *I already have a boyfriend. This whole time, I've been going out with someone else.*

Sam waited for me to respond, his expression naked with confusion, distress, and longing. I knew in my heart that I owed him the truth, but in a flash, I realized that if I *told* him the truth, he'd never forgive me. And selfishly, I wanted to keep his good opinion. I would cherish my memories of him, and I wanted him to do the same. He didn't have to go on loving me, but I didn't want him to hate me.

"Good-bye, Sam," I whispered.

"Elizabeth, don't go," he begged.

I started to walk away. He reached out for me, his hand just brushing my sleeve. I broke into a run. "Try to forget about me," I sobbed. The wind tore the words from me, tumbling them over the sand. "Some other girl will make you happier."

I ran to the car, half hoping Sam would follow and try to talk me out of leaving. But when I looked back over my shoulder, I saw that he'd remained on the beach. He'd turned his back to stare out at the gray, churning surf.

I climbed into the driver's seat and jammed the

key in the Fiat's ignition. The engine started with a roar. Gravel spit from beneath the tires as I backed up, a little bit too fast, from my parking place. Half blind with tears, I sped onto the coast highway.

I'd never return to this beach—ever. "Good-bye, Sam," I whispered one final time.

Supposedly time heals all wounds, so eventually I guess it will heal this one, but for now, my heart still aches. The hardest part is not being able to talk to anyone about this. I came close to confiding in Jessica the other day, but then I changed my mind. She'd insist on knowing every single detail of what happened between Sam and me, and I just don't want to expose those private moments to her curiosity.

So, the chapter's closed. I'll never know what might have been. I'm concentrating on looking forward rather than backward, which means repairing my relationship with Todd (though of course he doesn't even realize it's damaged). But I miss Sam, Diary—I can't pretend otherwise. I miss him so, so much.

Wednesday, 9:00 P.M.

Diary, I've never been so furious in my entire life. You will not believe what my utterly thoughtless sister has done this time. She's entered the Miss Teen Sweet Valley Pageant! A beauty contest! Prancing around in high heels and swimsuits. Can you imagine anything more out-of-date and sexist and demeaning? Ugh. Just thinking about it makes me ill!

Jessica's trying to justify it by pointing out that the Sweet Valley Chamber of Commerce is sponsoring the contest as a fund-raiser for a new community swimming pool, but she's batty if she thinks anyone's going to buy the story that she's entering out of civic spirit.

Naturally, I'm not the only one who thinks the beauty pageant is ridiculous. Most of my friends agree with me, so Enid and I decided to organize a protest committee. We recruited a bunch of people (including Dana, Olivia, Todd, Winston, and Maria) to help collect signatures for a petition. I don't know if we can stop the Chamber of Commerce from holding the pageant, but maybe we can keep it out of the S.V.H. auditorium. A beauty contest just sends absolutely the worst message to girls and to guys—the message that for women, looks matter more than substance. Forget talent and Miss Congeniality— nobody pays any attention to that stuff. It really comes down to how you look in an evening gown and a bathing suit. It just kills me!

So, you can picture the scene at the dinner table tonight when Jessica announced that she was entering the contest at exactly the same moment I announced that I was going to try to keep the pageant from taking place. I'm not sure who was madder, her or me! She stomped off right in the middle of the meal. Jessica can be so clueless, and most of the time it doesn't affect anyone but herself, but this is one occasion when she ought to sit down and really consider the implications of what she's doing. But she won't listen to reason. Her attitude is, who needs self-respect when you might get to wear a little gold crown on your head? How can I argue with something like that?

Friday, 11:00 P.M.

I have to say, Diary, even though I'm steamed about the beauty pageant, there's a good side to it. I have a cause to throw myself into, and you know me—I never do things halfway. I'm totally on the warpath! Which means I'm almost too busy and tired to think about Sam Woodruff. (Note the word almost!).

After school today, I canvased the Valley Mall with my petition. I got about fifty signatures—a pretty good start. While I was there, I bumped into Barry and Amy. I got the impression Barry might have signed the petition if it weren't for the fact that Amy's entered in the contest! I guess volunteering at Project Youth and dating Barry hasn't totally transformed her—she's still an airhead.

Speaking of airheads, Jessica was at the mall today too. She actually managed to sweet-talk the manager at Simple Splendor to loan her a formal gown. "It will be good publicity for the boutique if the winner of the Miss Teen Sweet Valley contest—me—is wearing one of their creations"—that was the line she gave them, and they went for it. She showed me the dress and got mad when I made fun of it, but I couldn't help laughing. It's a total princess affair: frothy and pink and covered with pearls. Can you stand it?

As if that wasn't enough activity for one day, tonight the protest committee *held a meeting at my house. We discussed our plan of action and painted signs to carry at a march in front of the Sweet Valley courthouse tomorrow morning. I was kind of tired and on edge and I'm afraid I took my mood out on Todd, but he was sweet about it, as always. . . .*

"What's with Jessica?" asked Todd as he reached into the takeout box for the last slice of pizza.

The protest committee had devoured the three pizzas I'd ordered in record time. In the middle of our pizza break, my sister had entered the basement. I thought she was coming down to ask for a slice, but instead she'd walked past us as if she didn't see us, carefully stepping over the cans of paint and pieces of paper board spread over the floor. After retrieving a record album from a stack of my parents' old sixties and seventies LPs, she marched back upstairs, ignoring Todd's offer to take some pizza with her.

I picked up a paintbrush, shrugging off Todd's question. "How should I know?"

"I didn't expect her to hang out and paint signs," Todd said. "I've just never seen her turn down Guido's pepperoni and mushroom."

"Maybe she's watching her weight for the pageant," I said sarcastically, jabbing my paintbrush

134

somewhat viciously into a can of bright orange paint.

Todd cocked an eyebrow. "Do I sense a family feud?"

"You got it," I confirmed.

"Who started it?"

"Does it matter?"

"Maybe. You seem really tense." Todd placed a hand on my back and rubbed gently. "I know you feel this beauty contest thing exploits women and all that, but Jessica's still your sister. Fighting with her always makes you unhappy. Why not agree to disagree?"

"Wait a minute." I paused in the middle of painting "No Beauty Pageants at S.V.H." on a piece of white cardboard in order to frown at Todd. "Whose side are you on?"

"Yours, silly," he assured me.

"But you think I should drop the protest and support Jessica's lofty ambition to become the first ever Miss Teen Sweet Valley?"

"I didn't say that." Todd laughed. "Of course I think you should go forward with the protest. I'm here, aren't I? But believing strongly in something doesn't mean you can't find common ground with someone who holds a different belief. You and Jessica don't have to become enemies over this."

I continued to scowl. Todd reached over and took the paintbrush from my hand so he could give me a hug. "Just talk to her, Liz," he urged. "You'll both feel a lot better."

I couldn't resist the hug. My mouth twitched a little—not quite a smile, but close. "You're right," I conceded grudgingly.

Todd's arms tightened around me. "Aren't I always?"

I pushed him away. "Chauvinist!" I kidded.

"Hey!" He held up a sign he'd painted earlier: "More Than Just a Pretty Face." "How can you call me that when I'm putting my tough-guy reputation on the line for women's rights?"

I'm really lucky to have a boyfriend like Todd. There are some macho guys at school who think the protest committee is dumb and wouldn't be caught dead marching around town with a "No More Pageants" sign, but Todd's self-confident. He likes having a girlfriend who's smart and thinks for herself. He's also just so totally level-headed and reasonable. He's right about this situation with Jessica: She and I should accept each other's different opinions. I plan to take the first opportunity to talk things over with her.

Monday, 4:00 P.M.

Guess what, Diary? I wrote a story about the beauty pageant for The Oracle

136

and it's being picked up by The Sweet Valley News! An editor called this morning to get permission to print it in the evening edition—she described my article as "concise and well-written." Isn't that awesome?

The only problem is, I'm afraid this will dig the canyon between Jessica and me even deeper. When I got the phone call, I was so excited, I rushed right into Jessica's room without even thinking. I'm just so used to sharing good news with her—for a second, I forgot we were fighting. Needless to say, she wasn't happy at the thought of the whole town reading my article, or "sermon," as Jessica snidely referred to it. (The piece basically trashes the beauty pageant and says that the girls entering it are traitors to their gender. Do you think that's too extreme? I don't!)

So much for making peace with my sister. I've tried a bunch of times to take Todd's advice and talk to her, but she won't meet me halfway. She says I'm being stubborn and unfair, but she's ten times more stubborn than I am!

Tuesday, 8:00 P.M.

Jessica has been late for dinner every night this week, and when she comes

137

home she's exhausted. Since we're offi-
cially not speaking, I can't ask her what's
up, but I think it has to do with the
beauty pageant. Mom knows something,
but she's keeping her lips zipped. Jess is
probably taking charm classes, or maybe
she's off somewhere rehearsing her an-
swers to the judges' questions, such as, "If
you were head of the United Nations,
Miss Wakefield, what would you do to
make the world a better place?" Jessica:
"I'd ensure that everyone has access to a
wide range of salon-quality hairstyling
products." Ha!

Wednesday afternoon

This beauty pageant business is turn-
ing into the War of the Wakefields.
Believe it or not, Jessica and I got to de-
bate the subject for a local TV news
program—we'll be on the air tonight! A
reporter who'd read my article in The
Sweet Valley News *noticed Jessica's*
name on the list of pageant contestants
and decided that interviewing two sis-
ters on opposite sides of the issue would
make a good story. He talked to us at
school today, during study hall. I think
I was very articulate and persuasive.

Jessica, on the other hand, was all dimples and charm, simpering at the camera every chance she got. That's exactly the sort of attitude that undermines young women's confidence in their own intelligence. Not that Jessica didn't speak well, because she did. She has this standard line down, about how pageants reward "intelligence, poise, talent, and hard work, as well as beauty." Yeah, right. Tell me about it. I countered by arguing that millions of little girls watch beauty pageants on TV and because of that they develop totally warped perceptions of how they should look and what they should strive for. That shut Jess up for a minute or two!

I can't say I "won" the debate, because it wasn't really a debate—just an exchange of views. Hopefully it will inspire more people to protest the pageant. Jessica, of course, hopes it'll build more support for the pageant. We'll see fairly soon because the pageant's scheduled for this coming Saturday night!

Later on Wednesday

After dinner tonight, the whole family gathered around the TV in the family room to watch Jessica and me on the local news. Steven was down from college for the evening, and he and Mom and Dad clapped and whistled and cheered when Jess and I appeared on screen. I could tell Jessica was a little nervous, and so was I, but we both ended up feeling pleased with our performances. She thought she looked pretty and I thought I sounded smart and sincere. In a nutshell, that's the difference between us!

Afterward seemed like a good time to hold peace talks with Jessica. There we were, actually in the same room—a rare occurrence these days! But Jessica doesn't seem interested in a cease-fire. . . .

When the interview was over, my mother turned off the television. "There's cold chicken and salad in the kitchen for anyone who wants it," she announced.

Steven and Dad trailed Mom out of the family room. Jessica started to follow them. "Jess, wait," I said. "Can we talk for a minute?"

Jessica stopped in the doorway, then turned to face me, her expression blank. I noticed for the first time that she was wearing a leotard and sweats. She looked like she'd just come home from a workout, but it was way too late for cheerleading practice. "What?" she asked curtly.

140

"Sit down," I invited, patting the sofa cushion next to me.

She narrowed her eyes suspiciously, then perched on the arm of the sofa with her legs and arms crossed. Her body language was as hostile as it could be, but I decided to forge ahead anyhow. "Jess, don't you think this cold war is getting out of hand?"

"I'm just minding my own business," she said, her tone still frosty.

"Well, the atmosphere around here is really awful," I noted. "It's my fault too. But I'm ready to call a truce if you are."

She raised her eyebrows. "You mean, you're calling off the protest?"

I shook my head. "I have to do what I think is right. So, no, I'm not calling it off."

Jessica rose to her feet, glowering once more. "Then what is there to talk about?" she snapped.

"I guess I just want you to know that I'm sorry if I've hurt your feelings by taking a stand against beauty pageants," I said, still trying to keep a cordial tone. "I know you're mad about it, but you shouldn't take it personally."

"I shouldn't take it *personally?*" Jessica laughed bitterly. "That's a good one, Liz. I shouldn't take it personally that you attacked me in your newspaper article and then tried to make me look like a fool on TV!"

"That's just the point," I exclaimed. "I wasn't

attacking *you*. I'm against the idea of beauty pageants. It's not personal."

"It *is* personal," Jessica insisted as she marched toward the door. "The beauty pageant isn't just an idea. It's a real event with real people involved, and one of them happens to be your sister, but you don't care about that. You just care about your stupid self-righteous principles." She glared at me, her eyes dark with anger. "It must be a real burden, Saint Elizabeth, to feel so perfect and superior that you have to try to reform the whole world."

Before I could respond, she stomped from the room. I sat for a few moments, stunned, listening to her footsteps pound up the stairs. Of course, I was still completely irritated with her, but now some new emotions crowded onto the scene. *Is that what she thinks?* I wondered. *That I'm doing this because I think I'm better than her and everyone else?*

> *Obviously, I'm not a saint, Diary. Far from it. Have I been acting like I think I'm one, though? OK, let's analyze the situation. Here it is in a nutshell: I believe that I'm right and Jessica's wrong about the subject of beauty pageants. But I'm not willing to let it rest at that. I want to change her mind so she thinks like me. Is that self-righteous? Maybe!*

I suppose the real question is, Why am I so obsessed with this beauty pageant? Am I taking the moral high road to compensate for cheating with Sam?

I still feel really guilty about that, and about the fact that I still think about him. I was counting on it being "out of sight, out of mind," but that's not how it is. Every time I'm out with Todd and my other friends, at the Dairi Burger or wherever, I find myself hoping I'll see him. I wish Jessica and I weren't fighting—I'd love to be able to pour my heart out to her. Instead, this secret is going to keep gnawing at me.

Thursday, 8:00 P.M.

Despite how hard the protest committee's been working, we haven't been able to drum up that much public support for our cause. I was starting to get kind of discouraged, and kind of burned out too. But this afternoon, I took one last stab at it and went to the town library to do some research, and believe it or not, I think I may have found out how to put a stop to the beauty pageant once and for all!

It turns out there's a town rule that outside organizations can't hold money-raising

143

events at a school facility without writ-
ten consent from the school superinten-
dent. And it just so happens that the
Chamber of Commerce couldn't have
gotten the superintendent's signature be-
cause he's been out of the country at
an education summit in France for the
past few weeks. It's a technicality, but
it should be enough. Rules are rules,
after all!

When I got home from the library, I
headed straight for the phone to call The
Sweet Valley News and give them the
scoop. Before I dialed the number,
though, I saw something that made me
think twice about what I was about
to do.

After gathering up the notes I'd taken at the library, I headed for the kitchen to look up the
newspaper's number in the phone book. As I
passed by the living room, I spotted Jessica. She
was busy dancing and didn't notice me. I almost
kept walking, but then on an impulse, I stopped.
Peeking around the door frame, I watched her for
a minute.

Years ago, Jessica and I had taken modern
dance lessons. Neither of us had been a total
klutz, but we hadn't been particularly talented
either. But the routine Jessica was practicing

now was pretty sophisticated and she was managing the moves with grace and precision. When and where had my twin learned to dance like this?

Without thinking, I burst out, "Jess, that's great! Have you been taking lessons or something?"

She stopped dead and turned to look at me, her face red with exertion and possibly embarrassment too. I don't think she wanted me to see her. "As a matter of fact, yes," she said stiffly, grabbing a towel from the back of a chair and wiping the perspiration from her neck.

"Why?" I asked.

"If you must know, I'm dancing for the talent section of the pageant," she told me, her tone cold. "Now, if you don't mind, I need to run through my routine one more time before my lesson with Mr. Krezenski. This is my last chance to get his input before the pageant."

She turned her back on me and hit a button on the stereo, starting the CD over. I respected her request for privacy and disappeared down the hall. In the kitchen, I sat for a long time in front of the unopened telephone directory. *So that's where she's been going every afternoon*, I thought. Mr. Krezenski, who'd once been a famous dancer, ran the most prestigious dance academy in town and had a reputation as a strict, challenging instructor. Jessica certainly had improved—obviously she'd been working incredibly hard. No wonder she always looked tired. Taking a demanding modern dance class on top of cheerleading practice!

I knew that with one phone call I could crush Jessica's dream of becoming Miss Teen Sweet Valley. Ten minutes earlier, I might have done it. But now the phone book remained closed. While I'd been putting in a lot of hours organizing the protest, Jessica had been exerting herself too, and not just by getting manicures, trying on evening gowns, rehearsing smiles, and figuring out which hairstyle would look best with a crown. I recalled what Jessica had said to me the night before: "The beauty pageant isn't just an idea. It's a real event with real people involved, and one of them happens to be your sister . . ."

I heard the sounds of modern dance music coming from the living room. *I can't ruin it for her,* I realized. I thought of the slogan on the sign I'd carried during the protest march in front of the Sweet Valley courthouse the previous weekend: "More Than Just a Pretty Face." That was my sister, all right. She was beautiful, but she was strong and motivated and smart too. How could I deny her the opportunity to demonstrate her talent to the world?

*   *   *

I went back and forth on the rules issue all day today, Diary. I didn't tell anyone else on the protest committee about what I'd discovered, so the decision was mine alone. But I finally ended up following my heart over my head. I still believe one hundred percent that beauty pageants are old-fashioned and sexist. But I can't ignore the argument for the other side, because the evidence is living and breathing in my own house. Jessica says beauty pageants give people a chance to shine, and she's proving the point by throwing herself into these modern dance classes. Maybe she's just doing it to win a crown and some dumb prizes, but just because I don't crave a shopping spree at the mall doesn't mean it's not valid for her to want that.

So, I'm throwing in the towel. The anti-pageant committee is officially history, and tomorrow night, some lucky girl will be crowned Miss Teen Sweet Valley in the S.V.H. auditorium. I have to admit, it still turns my stomach to think about it. Jess will have a cheering section—Mom, Dad, and Steven are going—but I'm not sure I can sit through it. For all I know,

147

Jessica won't even want me there, after all that's been said and done these last few weeks.

Sunday morning

The Miss Teen Sweet Valley pageant took place last night, Diary, and it worked out differently than anyone, including me, could have expected. First, I went after all. Todd and I were set to go to a movie, but on our way to the theater, I made him turn the car around. I just couldn't skip the pageant, knowing how much it meant to my sister. Despite our differences, I've always been her biggest fan and she's always been mine—if the roles were reversed, I'm sure she'd have swallowed her pride and principles and cheered me on too.

Well, it turned out to be a good thing I went because Jessica needed me for more than just moral support. She was the last contestant to perform during the talent section, and she had some tough acts to follow. Sharon Jefferson played an exquisite Mozart piano concerto, and Maggie Simmons, who's an outstanding actress, acted out a soliloquy from Romeo and Juliet. Jessica was right up there with the best of them. She danced beautifully, but toward the end of her routine, she had some bad luck. Maybe she was nervous—maybe she was just trying too hard. Either way, she fell. She recovered quickly and finished the routine gracefully, but I could tell she was devastated. I ran backstage to find her afterward, and she was crying her eyes out. She'd already changed into shorts and a T-shirt and declared she was too humiliated to finish out the pageant.

That's when I heard some pretty odd words coming from my lips. I actually tried to persuade Jessica to put on her swimsuit and get back out there to strut her stuff with the rest of the girls! Jess was as amazed as I was at my turnaround. But standing in that dressing room with her, I recognized something with absolute clarity. My sister is a girl of incredible character, strength, and talent. When she does something, she doesn't do it halfway—she throws herself into it wholeheartedly and strives for nothing less than success. I was really proud, watching her perform, especially after she made that mistake. She didn't give up—she pulled herself together and danced on. At that moment, my twin sister was a great role model for any young girl. We should all be that dedicated and determined.

So, all of a sudden, I'm using all my eloquence to argue for the other side of the subject. But I couldn't talk Jessica into putting on the swimsuit. She was too embarrassed about having fallen in front of an auditorium full of people. She ran off, leaving me holding the bag . . . literally. And in her dance bag was . . . the swimsuit. Can you guess what I did, Diary? Yep, the same thing I've done before when the chips were down. Me, Elizabeth Wakefield, the girl who's been proclaiming far and wide that beauty pageants, particularly swimsuit competitions, are sexist and outdated, shimmied into Jessica's skimpy turquoise one-piece, slipped on a pair of high heels, touched up my makeup, tousled my hair so that it looked like my sister's, and pranced out onto the runway along with the other pageant contestants. That's how much I love my sister!

Jessica was still lurking backstage, and when she saw what I did, it gave her the boost she needed to rejoin the competition. While she zipped up her pink evening gown, I stripped off the swimsuit and got back into my own clothes. I rejoined my family in the audience, and no one was any the wiser. And I don't regret it even the tiniest bit, because, guess what? Jessica won! Yes, my twin sister is Miss Teen Sweet Valley! And I really do believe that she didn't just win because she was the prettiest girl in the contest, although if I may say so myself, she was. She answered the judges' questions with wit and intelligence, she danced with grace and skill, and she held onto her poise except for her little collapse backstage, which only I witnessed.

I had to laugh, though, because after the fact, she ended up feeling a little let down by the whole experience. I guess wearing a crown wasn't quite as exciting as she expected. As for the prizes, for some reason Jessica thought she was going to get $1,000 and a whole new wardrobe—instead, she won a set of Wide World encyclopedias, a free haircut, some free movie rentals, and a gift certificate to a local bowling alley!

What we both ended up winning, though, which was more valuable than any prize, was each other. I have my sister back. . . .

After the pageant, my family went out for pizza with some of Jessica's friends to celebrate the big victory. Jessica wore her pink dress and Miss Teen Sweet Valley sash and tiara, so we got plenty of attention everywhere we went. I think that was some consolation, but I could tell Jessica was disappointed by the low-budget prizes, and maybe by something else.

At home later, I followed my sister to her room. She'd left her door ajar for the first time in weeks—an invitation to come in and talk. "Knock, knock," I said.

"Come in," she called, her voice muffled.

Jessica was lying with her face buried in the pillow. "Now that we're alone, you can say it," she told me.

"Say what?" I asked, sitting cross-legged on the rug next to her bed.

"I told you so," Jessica replied. "Isn't that what you're thinking?"

"No, it's not," I said honestly. "Do *you* think tonight proved that I was right?"

Jessica sat up, pulling the pillow onto her lap and hugging it. "Kind of," she admitted.

"How come?"

"I just got this funny feeling, when Chrome Dome opened the envelope and announced that I was the winner. Instead of feeling psyched, I felt . . . I don't know. Like I'd cheated or something. And I don't mean because you stood in for me in the swimsuit competition. I mean, because Maggie and Sharon were ten times better than me in the talent section, and they looked nice in their swimsuits and evening gowns too, and they answered the questions really well. I think I won because of my looks."

Jessica made this revelation in a near whisper, with an expression of terrible guilt. I burst out laughing. "Of course you won because of your looks, silly!" I exclaimed. "It was a *beauty* pageant! But you didn't *just* win because of your looks. You spoke well, and you danced beautifully—even Mr. Krezenski said so."

Jessica's dance instructor had been in the audience and had congratulated her after the pageant. "So, I shouldn't feel bad?" she said hopefully.

"Of course not. You should feel great. You set out to win the crown and you did."

"But beauty pageants are demeaning," Jessica countered, quoting me. "They don't recognize the whole woman, inside and out."

"Sure they do," I responded. "You had to demonstrate talent, poise, and intelligence. There was definitely an emphasis on the physical, but your 'whole woman' got a chance to shine. You scored points in every category, Jess."

A slow smile spread across my sister's face. "I looked pretty good, didn't I?"

I grinned back. "Totally hot."

"You were hot too." Jessica's blue-green eyes

twinkled. "Admit it, Liz. When you were parading around in that swimsuit, you liked being the center of so much attention and admiration."

"I hated it," I insisted.

"Liar."

I laughed. "OK. I liked it a little. Just a little."

My sister and I smiled at each other. "So, the family feud's over," Jessica observed. "Aren't you relieved?"

"You bet."

"Would you say we were both part right and part wrong?" she asked.

I considered for a moment, then nodded. "That sounds fair."

Jessica bent over the side of the bed to give me a hug. "Thanks for being there for me, Liz. You're the best sister in the whole world."

I squeezed her tight. "You too."

Jessica sat back. "What can I ever do to repay you?"

"You don't have to repay me," I said. "That's what sisters are for."

"But there must be something . . ." Jessica tapped her cheek with her index finger. Then her eyes lit up with mischief. "I know! How would you like your very own personal set of Wide World encyclopedias?"

I called Todd just now to tell him
about the pageant, but I left out the part

about filling in for Jessica. That will be her and my secret. And do you want to know another secret, Diary? I was lying when I told Jessica I hated participating in the pageant. I enjoyed it. Sure, I felt self-conscious—I was half naked! But it was fun too, acting glamorous and confident about my good looks. That doesn't mean I don't want to be valued as a whole person, for qualities more important than just appearance. I'm not going to chuck my dream of being a writer and try to be a supermodel. But it's kind of nice, as I told Jessica, to score points in every category!

Wednesday, 7:30 P.M.

Things at home are peaceful now that Jessica and I are friends again. I hadn't realized how lonely I was. Fighting with my sister also made it even harder for me to stop thinking about Sam. He still crosses my mind once every twelve or thirteen seconds, but it's getting better. Sort of.

So, things with Jessica are back to normal, but unfortunately, I can't say the same about things with Todd. I know I should be trying to spend more time alone

155

with him—it's the only way to recapture the old passionate feelings. Instead, I keep making excuses for us to be part of a crowd rather than doing things alone as a couple. Todd finally got fed up with me being so busy. He practically made me sign a contract promising that I'd start setting aside more time for him. . . .

"A table for two," Todd commented as we placed our lunch trays on a table in a relatively quiet corner of the S.V.H. cafeteria. "Won't last long, though," he predicted.

I didn't expect it to either. We almost always ate with a gang of friends: Enid, Penny, Winston, Aaron, Olivia, Maria, Ken. Sometimes it was Todd's basketball teammates, sometimes my *Oracle* friends. "Let's sit with our backs to everyone," I suggested as I pulled out a chair. "Or we could make out. Then people would leave us alone!"

Todd grinned. "You wouldn't do that, not in front of the whole cafeteria."

"We could *pretend* to make out," I amended.

"Maybe we'd better stop talking about it," said Todd as he unwrapped a sandwich the size of a whole loaf of bread. Have you ever noticed how much guys can eat and never gain a pound? "It only reminds me of how long it's been since we drove up to Miller's Point."

I felt a stab of guilt, which had become a very familiar sensation lately. Even though I was trying hard to put Sam out of my mind, I hadn't been entirely successful. I found myself fantasizing about him at very inconvenient moments . . . such as when Todd was kissing me. For that reason, I'd taken to avoiding intimacy with Todd. "Well," I said, popping the top on a can of soda, "we'll have to do something about that this weekend."

"OK, then promise me," Todd declared, grabbing my hand and holding it tight.

I blinked. "Promise you what?"

"I'll have you all to myself this Friday night *and* Saturday night. And from now on, we'll have at least one romantic date during the week, and eat lunch alone, just the two of us, at least once a week too."

Before speaking, though, I stared into my boyfriend's dark brown eyes. They were glowing with a simple and uncomplicated desire: to be with me, the girl he loved. *I owe it to him to keep trying,* I thought. And I owed it to myself too. Wasn't that why I'd broken up with Sam, to preserve my relationship with Todd? I was still feeling the pain of the split, and Sam probably was too. If I let myself drift further from Todd, if I let *this* relationship fail too, then all that suffering would be for nothing.

"I promise," I told Todd.

He slipped an arm around my shoulder and pulled me close to him. "You won't regret it." Brushing my lips with his own, he added, teasingly, "Now, how about that pretend make-out session?"

For about thirty seconds, Diary, Todd and I were in utter harmony. Then Roger Barrett-Patman sat down to eat with us. Todd and I had just agreed to take a bike ride together after school to Secca Lake to swim, lounge around, kiss, talk, all that jazz. But Roger seemed really stressed out, so I invited him to come along.

You should have seen the dirty look Todd gave me! But Roger's a good friend of mine and I don't turn my back on my friends. Especially someone as sweet and generous as Roger. Part of the reason he's running ragged is because track practice is really intense these days—the team is gearing up for the all-county meet in a month and a half. On top of that, for the next few weeks Roger is going to be sort of babysitting this thirteen-year-old boy named Mitch Ferguson. You know Roger's whole story, how he never knew his father, but then, after his mother died a while back, he found out that Mr. Patman's brother was his father, so he moved in with the Patmans? Well, this Mitch kid's mother was a close friend of Roger's mom. Apparently, Mitch's dad died a few years ago and now Mrs. Ferguson is having a hard time controlling her son. He's running around with a bad crowd at his school in L.A. and just got suspended for drinking. At the age of thirteen! His mother decided a change of scenery would benefit Mitch, and so would hanging out with Roger, who would be a good role model. I really commend Roger for taking so much responsibility on his shoulders. Mitch sounds like a sad case. If anyone can make a difference in his life, it'll be Roger.

Todd wasn't quite as sympathetic, though. When Roger invited us to a cookout on Friday to welcome Mitch, I said yes, naturally. Todd had no choice but to go along with the plan, but after Roger took off and we were alone again, Todd let me know how he really felt about it. . . .

"Thanks for the bruise on my shin," I said to Todd when Roger was out of earshot.

"Sorry," Todd apologized. "It was supposed to just be a nudge, not a kick."

"Why even a nudge?" I wondered. "What's wrong with going to a cookout at Roger's?"

"Friday night, Liz," Todd said, in a tone that made it clear he expected those three words to explain everything.

I shook my head. "I still don't get it."

"Five minutes ago, you promised we'd be alone this weekend," he reminded me.

"I know." I placed a hand on his arm. "And I really want us to have some time to ourselves. But Roger asked us to the cookout as a favor to him, to help him make Mitch comfortable in Sweet Valley. We can't blow him off."

"OK," Todd granted, "but then, when Roger mentioned the party on Saturday night after the track meet, you said yes to that too!"

I wrinkled my nose. "I didn't really say yes. I said *maybe* we'd stop by."

"You said we'd *probably* stop by," Todd corrected me.

"So we probably will!" I exclaimed, growing impatient with his attitude. "And why not? All our friends will be there. Besides, since I'm covering the track meet for *The Oracle*, I'll want to talk to everybody afterward. It doesn't have to take up our whole evening."

Todd sighed. "I guess I'm just disappointed," he admitted. "I know I see you every day at school, but still, I miss you."

The words stole right into my heart. "I miss

you too," I said softly. "I promise we won't stay long at Roger's or at the track team party."

"We both have a lot going on in our lives," Todd acknowledged. "You have other friends and other interests besides me, and I wouldn't have it any other way. But how about we make each other priority number one for a while?"

I couldn't say no, especially since Todd was holding my hand under the table. He pressed my fingers and I pressed back. "Priority number one," I agreed.

At first, I couldn't believe Todd was making such a big deal about Roger's cookout and everything else, but I ended up seeing his point of view. He doesn't want us to take our relationship for granted, and he's right, although it may be too late. I've been taking him for granted for a long time now, and that's what opened the door to having feelings for another boy. But Todd will never know how close he came to losing me. I'm going to make good on my promise. From now on, he's priority number one.

Saturday, 10:00 A.M.

Well, last night was a disaster. There's really no other word to describe it. And it

*was all Todd's fault! No, that's not entirely
fair—I have to admit, it was an awkward
situation. But Todd behaved really imma-
turely. It was like having two thirteen-
year-olds at the party! What's gotten into
him?*

"I forgot that a party at Roger's is the same
thing as a party at Bruce's," Todd muttered under
his breath as we stepped over to the table where
Roger had set out some snacks and drinks.

Bruce himself had answered the door when
we arrived. After escorting us to the poolside
patio where Roger was entertaining his guests,
Bruce had disappeared back inside the Patman
mansion. "He's made himself scarce," I pointed
out to Todd. "Luckily."

Todd poured us both some lemonade. "It's not
even a party, really," he went on. "Just Annie and
Tony and the kid. How are we going to make a
quick getaway?"

"We might not want to." I gave him a quick
hug around the waist. "Give it a chance. This
could be fun."

As we rejoined Roger and the others, though,
I didn't have a good feeling about the night ahead
of me. Todd wasn't in the best mood, and I knew
it was because I'd corraled him into going to this
cookout. And he was right—there were fewer
people at Roger's than I'd expected. Roger must

have decided it was better not to overwhelm Mitch.

Todd and I sat down at the table with Tony Esteban, Annie Whitman, and Roger and his houseguest. Tony was on the track team with Roger. He was Sweet Valley High's star sprinter and an Olympic prospect being recruited by a lot of colleges and universities. Annie was on the cheerleading squad with Jessica. *Are Tony and Annie together?* I wondered, eyeing the pair surreptitiously.

"So, Mitch," Roger was saying. "What kinds of things do you like to do for fun back home? Like, extracurricular stuff?"

Mitch, dressed in baggy black jeans and a ripped black rock concert T-shirt, was slumped in his chair in the exact same position he'd been in since Todd and I arrived. He had shaggy dishwater blond hair and a pierced nostril, but I could tell he wasn't as tough as he looked. His attitude was old, but his eyes were young, and at Roger's question, his cheeks turned faintly pink. "You mean, besides getting in trouble for drinking?" he asked with exaggerated sullenness.

Roger didn't rise to the bait. "How about sports?"

Mitch shrugged. "Skateboarding's OK," he muttered.

"Roger and I run track," Tony remarked.

"Tony holds the school record for the 220-yard dash," Todd put in.

"Really?" Mitch sat up slightly, eyeing Tony with what looked like interest. "Man, you must be fast."

"Yeah," Tony said.

"Like, are you just born that way?" Mitch wanted to know. "I mean, fast?"

Tony laughed. "No way. I work my tail off. Tell him what practice has been like lately, Roger."

Roger launched into a description of that afternoon's workout. "Which reminds me, I haven't eaten since lunch and I'm starving," he concluded. "The burgers are probably ready to be flipped."

"Tell you what." Todd jumped to his feet. "Liz and I will handle the grill. You guys sit tight."

"You sure?" asked Roger.

"No sweat," Todd assured him.

Todd hustled me over to the big gas grill where a dozen hamburgers and hot dogs were sizzling. "I'm onto you," I told him, smiling. "You're just trying to get me alone."

"So, shoot me," he said with a sly grin.

Grabbing a spatula, Todd expertly flipped the burgers. Then he hung the spatula back on its hook and reached out for me. With the lid up, the grill pretty much blocked us from view. "This is really romantic," I said with a giggle.

"Ssh," Todd whispered, nuzzling my neck.

We were about to kiss when someone cleared his throat loudly. Todd and I both jumped. Bruce Patman stood behind us, a platter in one hand. "Do you mind?" he said snidely.

Todd and I stepped aside so Bruce could place a single salmon fillet on the grill. "Burgers and dogs aren't good enough for you?" Todd couldn't resist saying.

"Actually, no, they're not," Bruce drawled.

"I've seen you eat enough of them at the Dairi Burger," I commented.

"When I'm with the masses and there's nothing else on the menu, I sometimes order blue-collar, middle American cuisine," Bruce conceded.

Bruce is so snobby that he's almost a caricature, and Todd and I had to laugh. "So much for making out behind the grill," I said to Todd as we strolled back around the swimming pool.

"I'm not giving up," Todd declared. "This estate is huge. There's got to be someplace we can sneak off to."

When Roger started a game of croquet after dinner, Todd intentionally whacked my ball into the bushes so the two of us had to scramble through the dense foliage to look for it. As we were about to kiss, though, someone else's croquet ball sailed into the shrubbery. Both Tony and Mitch waded into the rhododendrons to hunt for it. "Getting kind of crowded in here,"

Todd grumbled as he reached over to retrieve my ball.

We tried again later to steal a moment alone while Roger was giving Mitch a tour of the Patman tennis court, which was carved into the side of the hill below the house. Todd pulled me away from the others. He'd just wrapped his arms around me when we were suddenly illuminated by a blinding beam of light. We jumped apart guiltily.

"Hey, none of that," Roger called out jokingly as he continued to flip a variety of switches to show Mitch how to adjust the court's floodlights.

I laughed, but Todd was glowering. "This is really getting to be a drag," he muttered to me.

"Todd, ssh," I said, shooting a glance at Tony and Annie, who politely pretended they couldn't hear us.

"Why can't we have some privacy for once?" Todd wanted to know.

I took his arm. We walked around the far side of the tennis court. "Because we're at someone else's house," I reminded him. "This is a party!"

"Then let's leave," he suggested.

"Todd!" I couldn't believe he was acting like such a baby. "That would be really impolite. We haven't even had dessert yet, and Roger bought a whole bunch of homemade ice cream from Izzy's Incredible as a special treat for Mitch."

Grudgingly, Todd agreed to stay through dessert, which Roger served on the patio. While Roger was scooping ice cream, Mitch went inside to put on some music. Suddenly, the nighttime quiet was shattered by screeching, tuneless heavy metal.

"What is this crud?" Todd hollered when Mitch reapppeared.

Mitch dug his hands deep in his pants' pockets and glared at Todd. "It's my favorite band," he retorted.

"I kind of like it," Tony admitted.

"You could turn down the volume a bit, though," Roger suggested diplomatically.

Mitch didn't budge. "Yeah, it's cool but too loud," Tony said. This time, Mitch obliged.

Peace didn't last long. Roger passed around bowls piled high with ice cream. Mitch peered at the contents of his bowl, then pushed it away. "Lame flavors, man," he said rudely.

I heard Todd draw in his breath as if he was about to say something, so I jabbed him in the ribs with my elbow. Mitch was being a brat, but it wouldn't help matters for Todd to keep antagonizing him.

I spooned into my ice cream. "Delicious," I told Roger. "Mint chip is my favorite."

"Mine too," Annie piped in.

Todd ate his ice cream in silence, a stony expression on his face. I sighed inwardly. At this

167

point, even if we left the cookout early, it didn't look as if there was much chance of salvaging the evening. *So much for reviving our romance,* I thought.

Todd apologized when he drove me home, but it didn't make up for the way he acted at Roger's. I'm not sorry we went to Roger's—that's what friends are for. I have to say, though, I don't envy Roger having to deal with Mitch. Getting through to that kid isn't going to be easy. Although Tony did seem to make an impression on him. Before we left the Patmans' last night, I heard Mitch telling Tony that he plans to go to the track meet today to watch Roger and Tony compete. He actually sounded semienthusiastic!

So maybe there's hope for Mitch. I'm not so sure about Todd and me, though!

Sunday, 3:00 P.M.

Dear Diary,

A crummy thing happened at the track meet against Big Mesa yesterday. Tony fell in the last few meters of his top event, the 220, and hurt his knee. It was scary, seeing him lying on the

168

track, not knowing how badly he was injured. We all ran down to see if he was OK—Annie got to his side first, of course. One thing was kind of weird, though. Mr. Esteban, Tony's dad, rushed over too, but instead of being worried about Tony like the rest of us, he was mad that Tony had blown his chance to make a good showing in front of Burr Davidson, this sports talent scout who had supposedly come to the meet to watch Tony run. According to Annie, Mr. Esteban puts a lot of pressure on Tony. There's poor Tony, in incredible pain, and he has to apologize to his dad for tripping.

S.V.H. won the track meet anyway, but Tony's accident put a damper on everybody's mood. One second, Tony was running strong and smooth, and the next, he was tumbling to the ground. The thing is, every time I think of seeing Tony's body lying crumpled on the track, I think of Sam. What if Sam ever gets into a dirt-bike racing accident?

I know that I should be worried about Tony right now, not Sam—it's just that I never really considered how dangerous dirt-bike racing must be. Now I can't think about anything else. If anything

were ever to happen to Sam, I'd be devas-
tated. But since we're not in touch any-
more, I wouldn't even know. For all I
know, right at this very minute, he's risk-
ing his life in a race!

I have to know, Diary. I have to see
him again.

Sunday, 6:00 P.M.

Just time for a quick scrawl. I did it,
Diary. I called him. He's meeting me at
the beach in half an hour! I know it's
wrong, but I don't care.

Sunday, 11:00 P.M.

I saw Sam, and it was unbelievable.
Our feelings for each other are stronger
than ever. I can't deny it any longer. I love
him and I told him so. There's no going
back now. . . .

I was so nervous and excited that I drove
through two stop signs on my way to the beach
and got there five minutes early. I checked my
watch every thirty seconds or so as the minutes
ticked by. Six-thirty came and went, then six-forty.
At ten minutes before seven, I was on the verge
of bitter, disappointed tears. *He changed his*

mind—he doesn't want to see me again, I thought, sniffling. And who could blame him? I'd broken up with him with no explanation, and now, out of the blue, I'd called him up, again without an explanation, and asked him to meet me. What must he think of me?

It was windy, so I stood in the shelter of a sand dune, hugging myself to keep warm. *Five more minutes,* I decided, close to despair. I'd wait until seven o'clock and then go home.

The roar of surf and wind obliterated all other sounds. So when someone spoke right behind me, I nearly jumped out of my skin. "You always forget a sweater, don't you?"

I whirled around. Sam stood with his hands stuck in the pouch pocket of his hooded Bridgewater High School sweatshirt, his curly blond hair tousled by the wind. I held my breath, praying he wasn't angry at me, waiting for him to smile, and when he did smile, it was as if the sun was rising instead of setting. The whole world felt flooded with warmth and promise. "I've missed you, Elizabeth," he said, his voice husky.

Then, somehow, we were in each other's arms, embracing tightly. "I've missed you too." My voice was wavering with emotion.

Sam slid his hands up my arms, then cupped my face in his hands. "I can't believe how good it feels to see you, to hold you," he whispered. "Promise me."

"What?" I whispered back.

Instead of answering, he put his mouth on mine. We kissed with all the passion that had been suppressed during weeks apart, weeks of longing. When we drew apart, we were both breathless. "Promise," Sam repeated, "that you won't leave me again."

I wanted to do it, to say the words that would make him happy. It would be so easy. *I won't leave you, Sam. We belong together. I'm yours and yours only.* But I couldn't. It was impossible, because making such a promise to Sam meant that I'd decided once and for all to break up with Todd. "I—I can't," I stammered.

Pain shadowed Sam's face. He didn't let me go, but I felt his whole body stiffen. "Then why are you here?" he asked.

Before I had time to consider the consequences of the words, they spilled from me. "Because I love you."

Sam stared down at me. In his eyes, joy replaced the unhappiness that had been there an instant before. "Then why can't we be together? Why can't we talk about the future?"

"We *can* be together," I told him, "but it has to be like"—I waved an arm at the windswept, deserted beach—"like this. Just you and me, here, today. I can't make any promises about tomorrow. If you can accept that . . ."

For a moment, Sam hesitated. I knew it would

make my life easier if he said no, he didn't want to see me under those circumstances. I also knew that it would break my heart.

Finally, after what seemed like an eternity, he put a hand to my face, gently brushing a wind-blown strand of hair from my forehead. "All right," he told me. "If that's how it has to be, we'll take it one day at a time."

He held me hard against him, sheltering me from the wind. As we kissed, I wondered if he could feel my heart singing, soaring like the seagulls wheeling in the air overhead. I could feel his, beating strong and sure, and at that moment, I wanted nothing more for the rest of my life but to be held close to that generous, loving heart.

Monday, 5:30 P.M.

I just put a pot of homemade spaghetti sauce on the stove to simmer—it's my night to cook. It feels really weird to be doing ordinary things like going to school, proofreading articles for the next issue of The Oracle, *walking Prince Albert, doing laps in the pool, chopping garlic and tomatoes. It's like I'm floating above my body, watching myself go through the motions of my usual life. But in reality, I'm leading this secret, wonderful existence*

*where I'm in love with an adorable boy
from Bridgewater named Sam Woodruff.
But no one in the world knows about it,
not my twin sister, not my best friend, nobody.*

*I'm walking a tightrope, Diary, with-
out a safety net. Will I fall? If I make it
to the end, what's waiting there for me?
When I imagine breaking up again with
Sam, I want to die, but I can't bear the
thought of telling Todd it's over either.
I'm taking things one day at a time, the
way Sam and I agreed. One hour at a
time.*

Tuesday evening

*Sam and I saw each other this after-
noon, but just for an hour and a half. He
has a big test coming up, so we brought
our books and studied together at a coffee
shop in Bridgewater. It was really fun,
hanging out with him in such a casual
way. It felt so comfortable, like we were a
steady couple. Is that what I want? To be
Sam's girlfriend, to be his exclusively?*

Wednesday, 8:00 P.M.

*I still have Sam on the brain. And
every time I think of him, I tingle all over!*

174

Todd asked me to spend the afternoon with him, but I really didn't want to be alone with him, so I dragged him along to play miniature golf with Roger, Mitch, Tony, and Annie. It was not a particularly fun outing. Todd was ticked at me for inviting four other people along on our "date," even though I pointed out that it was Wednesday afternoon, not Saturday night.

Mitch, predictably, acted totally obnoxious. Roger's worried. The visit just isn't going well. He confided to me that he found an empty beer bottle in Mitch's room—he knows he should say something to Mitch, but he's afraid Mitch won't listen. So I suggested that he ask Tony to talk to Mitch. That's the only good thing that came out of this afternoon—Mitch has really bonded with Tony. I think it's because Tony doesn't put up with Mitch's attitude—he tells Mitch right to his face to shape up. You know, in a good-humored way, but he's serious. Mitch seems to respect that.

Driving home, Todd and I bickered the whole way. He wanted to know if I was going to invite the whole S.V.H. junior class along next time we go out. "Maybe we could charter a bus to Miller's Point," he suggested in this really sarcastic way. I came pretty close to blurting out that, if he doesn't stop being so possessive, there might not be a next time.

Thursday, 5:30 P.M.
Dear Diary,
I almost can't see to write, my eyes are so swollen from crying. It's all over. Sam saw me kissing Todd and I know he'll never forgive me. . . .

Todd and I went to the Dairi Burger after school, like we still always do a couple of times a week. It's the most popular hangout in town. On this particular day, Jessica was sitting in a big booth with some of the other cheerleaders. Tony and Annie were at the restaurant, and so were Andrea and Nicholas. Winston was entertaining a table full of friends: Maria, Aaron, Ken, Terri, DeeDee, and Bill. In fact, the Dairi Burger was so busy that by the time Todd and I arrived, the only two seats left were at the far end of the counter.

"We *could* squeeze into Jessica's booth," I suggested.

"Let's take the counter," Todd replied. "It'll be more private."

I didn't argue. Privacy is a big issue with him these days, or rather the fact that we never have any. If sitting at the Dairi Burger counter was going to make Todd happy, I was all for it!

We made our way through the crowded restaurant, waving to our friends as we went, then sat down side by side on stools at the counter. As I picked up the plastic-covered menu, I swiveled to face Todd. "This is kind of fun," I admitted. "We *never* sit at the counter."

Todd swiveled his stool too. We were so close together, he had to sandwich one of my knees between his own. "That's because it's never just the two of us."

"It's kind of like being on an old-fashioned date at the soda shop," I commented.

He smiled. "Buy you a malt?"

I smiled back. "Hey," I said, tilting my head to one side.

"Hey, what?" He brushed some strands of hair away from my face.

"Hey, this is fun."

"You already said that."

"I know. But I *mean* it." I was still smiling broadly.

"I've been kind of a grump lately, huh?" Todd said wryly.

"Kind of," I agreed.

We both laughed. "The thing is, this is all I want." He put a hand on my knee and squeezed. "Just to be with you like this. I don't need all your

177

attention all the time, but every now and then, it's kind of nice."

Out of nowhere, a wave of nostalgia washed over me. "Remember our very first Dairi Burger date?" I asked Todd.

His eyes twinkled. "Do I! As I recall, we had a booth all to ourselves. We split a hot fudge sundae and you got a cute little dab of whipped cream on the tip of your cute little nose."

"And you kissed it off," I said.

"Right." He touched my nose with his fingertip. "I kissed you there and then . . ." He gently touched my lips. "I kissed you here."

"Right in the middle of the restaurant," I said softly. "Where everyone could see."

"I didn't care," Todd told me. "I was madly in love."

"You were?" I asked softly.

"I was. And I still am."

As we gazed deeply into each other's eyes, something magical happened. It was almost as if time ran backward. For a few moments, Todd and I were a little bit younger. He was new at school. We hadn't known each other long and our feelings were brand new and unexplored. One thing was already clear, though—I was the luckiest girl in Sweet Valley to be dating him. He was smart, fun to be with, thoughtful, generous, incredibly good-looking . . . a dream come true. *And I'm on the verge of throwing it all away*, I thought with a pang.

"I love you, Todd," I whispered, my eyes brimming with tears.

"Hey, don't cry about it," he teased, putting his lips on mine.

We kissed for a long, sweet moment, pulling back from each other reluctantly. Todd sighed happily. "See how good it can be, Liz, if we take the time to—"

He never got to finish his sentence. As I turned away from Todd, I saw someone staring at me from across the restaurant. Someone in a Bridgewater High School sweatshirt.

Sam.

He was standing just inside the door to the Dairi Burger. *How long has he been there?* I wondered, turning pale. Long enough, apparently. For a split second, our eyes locked. Then, his face twisted with pain, Sam turned on his heel and bolted outside.

Todd still had an arm around me. I wrenched away from him and jumped down from the stool. "Liz, what's the matter?" he asked. "Where are you going?"

I didn't answer Todd's questions. Without looking back, I ran toward the door. I don't know what I planned to say to Sam, if I caught up with him, or what I'd say to Todd if he followed me outside and saw me with Sam. As it turned out, it didn't matter. As I dashed out to the parking lot, I could hear the receding roar of the dirt bike's engine. All that was left behind was a cloud of dust. Sam was gone.

It was the worst moment of my life, Diary. I was so upset and confused, I couldn't think straight. I was crying my eyes out, and I absolutely could not go back inside the Dairi Burger, with everybody staring and wondering what my problem was, and Todd wanting to know why I'd taken off like that. So I just climbed into the Fiat and drove home all by myself. I know it was childish. And I won't be able to hide forever. I'll have to explain myself, especially to Todd. What am I going to say?

Friday, 8:00 P.M.

Well, I've really done it this time. For a while there, I had two boyfriends, and now it looks as if I might end up with none. I've hurt both the guys I love. I keep trying to call Sam, but he won't talk to me. Meanwhile, Todd doesn't understand why I ran out of the Dairi Burger yesterday right after he kissed me, and I don't blame him for being confused. I made up this feeble excuse

180

about suddenly not feeling well, but he saw right through it. "Look, Liz," he said when I called him to apologize later, "if you're not as psyched about this relationship as I am, just tell me." I don't even remember what I said, but whatever it was, it must not have satisfied him. I tried to make it up to him today after school, but he blew me off. He didn't even kiss me good-bye. . . .

Even though Todd had avoided me during lunch and study hall, I was trying hard to pretend to the world—and to my nosy sister, who'd witnessed the strange scene at the Dairi Burger—that nothing was wrong. *We haven't broken up, after all,* I thought as I hurried to Todd's locker after the final bell. *We're still a couple . . . aren't we?*

Todd wasn't alone. Aaron and Winston were lounging by his locker, backpacks slung over their shoulders. I bit my lip. I really didn't want to approach Todd in front of other people, but it didn't look like I had a choice.

"Hi, Todd," I said with forced cheeriness.

"Liz," he said, his expression blank and unreadable.

"Um, so, do you want to make plans for tonight?" When he didn't respond right away, I felt myself blush. "I mean, we keep talking about

181

doing something, just the two of us, and I thought maybe we could—"

Todd slammed his locker shut. "I've got a meeting tonight."

"Oh?"

"About organizing the new kids' basketball league. Remember?"

His tone was mildly accusatory. Had he told me about this? I vaguely recalled a conversation where Todd had talked enthusiastically about *something*. "Oh, yeah," I bluffed. "Right. The kids' basketball league. Well, what about tomorrow?"

"I don't know what my schedule is," Todd's voice was bland and devoid of emotion. "I gotta get going. I'll call you later, OK?"

"Sure." I shot a glance at Winston and Aaron, wondering how this appeared to them. Winston scuffed his feet. Aaron dropped his eyes. They both looked embarrassed. "Well, see ya, guys," I said, still managing to sound perky.

"See ya," Aaron replied.

"Bye," said Winston.

"So long," was all that Todd would say.

I lingered, waiting for Todd to kiss me, as he always did when we parted. I didn't expect a loving smooch—maybe just a peck on the cheek for appearance's sake. But I didn't even get that. Without another glance at me, he sauntered off down the corridor toward the locker room with his friends.

I was left standing alone, feeling like a fool. Feeling *worse* than a fool. My heart ached unbearably. Todd was giving me the cold shoulder—maybe he was even considering breaking up with me. And I had no one to blame but myself.

Saturday, 2:00 P.M.

I'm skipping the S.V.H. track meet today even though Tony Esteban's knee is better and he's entered in the 220—everybody will be there to watch him compete. But I finally got through to Sam. Mr. and Mrs. Woodruff must think I'm some kind of psycho, calling so much. Luckily, after about ten tries this morning, Sam picked up the phone. I told him I just wanted to explain, but before I could say a word, he said, "You told me that guy was just a friend. You've been lying this whole time. Was everything you said to me a lie?"

He sounded so, so hurt. I realized I couldn't make him understand over the phone—it was too cold and unfriendly. He didn't want to go to the beach, but he agreed to meet me at the coffee shop in Bridgewater where we had our last "date." Oh, Diary, when I think about how differently things might have turned out. . . .

Sam was sitting at a small round table on the sidewalk with a Styrofoam cup of steaming cappuccino in front of him. I eased into the other wrought-iron chair, glancing around us. "Couldn't we go someplace more private?" I asked.

Sam clenched his jaw. "This'll have to do."

His tone was cool and unforgiving—such a contrast to the amiable, affectionate manner he'd always shown me. Tears jumped to my eyes. *I deserve this*, I reminded myself. "Sam, I'm sorry," I croaked, reaching for his paper napkin and dabbing my eyes.

"I just don't understand." His words were careful and measured. Under the surface, obviously he too, was fighting a surge of powerful emotions. "Were you playing some kind of game with me?"

I shook my head vehemently. "No," I insisted. "It was never a game. I cared about you. I still care about you."

"But this other guy . . ."

"Todd," I said. "Todd Wilkins. My . . . my boyfriend."

Sam flushed. His jaw tightened again. "Why didn't you tell me the truth right from the start? Why did you let me think you were available?"

These were questions I'd been trying for

weeks to answer myself, unsuccessfully. "Because . . ." I struggled to find the words to express my motives. "Because I *liked* you," I said finally. "So much. And I knew if I told you I already had a boyfriend, I'd never get to know you."

Sam fiddled with the plastic spoon in his coffee cup. "And Todd? Did you tell him about me?"

I shook my head, ashamed. "No."

"So, you decided to have it both ways," Sam accused harshly.

I blushed. "It wasn't a decision. I *couldn't* decide—that was the whole problem. When I was with you, I was so happy. I'd start thinking about breaking up with Todd. But then, when I was with *him* . . . We've been together for so long, and we're such good friends. . . ."

My voice trailed off. There was nothing I could say to make my behavior appear in a better light. I'd cheated on Todd and two-timed Sam. That was all there was to it.

Sam stared at me. His face was wooden; only a slight redness around the rims of his eyes gave him away. "I really fell for you, Elizabeth," he told me. "I remember thinking, that first time we talked on the beach, 'This is my lucky day. I've found her. The girl of my dreams.'" He laughed bitterly. "Now I wish we'd never met."

"I'm sorry." A tear spilled down my cheek. "I didn't mean to mislead you."

"Yes, you did." Sam pushed back his chair. "That's what hurts the most. Yes, you did."

"I'm sorry," I said again. "I really am. Will you—can you forgive me?"

Sam got to his feet. I remained sitting, my shoulders hunched, looking up at him with desperate unhappiness. "Good-bye, Elizabeth," he said hoarsely. He walked away without another word.

For a few minutes, I sat alone at the small table with Sam's abandoned cup of now-cold cappuccino, trying not to cry in front of all the other people who were suddenly crowding into the shop for their Saturday morning coffee, pastries, and newspapers. Then I trailed sadly back to my car. I knew I'd never forget the look in Sam's eyes, and the note in his voice, as he said those final words to me—the last I'd ever hear from him.

Good-bye.

I've been locked in my bedroom all day—I don't think I've cried this much in my life. After so much lying, it was a relief to finally tell Sam the truth, but knowing that he'll never forgive me, that he'll always think I'm an awful person, hurts more than I can say. At the coffee shop, I saw myself through Sam's eyes, and I realize now

186

that what I did was terribly selfish. He's right—I was trying to have it both ways. I should have known that sooner or later the whole situation would come unraveled.

The hardest part, Diary, is that I feel as if I've not only lost Sam, but I've also lost the person I was when I was with him. I was a different Elizabeth Wakefield when I was around him: mysterious, whimsical, carefree. Now that girl is gone forever and I'm left with my same old very imperfect self. I can't go back and do things differently, though. I can't live my life over. All I can do is mourn what I've lost and then try to mend what's left of my life. I won't hurt Todd the way I've hurt Sam. I'll start treating him better, from this day on. But what if it's already too late?

Friday, 7:00 P.M.

It's been a long, lonely week. Sam is never far from my thoughts. It's so hard to let it go, knowing that his memories of me will always taste bitter. You know how when you read a good book, at the end everything wraps up just right? That doesn't mean there has to be a stereotypically "happy" ending, but there needs to be closure. The story has to feel finished and satisfying. The way things worked out with Sam, I have exactly the opposite feeling. It's just so depressing. I can't change the ending to the story, no matter how much I wish I could. I have to live with it the way it is.

At least things are a teeny weeny bit better with Todd. We both had a really busy week at school, but I'm trying double hard to make time for him, and I think he appreciates my efforts. He's still kind of standoffish, though. So I've come up with a plan to sweep him off his feet and prove my love. It was Jessica's idea, to give credit where it's due. I'm going to kidnap him! Actually, Annie and Enid are going to kidnap him next weekend, and drive him someplace—we haven't figured out where yet—and I'll be waiting to have a romantic dinner with him. I just want to show him, so there can be no doubt in his mind, that he matters to me. If we could just get away and have time together, I'm certain he and I can make things right. I've never stopped loving him and never will. I know that now.

Dear Diary,

I'm not the only one with boyfriend troubles. Annie just found out that Tony's taking steroids! Isn't that awful? She found this bottle of pills in his locker and knew it wasn't pain medication, since Tony stopped taking that a week or two ago. She had a bad feeling about the pills—I guess Tony's been acting weird lately—so she snuck one out of the bottles and gave it to her cousin Beth, who's a chemistry graduate student. Beth analyzed the composition of the pill and told Annie the bad news. Tony's taking steroids, probably thinking they'll make him stronger and faster. But they're illegal for athletes, and from what I've heard, can totally screw your body up.

Tony's recovery did seem kind of miraculous, now that I think about it. After just a couple of weeks on crutches, he started training again, and suddenly he was faster than ever. His first race back, he broke his own S.V.H. record in the 220! And Annie kept mentioning that he was acting differently too. Usually Tony is a mellow guy, but lately he's been short-tempered and hypercompetitive with his track teammates, even Roger. Plus the other night, when a whole bunch of us were out bowling, he totally snapped at Mitch, who you know thinks that Tony walks on water.

Understandably, Annie's really upset. She's worried that Tony's going to hurt himself, and his behavior is threatening their relationship too. I've learned the hard way how destructive it can be to sneak around, so I advised her to get it all out in the open—to tell him that she knows about the steroids and urge him to seek some help, maybe at Project Youth. She's planning to talk to him tonight. I wonder how it's going.

Wednesday, 5:00 P.M.

Annie told me during lunch today that she confronted Tony about the steroids last night, but he just completely denied that he was taking anything other than prescription painkillers. Needless to say, Annie's more worried than ever. She has this feeling, though, that Tony wasn't out-and-out lying to her. She thinks he might not know what the pills are—someone may have given or sold them to him without telling him they're dangerous. I think that's a good guess. I mean, Tony's one of

190

the most clean-cut, straight kids I know.
It's so hard to believe he'd knowingly do
anything illegal.

Anyhow, Annie told Roger the whole
story too, and the three of us put our
heads together to figure out what to do
next. Roger's the one who came up with
a plan. He suggested that Annie ask her
cousin to whip up some fake sugar pills
that look just like the steroid pills. Annie
could substitute the "placebos" for the
real thing. At first, both Annie and I
were skeptical. Wouldn't Tony immediately feel different and realize there'd
been a switch? But according to Roger,
part of the steroids' effect might be psy-
chological. Tony believes the pills make
him faster, and so they do. Annie decided it was worth a try. I really hope
the fake pills work, for her sake and for
Tony's sake.

As for my love life, the plan for
Saturday is all set. Enid and Annie are
going to tell Todd that my car broke down
and I need help, and then "kidnap" him
and take him to Castillo San Angelo,
where I've made dinner reservations for
two. I know what you're thinking, Diary.
"Castillo San Angelo . . . didn't you go
there once with Sam?" It's true, I did, and

I wouldn't have chosen it myself, but Annie bought this guidebook to romantic destinations in southern California, and that's where she and Enid decided I should take Todd. I couldn't exactly tell them why it didn't suit me! Now that the time is getting closer, though, I actually think it'll be fine. I need to get over Sam. I can't hold anyplace—the beach, Castillo San Angelo—sacred to him. Todd and I will go there together and make new memories that I'll treasure even more than my memories of Sam.

                             Saturday, midnight

Dear Diary,

    It worked! Todd and I had an unbelievably romantic evening together at Castillo San Angelo. The funniest part about it was that the whole time that I was planning to kidnap him, he was planning to kidnap me too!

    Here's what happened: At about six o'clock, I'd just stepped out of a bubble bath and into my new floral halter dress when Winston Egbert, of all people, rang my doorbell. He gave me this story about how Todd had gone for a ride on a friend's motorcycle and had a minor accident. Instantly, I was frantic with worry—too worried to think about how odd the whole thing was. Winston told me to hop in his car, so I did. We headed up the coast, and when we stopped for gas, Winston popped a blindfold over my eyes and told me he was whisking me away to a secret destination, on Todd's orders!

I'd never been so confused in my life. How could Winston be kidnapping me on Todd's orders, when Todd was being kidnapped by Enid and Annie on my orders? I thought for sure the whole night was going to be ruined and I demanded that Winston let me go so I could drive to Castillo San Angelo and meet Todd, but Winston absolutely refused. Imagine my amazement when we finally stopped, and Winston took off my blindfold . . . and we were at Castillo San Angelo!

It turns out that Winston had borrowed Annie's Romantic Getaways guidebook, claiming he wanted to help his parents pick out a special restaurant for their anniversary. In reality, he was helping Todd find a romantic place to take me and, coincidentally, Todd ended up choosing the same one I did. So, Annie and Enid pulled up at Castillo San Angelo with Todd just as Winston and I arrived. We all spent a few minutes laughing and comparing notes, then those three took off in Annie's car, leaving Winston's car for Todd and me. I was so relieved and happy that the plan worked out after all. Happier than I've been in a long, long time. . . .

"Elizabeth Wakefield." Todd shook his head with mock disbelief. "A law-abiding citizen like you. Who'd have thought you'd resort to kidnapping to get a guy's attention?"

The Castillo San Angelo setting couldn't have been more romantic. Todd and I sat on the terrace at a table for two that was draped in a snowy white cloth and sparkling with votive candles.

"What about you?" I countered. "Talk about a desperate move. Kidnapping your own girl-friend!"

We were both still wearing ear-to-ear grins. "I knew I was in trouble when Annie threatened to gag me with one of her S.V.H. cheerleading pom-poms," Todd related.

"That's nothing," I said. "Winston blindfolded me with a pair of magenta pantyhose!"

We both giggled. "We have pretty nice friends," I noted.

"Yeah," agreed Todd. "They must really like us if they'd go to such crazy lengths to help us stay together."

My expression grew more serious. "Were you really worried? I mean, about us?"

Todd shook his head. "Not worried so much as frustrated. I guess I had faith we'd iron things out eventually. But I didn't want to wait forever for that to happen. I realized I had to take drastic action."

"I'm glad you did."

"I'm glad *we* did." Todd smiled.

We prolonged dinner for hours, and when the delicious, elegant meal was over, we lingered on the terrace, dancing cheek to cheek to the music of the jazz quartet. "I feel a million miles away from Sweet Valley," Todd murmured, his lips close to my ear.

"Me too." I whispered.

"Let's never go back," he said huskily.

"OK." I rested my cheek against his broad shoulder and felt safe and secure.

"I mean it." His arms tightened around me. "Let's hold on to this feeling."

I tilted my head back so I could look up into his warm, brown eyes. "I'd like to," I said honestly.

"It takes work sometimes," Todd said. "That's what people don't always realize. They think being a couple is easy."

"And usually it is," I pointed out.

"But the couples that last really have to be dedicated."

I stood on tiptoes to kiss him softly on the lips. "We're going to last," I predicted. "I think we're a *great* couple. Don't you?"

"I sure do."

"I love you, Todd Wilkins."

"I love *you*, Liz Wakefield."

> *We continued to dance, not talking, just content to be in each other's arms. It was a perfect night—I'll never forget it. Sweet dreams, Diary.*

> *Sunday, 3:00 P.M.*

> *This has been a lazy, happy day. Todd came over for brunch and we sat by the pool for the longest time reading bits of the Sunday paper out loud to each other. It was so cozy and comfortable and fun. Escaping to Castillo San Angelo last night was definitely a healthy thing for us to do. Getting away from the usual scene gave us a chance to get to know each other again, to remember why we fell in love way back when . . . and to fall in love all over again.*

> *Monday, 5:30 P.M.*

> *It ended up being a good weekend for Annie and Tony too. They were on the*

verge of breaking up because Tony had been acting so strange, but now they're back together because Tony stopped taking steroids! It turns out Annie was right—at first, he didn't know what was in the pills. Some guy at his health club told him they were "magic vitamins." Tony was kind of suspicious, but he really wanted his knee to heal fast so he could race in the all-county meet and maybe qualify for the Olympics, so he went against his own better judgment and took the pills.

Well, after Annie confronted him, Tony found out that the guy at the gym had gotten busted for selling steroids. I guess it was a real wake-up call. Then and there, Tony decided to throw away the pills and confess to his father and to Coach Featherston. Annie confessed too—that she'd substituted placebos for the steroids. She was worried Tony would be mad at her for doing that, but he saw it for what it was: proof of her love and concern for him. Tony knows he's jeopardized his chances of running in the all-county track meet—he has to take a blood test, and if there are any traces of steroids, he won't be allowed to compete. But now his priorities are straight again. Winning races isn't the only thing that matters. Self-respect and fair play are more important. You never come in first when you take drugs. You hurt yourself and the people around you too.

I'm really glad for Annie and Tony. They're a cute couple. At school today, they both had that falling-in-love glow. I think Todd and I are glowing a little bit too, even though we've been going out for a long time. Saturday night definitely recharged our romantic batteries. I have to admit, though, that my memories of Sam haven't completely faded. He lent me one of his sweaters the night we first kissed, and I still have it. I hid it in the back of my closet, but for some reason, I keep getting it out. When I look at it, and touch it, it brings him so close. Maybe if I think about him tonight before I fall asleep, I'll dream about him one last time—dream up a happy ending for us.

Wednesday, 7:00 P.M.

I did dream about Sam last night, Diary. It was a sad dream, but beautiful too. . . .

The dream was like dreams often are—realistic in some ways, fantastic in others. Sam and I were on the beach, and it was *our* beach, the one where we'd always met, but in my dream it looked familiar and strange at the same time. Instead of foamy white ocean waves crashing onto the shore, the water was smooth and gilded, like molten gold. The whole scene was incredibly peaceful and quiet. Sam and I were the only two people there.

In my dream we were walking side by side, not touching or talking. Even though no words passed between us, we understood each other perfectly, and I knew that he'd forgiven me for leading him on and lying about Todd. We walked to the end of the beach and then we stopped. I was cold, so Sam wrapped his sweater around my shoulders—the same sweater that he'd once wrapped around me in real life. Then he bent over to kiss me lightly on the forehead.

When he turned away, I wanted to ask him to stay, but I didn't. Instead, I watched him leave, and that's when I noticed that there was another girl down the beach, who appeared to be waiting for him. A slim, blond girl with laughing, blue-green eyes. A girl who looked an awful lot like me. Jessica!

My twin sister held out her hand to Sam. He took it without hesitation. They looked back at me, as if they expected something from me—

some sign that it was OK. I nodded and they both smiled. Then they walked away across the sand, leaving me alone beside the tranquil gold water.

Isn't that a strange dream, Diary? I'm dying to tell Jessica about it, but I can't unless I also want to tell her the whole long story of Sam, and at this point, even though part of me longs to tell all to my sister, I think it's best for my secret to remain a secret.

Anyway, Jessica would just analyze the dream to pieces. She saw a TV show the other night about the power of dreams, and ever since she's been playing Sigmund Freud, trying to interpret everyone's dreams. She's convinced she's about to meet her true love because she's had the same dream three times in a row. Ironically, it's about meeting a gorgeous guy at the beach! Isn't that funny? Sometimes being identical twins is too bizarre. Even when we're sleeping, our brains are somehow connected. I think that's why I dreamed about Sam and Jessica. She's been talking so much about dreams lately, she showed up in one of mine.

As for the rest of it, I think my dream

means that I've finally come to terms with saying good-bye to Sam. It's the closure I've been waiting for.

Saturday night

Speaking of closure, you'll be happy to hear that Tony Esteban won the 220 at the all-county track and field meet today. He's drug-free and faster and happier than ever. We're all really proud of him.

And remember Roger Barrett-Patman's thirteen-year-old buddy Mitch? He's back home with his mom in L.A., but he visited Sweet Valley again to watch Tony's meet. I think he's going to be OK, and Tony can take a lot of the credit for helping him straighten out.

Friday, 8:00 P.M.

Dear Diary,

I'm going to soak my bones in a deep, hot bubble bath and then crawl into bed early. This has been a long, busy week. I'm writing a feature article for The Oracle about dating at S.V.H.—what attracts boys and girls to each other—and it involves a lot of extra work and research.

I distributed a questionnaire at

school asking people to rank the qualities they look for in the opposite sex: looks, personality, sense of humor, intelligence, popularity, fashion sense, etc. Next, I have to sort through all the responses and make a chart to show how guys and girls value different things. I know a good journalist shouldn't make up her mind before all the votes are in, but I'm pretty sure I know what I'll find. I think guys are way more concerned with a girl's appearance—I think they put that first and don't much care about anything else. Girls, meanwhile, are a lot more discriminating. We want to go out with someone we like and respect, not just someone who's studly.

Just today at lunch there was a scene in the school cafeteria that exactly proved my point. Do you know Scott Trost? He's a sophomore, the back-up quarterback for the Gladiators—tall, pretty good-looking. He dated Amy Sutton for a while, back when she was in her a-different-guy-every-week phase. Anyway, at lunch, Scott and a bunch of his football team friends were sitting at the table next to Todd's and my table. We couldn't help overhearing them because they were talking and laughing loudly. Scott was the *loudest—he was bragging that he could get any girl at school to go with him to the spring dance. He actually snapped his fingers and said, "anyone I want, just like that." Ugh! It made me want to barf. And the worst part was that Todd didn't even think Scott's attitude was that outrageous. He actually stood up for that arrogant jerk!*

"There goes my appetite," I grumbled, stuffing the second half of my tuna salad sandwich back into my lunch bag. "Come on. Let's go outside and get some fresh air."

I stomped outside to the courtyard adjacent to the cafeteria, Todd jogging after me. "Why the sudden exit?" he asked.

I tossed my book bag on the grass and sat down next to it. "I couldn't stand to listen to Scott Trost for a single second longer," I explained. My eyes flashed. "Wasn't that a sickening display of male chauvinism?"

Todd laughed. "I guess it was. Yeah, it was textbook."

"It's not funny," I declared. "The way he was talking about the girls at this school, like we're all empty-headed Barbie dolls waiting breathlessly for Ken—or rather, Scott—to ask us out!"

"Don't take it so seriously," Todd advised, still smiling. "It's just guy talk."

I frowned. "What do you mean, 'just guy talk'?"

"I bet Scott doesn't really feel that way. His buddies were giving him a hard time about not having a date for the dance yet. He was just acting macho to impress them."

"So you're trying to tell me Scott Trost is really a perfect gentleman," I scoffed.

"No, I didn't say that either. But Scott's not always an arrogant jerk. In fact, he can be a pretty nice guy. He just acts differently around his friends. A lot of people are like that, haven't you noticed?"

Todd's tone struck me as more than a little patronizing. "Yes, I guess I have observed one or two things about human nature over the years, thank you very much," I replied indignantly.

Todd appeared to find this conversation incredibly amusing. "You're cute when you're mad," he said.

"That's just the kind of remark that makes me want to scream, Todd Wilkins, and you know it!" I snapped.

He laughed. "OK, OK, I take it back. But I don't take back the stuff about Scott. He's an all-right guy."

"Let me get this straight." I folded my arms across my chest and glared at my boyfriend. "You think it's just fine and dandy for Scott to boast at the top of his lungs that he can get any girl at school to go out with him, and for all those other guys to egg him on. You think that's admirable behavior."

"I won't let you put words in my mouth, Liz," Todd told me. "I said it's *understandable* behavior." With a careless shrug, he fell back on his original—and in my opinion, utterly lame—argument. "Guy talk."

The bell rang, signaling the end of lunch period—and the end, for the moment anyway, of Todd's and my heated discussion. "Well, if I were you, I wouldn't be so proud to belong to your gender, then," I told him. I gathered up my belongings and hopped to my feet.

Still grinning, Todd walked me back inside. "See you after school?"

"I'll be at the newspaper office, working on my article."

"Don't let this Scott Trost incident slant your interpretation of those questionnaires," Todd advised.

I arched my eyebrows. "I'm *completely* unbiased."

"Good." He dropped a kiss on my cheek. "So long, gorgeous."

I know Todd was just teasing me with that "gorgeous" comment, but I still wanted to smack him. I guess he made a joke of the Scott Trost thing because otherwise he'd have to admit that Scott is a pathetic but true reflection of typical S.V.H. male attitudes. I don't know, Diary. Things are basically good between us again, but even so, sometimes (like today!) I feel as if Todd and I are on completely different wavelengths.

Monday, 7:30 P.M.

I finished my "Dating at Sweet Valley High" story for The Oracle—it'll be on the front page of this week's paper. Just as I predicted, most guys who answered the questionnaire rated looks as the most important thing about a girl. Of course, when I showed the chart to Todd, he said it might be scientific, but it still wasn't accurate. In his opinion, it exaggerates the differences between boys and girls—he thinks looks matter to everybody. He also said that the results might be skewed because guys who were hanging out together filling out the questionnaires wouldn't want to sound too sensitive in front of their friends. So they wouldn't answer the questions with their honest responses—The "Scott Trost Effect," Todd dubbed it. Nice try,

Wilkins! I'm standing by my research.

On the homefront, I think my sister is going nuts. As I've mentioned, her latest obsession is interpreting dreams. This is so typical. She's read one book on the subject so now she thinks she's an expert. Believe it or not, she plans to go into business and charge for her services—she put up flyers at school advertising "Dreams Unlimited." Isn't that a hoot? Her goal is to save up enough money for a trip to Maui because now she thinks the guy she keeps dreaming about is a Hawaiian surfer named Jackson. I'm telling you, Nuts with a capital N. I'm sure "Dreams Unlimited" will turn out like all her other previous money-making schemes—a total disaster.

Wednesday, 5:00 P.M.

Dear Diary,

Sometimes truth is stranger than fiction. You would not believe the scene that took place today in the cafeteria. Claire Middleton and Jean West are actually fighting over Scott Trost! Here's how it all started. Just yesterday, Claire confided in me that she had a new boyfriend. When she told me it was Scott, I just about keeled over. Claire is such a smart, pretty, cool girl—remember when she became the first girl in history to try out for the Sweet Valley High football team? And she won a spot? I have so much respect for her. Anyhow, I was shocked that Claire would fall for a guy like Scott, but what could I say? I had to pretend I was happy for her.

But then I heard from Jessica that Jean West, who's on the rebound from her breakup with Tom McKay, has a new boyfriend too. And who's the boy of Jean's dreams? None other than Scott Trost! At that point, I couldn't keep my mouth shut any longer. Jess agreed that it was our duty to tell Claire and Jean that Scott was two-timing them. Naturally, they were both pretty steamed. Then and there (it was lunch period), they decided to march into the cafeteria and give Scott a piece of their mind. When they accused Scott of taking advantage of them, though, instead of being embarrassed, he acted proud of himself. In front of the whole cafeteria, he had the nerve to suggest that Claire and Jean should compete for the honor of being his date to the "Love in Bloom" dance. And this is the insane part—they agreed!

Can you believe it? So, Scott's going

to take them out on alternate nights, and at the end of a week decide which girl he likes best. I am absolutely flabbergasted by this, Diary. I, as much as anyone, know that love defies all logic, but this is ridiculous. Why would two intelligent, attractive girls like Claire and Jean subject themselves to public humiliation for the privilege of dating that Neanderthal?

Friday, 6:30 P.M.

What a wild week at S.V.H. My article came out in The Oracle, and as I expected, everybody's talking about it. Talking about it and writing about it— you wouldn't believe how many letters to the editor Penny's gotten! Some people agree with me and some people don't. Not surprisingly, a couple of guys wrote in defending themselves against the accusation that boys are only interested in girls' looks. Every rule has its exceptions—I'm willing to grant that. One of the letters has really started me thinking, though. In fact, I brought it home with me because Penny plans to print it in the next issue of the newspaper and she wants me to write a reply.

The guy didn't sign it—it's anonymous—but he gave it a title: "Is It True That Boys See Better Than They Think?" Here's the part that impressed me: "Of course, if you ask a guy what it is that first gets him interested in a girl, he'll say it's her looks. But if we're honest with ourselves, we'll admit that we're all interested in how people look. The point is that beauty is in the eye of the beholder. Not only that, but everybody knows that what we see is never the whole picture. It's only after you're attracted to someone because of how they look that you can find out if you're really interested in them or not."

I've read that section of Mr. Anonymous's letter over and over, and I have to admit, not only is it well written and sensible, it's absolutely true. Since my article got printed, I've been having second thoughts about my conclusions. This whole catfight over Scott proves that girls can be just as shallow as guys. Jean and Claire simply can't like Scott because of his personality—his personality is nauseating! He's a cute jock and that's it. Claire and Jean aren't the only girls at S.V.H. who are obsessed with looks and social status either. There's Jessica and Lila and all their friends. They won't give a guy the time of day unless he wears the "right" style khakis and drives the "right" car and has the "right" haircut.

The flip side of the coin is that there are plenty of boys who aren't totally superficial when it comes to relationships. Mr. Anonymous sounds like one, and my very own Todd is another. Todd won't pretend that he doesn't think I'm adorable, and I'll be honest—I wouldn't want him to! But as he tried to convince me the other day, what keeps him interested in me isn't my looks. He loves me for the person that I am on the inside, and the fact that he can talk to me about things. Our relationship has depth because we both have depth. I have my own opinions and ambitions and dreams and so does he, and by sharing them with each other, we enrich each other.

Needless to say, Diary, this leads me right to the subject of Sam Woodruff. I can't pretend I didn't fall for him at first because of his looks. We were drawn to each other that way long before we'd exchanged a single word. Then I discovered there was a lot more to him, and that's when the attraction deepened. But I never got to know him all that well. Would the *attraction have lasted? Was there a foundation strong enough to build a long-term relationship on?*

Enough soul searching. I have to change my clothes—I'm meeting Todd at the Dairi Burger in forty-five minutes. Who'd have thought one little story for the school newspaper would be this thought provoking . . . for the S.V.H. student body and for the author?

Later Friday night

I just got back from my date with Todd and I'm shaking so hard, I can barely write. Guess who was at the Dairi Burger tonight? Sam! It's the first time I've seen him since that morning at the coffee shop, and he flat out ignored me. Of course, under the circumstances I didn't expect him to speak to me, but at least a glance . . . He wouldn't even meet my eye.

I can't stop crying, Diary. How could he act as if there was nothing between us? Did I mean nothing to him?

As usual on Friday nights, the Dairi Burger was hopping. All the tables and booths were overflowing and kids were talking loudly to be heard over the jukebox. Todd and I were at the center of the whole scene, sitting at a big round table with Jessica; Amy; Barry; Cara; my brother, Steven; Winston; and Maria. We'd all ordered burgers, shakes, and fries, and while we ate, Jessica was making us laugh by interpreting one of Winston's dreams.

"OK," Winston was saying as he stuffed a french fry into his mouth. "So, then, after I escape from the giant tarantula by climbing up Abraham Lincoln's face on Mount Rushmore, I'm all of a sudden standing on this train track with a big freight engine speeding toward me. I try to run, but I can't move. My feet are glued in place."

Jessica gasped. Cara giggled. "You're making this up," Maria declared, rolling her eyes at her boyfriend. "You did *not* dream this."

Winston held out his hands, palms up. "Would I lie?" he asked, all innocence.

"Go on, Winston," Jessica urged as she flipped through the pages of her dream interpretation reference book. "Trains in dreams are *very* interesting and *very* suggestive."

"More interesting than giant insects?" wondered Amy.

Jessica tapped a page in her book. "Trains . . . Aha, just as I thought! There's a sexual motif here."

Todd wriggled his eyebrows at Maria. "Sorry to be the one to break it to you, Maria, but

Winston's going to leave you for a girl named Amtrak."

Everybody at the table laughed except Jessica. "Do you mind?" she lectured Todd. "I'm trying to get to the root of Winston's subconscious life. This dream could provide real insight into his psyche."

"And this is a good thing?" Barry joked.

We all laughed again. Winston resumed relating his dream, which became more and more absurd. Just as Jessica was looking up the meaning of purple poodles, the door to the Dairi Burger swung open, and three more customers walked in.

I was facing the entrance, so I saw them right away. First came April Dawson and her boyfriend, Michael Harris, both students at Sweet Valley High. They were with a friend, and when I saw who it was, I dropped my fork on the table with a clatter.

Sam.

A thousand different thoughts chased through my brain in dizzy circles. *He's here looking for me. No, of course he wouldn't do that. It's just a coincidence. But he had to know I might be here. How does he know April and Michael? Oh, right—they all race dirt bikes. Has he noticed me? Do I have time to hide in the girls' room? I don't think he's spotted me yet. No, he sees me. He definitely sees me.*

My face and neck were as red as a boiled Maine lobster. I grabbed my water glass and took a big swig. "Are you all right, Liz?" Todd asked, concerned.

"I, yeah, uh . . . I just choked. On a french fry." I hoped Todd didn't pick up on the fact that I'd finished my fries five minutes ago. I drained the rest of my water. "I'm fine," I assured him hastily.

April, Michael, and Sam were weaving their way through the crowded restaurant, heading for a booth that had just opened up in the back. Their path was going to take them right past the table where Todd and I were sitting, and as they approached, I held my breath. Would Sam say hello to me? If he did, how should I react? Everyone would want to know how I knew him. What story should I tell? When Sam's and my eyes met, would it be obvious to the whole world that we'd once been in love, briefly but deeply? Was the chemistry still there—would we be able to hide it?

At that instant, I was glad the Dairi Burger was so noisy. Otherwise, everyone would have heard the pounding of my heart. I watched Sam covertly while I pretended to listen to Winston. Then the moment came.

Sam walked alongside the table, almost close enough for me to touch. I glanced up at him, in a casual fashion. And then, the worst possible thing happened.

Sam didn't even look at me. Or rather, he looked at me but his eyes slid right past me as if I were a complete stranger, as if he'd never seen me before in his life. His gaze didn't linger on Todd either. Instead, for the second or two it took for him, Michael, and April to go by, Sam stared directly at . . . my sister.

Jessica was too busy leafing through her dream book to notice that a good-looking guy was checking her out, but *I* noticed. My cheeks, which a moment before had been scarlet, were now pale with hurt and disappointment. Breaking off my romance with Sam had been so hard. Seeing him brought it all back, and once again I felt my emotions pulling me in conflicting directions. *I could be with Sam instead of Todd tonight. Did I make the right choice?*

Todd couldn't know what I was thinking of course, but he picked that precise instant to reach over and take my hand, and when he did, certainty returned to my sad, puzzled heart. Yes, I'd made the right choice. But I still wanted something from Sam, and all of a sudden, I wanted it more than anything in the world. Just a glance, a smile, a sign that we'd once shared something that he still secretly treasured, as I did.

I didn't get what I wanted. I watched Sam's broad, stiff back as he walked away, struggling to hide my pain from Todd, Jessica, and the others, to keep my eyes dry and emotionless. I wanted to cry, though, as I remembered my recent dream. In it, Sam walked away from me, and I was sad, but it wasn't all bad because I felt he'd forgiven me and would remember me with affection, not bitterness. In real life, though, it looked as if I was going to be denied that consolation.

Clearly, Sam Woodruff hadn't forgiven me, and for all I knew, he never would.

My dream was a lie. Of course Sam's still mad and hurt. After the way I treated him, how could I expect anything else? And in front of Todd and all my friends, he couldn't exactly acknowledge me. Maybe I should be thankful that he didn't—he really could have blown it for me if he wanted to, if he wanted revenge. But he wouldn't do that. Sam is a sweet, decent guy. It did feel like punishment, though, Diary, the way he looked at Jessica instead of at me. I think he did that on purpose—I think he knew it would hurt me. Or maybe he was just struck by Jessica's exotic outfit—she was wearing a wraparound Hawaiian print skirt and matching top, part of her ready-to-meet-Jackson-in-Maui theme. Good ol' Jessica. Sometimes I really appreciate the comic relief she brings to my life.

This past weekend ended up being kind of quiet, which meant I had too much time on my hands, which meant I thought a lot about Sam. Running into him the other night at the Dairi Burger was pure torment, but I suppose it's what I deserve. I just wish that he wasn't friends with April and Michael—it will be too awful if he starts turning up regularly at Sweet Valley High hangouts.

Speaking of which, Scott Trost is also going to get exactly what he deserves. Get this: From the very beginning, Jean and Claire's contest to see who gets to date him has been a setup! A couple of weeks ago, they both unexpectedly got very romantic love letters in their lockers . . . from Scott. It's really too insulting—he didn't even bother writing an original letter to each girl; he just wrote a different name on top! What a creep!

According to Claire, when she and Jean found out about his double dealing, they decided to confront Scott publicly and really embarrass him. When he didn't act at all embarrassed, and in fact proposed the competition, they accepted his terms. What Scott doesn't know is

218

that he's not the one in the driver's seat. When he announces the "winner," his date for the Love in Bloom dance, she'll turn him down flat in front of as many people as possible. Scott will end up without a date for the dance, and after that, no girl in her right mind will ever agree to go out with him! I really can't wait to see this. I definitely plan to have a front-row seat in the cafeteria on D-Day (Dump Day!).

Tuesday, 5:00 P.M.

I'm not the only one whose dreams aren't coming true lately. Jessica's Dreams Unlimited business has gone down the tubes. All of her customers are demanding their money back because her interpretations and advice are turning out to be totally off base. Not only that, she was just flipping through one of her old magazines and she saw an ad for Hawaiian vacations with a photo of a beautiful beach, and on the very next page an ad for Jackson's Funtime Fashions . . . and the model in the clothing ad looked exactly like "Jackson," the guy in her dream!

So that explains that dream. She must have just remembered the images from *those advertisements while she was dreaming—and she thought she was predicting her fate and her future with "Jackson"! Needless to say, she's taken her dream analysis books back to the library and has stopped wearing tropical outfits. She's devoting all her energy to finding a date for the spring dance, which is only a week and two days away. I'll say one thing for my sister, she always bounces back fast!*

Wednesday, 8:00 P.M.

Diary, if I forget again, please remind me never to undervalue Todd's opinions. Remember the letter to the Oracle editor, from Anonymous? Well, guess who wrote it? Yep. My boyfriend! I was kind of steamed when I found out, because Todd had slyly gotten me to admit that "Anonymous" made a lot of good points. I felt pretty duped. But after I cooled off, I wrote a response that Penny printed side by side with Anonymous's letter in this week's paper. Todd and I are on the same wavelength, which is how I can love him so much even when my heart is still breaking over someone else.

I should be studying for a math test, but I have to write about what happened at school today. Jean and Claire carried out their plan to waste Scott. What a spectacle! They did it during lunch period and the cafeteria was packed—everyone knew Scott was going to make his little announcement and no one wanted to miss the show.

Well, it was even better than they expected. Scott was strutting like a rooster—he played right into Jean and Claire's hands. I would have wanted to throw up when he said, totally grandstanding, "My date for tomorrow night's dance is Jean West," but I knew Jean wasn't going to react with joy and gratitude the way he expected. She kind of went overboard, though. She threw a carton of milk all over Scott and shouted, "I wouldn't go out with you if you were the last boy on earth!" and then stormed out of the cafeteria. Scott lost his cool for about a tenth of a second, and then turned to Claire, assuming she'd be happy to take Jean's place as his date. She gave the same answer. "No way!"

The kids in the cafeteria cheered. Scott

was mortified, to put it mildly. And I have to admit, Diary, that even though I was primed to enjoy Jean and Claire's revenge, I found myself feeling a little bit sorry for Scott. I felt even more sorry for him—and for Jean—when I talked to her later. It turns out, despite the whole contest thing, Jean ended up having fun on her dates with Scott. She didn't want to go through with the scene in the cafeteria, but she couldn't admit to Claire that she'd fallen in love with the enemy. . . .

I knew something was wrong when Jean ran out of the cafeteria. She was supposed to be savoring Scott's humiliation, the way Claire was, but instead she'd left in tears. What was going on?

There was only one way to find out. When Claire had said her piece and lobster-red Scott was receiving grief from his football teammates, I dashed off in search of Jean. On a hunch, I ducked into the nearest girls' room and, sure enough, there she was.

"Jean, what's the matter?" I asked, taking a pack of tissues from my purse and handing them to her. "Don't you feel better now that you gave Scott a taste of his own medicine?"

She started to dab at her eyes, then gave up and burst into tears again. "No," she wailed. "I don't. I feel a hundred times worse."

I shook my head, mystified. "But Scott got totally burned. Wasn't that the point? You taught him that he can't treat girls like objects. You're a heroine, Jean!"

"You don't understand, Liz." Jean blew her nose. "I didn't want to teach Scott anything. I wanted to go to the dance with him!"

I stared. "What are you *talking* about?"

"I—I—" Jean stammered. She started to cry again.

I put an arm around her. "Come on," I said gently. "Let's go find a quiet place for you to pull yourself together, and then we can talk."

I herded Jean down the hall to a quiet nook, sat her down on a chair, and supplied her with more tissues. "OK, Jean," I said. "Spill the beans."

"It's Scott," she said, her voice still trembling. "It's Scott and me. I know I should hate him, but instead . . ." Tears welled up in her big green eyes. "I've fallen for him, Liz. Fallen hard."

"Oh, Jean." I reached out to pat her shoulder, not knowing what to say.

"I know you're wondering how I could like him," Jean went on, and I blushed, because I was wondering just that. "But you have to believe me, Liz. He's a different person when we're alone. It's like there are two Scott Trosts, the public one and the private one. Do you know what I mean?"

I nodded. I knew only too well what it was like to be two different people at the same time.

Jean's eyes grew dreamy and a soft smile curved her lips. "Claire said her dates with Scott were a chore—really boring. But he and I had a ball together. He's funny and considerate and not at all stuck on himself, the way he acts when he's in a crowd of his guy friends. We had the best talks. And he likes me too." Her smile faded. "At least, I thought he did."

"He *did* choose you over Claire," I commented.

"I knew he would," Jean said, "but I also hoped he'd admit to everybody that the contest was a stupid idea. That he'd apologize to me and Claire both. Instead, he went into that macho routine." Jean's eyes flashed with anger and betrayal. She was shredding the tissues to bits. "It made me so mad! There I was, worried about hurting him, because I'd promised Claire we'd get back at him together. But *he* didn't hesitate to hurt *me*."

I sighed, full of sympathy for her but not sure what advice to give. "This is really complicated," I had to admit.

"Actually, it's simple." Jean's lower lip trembled. "It's over between Scott and me."

I studied her intently. "Are you sure?"

"You were there," Jean said. "You saw what just happened, Liz. Do you think he could ever forgive me for embarrassing him like that? And should *I* forgive *him*?"

I couldn't help thinking about my own life, about Sam and me and the way he'd walked past me in the Dairi Burger without so much as a glance of recognition. "I can't tell you what to do or how to feel," I said slowly, "but if you really do care about each other, then yes, you'll forgive each other. You'll talk it over. You'll find a way to get beyond this."

Jean smiled wistfully through her tears. "Thanks for listening, Liz, but I just don't know." Her voice was sad and small. "What just happened in the cafeteria makes me think that I was wrong about him having another side. Maybe there is only one real Scott Trost, and he's not anyone I could ever truly care for and respect."

It just goes to show, Diary (and I should know this!), you can't judge a book by its cover. Things aren't always the way they appear on the surface. If a nice girl like Jean genuinely likes Scott (and Todd thinks he's an OK guy too), then he can't be as bad as he seems. I agree with Jean, though—it's hard to imagine they could work things out after that scene in the cafeteria. But I kind of hope they do. It would give me some vicarious satisfaction, since I can't hope for the same kind of reconciliation in my relationship with Sam, which isn't a relationship any longer, of course. So why do I keep sneaking his sweater out of my closet? I even wore it in my room for an hour last night while I was listening to music and writing poetry. I'm hopeless, Diary!

Friday, 6:00 P.M.

Jean just called, and she's ecstatic. She and Scott are back together! He came over to her house just now with a dozen roses and apologized for being such a creep. She assured me that she didn't make it easy for him. She demanded an explanation for why he'd behaved the way he did, and he said it was because there's this conflict between the inner Scott Trost— the person he is when he's with Jean, the person he wants to be all the time—and the outer Scott Trost, the guy who acts a certain way to impress his friends. He promised that she can count on him to be his best self from now on, not to be arrogant and mean, and he must have seemed sincere because it sounds as if at that point he and Jean fell into each other's arms and shared a big kiss.

I'm really rooting for them, Diary. I think it takes a lot of guts to turn over a new leaf the way Scott is. And I definitely admire how open those two are being with each other. I'm going to try to follow their example. I put Sam's sweater back in my closet, and this time, it's staying there. From now on, I'm not going to look for excuses to think about Sam—Todd's the one I want to dream about.

Which reminds me—it's time to hop in the shower and get ready for the Love in Bloom dance. Todd's picking me up in an hour!

Same night, very late

Just a footnote, Diary. The dance was dreamy. The Sweet Valley High gym was decorated with tons of colorful paper flowers and the Droids played all their best songs. Scott and Jean were inseparable—I've never seen a couple look more crazy about each other (except for Todd and me)! We danced to every song and the slow dances especially were incredibly, amazingly, deliriously wonderful. I don't know why, but I really felt like I was falling in love with him for the first time. When he drove me home, we dragged out our good-bye for an hour with countless kisses. Now I can't sleep because I'm still tingling from head to toe. I wish I could *have Todd's arms around me all night long!*

Saturday night, late

Todd and I went to the Beach Disco tonight with the gang, and we were having a wonderful time dancing under the stars . . . until I realized Sam Woodruff was there with some of his friends too. Diary, there was a time not too long ago when all I wanted was to be close to Sam, but now I wish he lived a thousand miles away! He didn't speak to me or acknowledge my presence in any way, but I was intensely aware of him. And I couldn't help noticing that he watched Jessica the entire time. In fact, at one point, I thought he was going to ask her to dance with him.

Just when I think my life is getting back to normal, Diary!

It was a perfect night for dancing under th
stars. And with Todd's strong arms around me
we swayed to a sultry slow song, I was in heaven

Over Todd's shoulder, I caught a glimpse
Jessica dancing with Steve Anderson. Steve ha
been her date to the spring dance, and they'd ha
a good time. He seemed like just the kind of gu
she was looking for: handsome, popular, a goo

dresser, a great dancer. Technically, he had it all. But I could tell just by watching them that one essential ingredient was missing: sparks.

"I hope my sister falls in love someday," I said out loud. "I mean, really in love. Not just this crush-of-the-week type of thing."

Todd pulled back slightly to smile down into my eyes. "What made you think of that?"

I nestled my head in the crook of his shoulder. "I just want her to be as happy as I am."

Todd hugged me closer. He didn't answer, and he didn't need to. At that moment, we were in such perfect sync, both mentally and physically, we didn't need words.

I wasn't sure I deserved to be so happy, but I didn't plan to waste precious moments dwelling on my imperfections and mistakes. It was starting to seem as if the girl who'd briefly dallied with Sam Woodruff was someone else, not me at all. *This* was me, the girl in Todd Wilkins's arms, the girl who had eyes for no one else. I belonged to Todd, and I never intended to stray from him again.

Then I saw something that jolted me out of my dreamy reverie. A powerful sense of *déjà vu* washed over me, momentarily stealing my breath away. A tall, broad-shouldered guy in a black leather jacket stood at the edge of the dance floor, his blond hair catching the light from a Japanese lantern in a nearby tree. Sam.

A few months earlier, Sam had come to the Beach Disco expressly to look for me. I remembered how I'd ditched Todd to sneak a dance with Sam. *What's he doing here?* I wondered. Was he going to make a scene? Would he march up and tell Todd how I'd betrayed him, betrayed them both? My panicked heart was beating rapidly and my skin prickled with nervous heat. *I have to get out of here,* I thought, suddenly feeling nauseous.

Mercifully, the song ended right at that instant, and the band announced that it was taking a break between sets. Seizing Todd's hand, I dragged him away from Sam. "I'm dying of thirst," I told him. "Come on. Let's get something to drink."

Todd tagged along obediently. Thankfully, he didn't seem to notice that my mood had altered. I felt safe at the crowded, noisy bar, especially when it became clear that Sam wasn't following me. He continued to stand at a distance, his eyes fixed intently on something. Or rather, on someone.

At first, I thought he was watching my friends and me. After a few minutes, though, it became apparent that Sam was watching one person in particular—the same person he'd stared at when he'd walked by my table at the Dairi Burger the other night.

Sam Woodruff couldn't take his eyes off of my twin sister, Jessica.

I sipped my drink, frowning. On the one hand, Sam wasn't the only guy at the Beach Disco who was checking my sister out. As usual, Jessica was dressed to kill, in high heels, a black leather mini-skirt, and a tight white top with a wide, scooped-out neck. With her long blond hair swirling around her, she was the sexiest, prettiest girl at the club. On the other hand, though, she wasn't just *any* pretty girl. Sam knew darned well she was my sister, and his interest in her couldn't be innocent and coincidental.

But maybe he's not really interested, I thought, getting a hold of myself. I was probably overreacting. There was no law that said Sam couldn't hang out at the Beach Disco with his friends, looking at girls. *As long as looking is all he does,* I decided.

The band started up again, plunging straight into a rocking dance tune. People began gravitating back toward the dance floor. Todd and I remained behind, though, finishing our drinks, and Jessica continued to chatter with some of her friends. I caught a few snippets of their conversation, which was extremely intellectual, as usual: ". . . the most adorable little rib knit . . . ," Amy gushed, waving her hands in excited emphasis. ". . . With a slit up the back . . . ," Lila added. ". . . And bright red lipstick!" raved Jessica.

I couldn't help smiling, but my amusement didn't last long. From across the room, I saw Sam straighten up and say something to one of his buddies. Then he began to make his way through the crush of people, his stride quick and purposeful. His gaze was fixed on Jessica—without a doubt, she was his destination.

My heart sank into my sandals. "He's going to ask her to dance!" I croaked, terrified.

"What?" asked Todd.

I couldn't let it happen. Putting my glass down with a clatter, I grabbed Todd's arm. "Come on," I urged, keeping my tone bright and playful as I steered him toward my sister and her friends. "This is a great song—we can't sit it out. Let's dance, everybody!"

In a somewhat crazed fashion, I hustled the whole gang back onto the dance floor and initiated a big arms-around-each-other circle dance. Todd was giving me funny looks, obviously wondering why I'd suddenly turned into the life of the party, but I really couldn't worry about it. I was too busy keeping an eye on my twin. Sam, meanwhile, had faded from view, but I couldn't relax my vigilance. *I'll bop till I get blisters,* I determined silently. Whatever it took to keep Jessica away from Sam!

Sam and his friends didn't stay late at the Beach Disco, so after a while I was able to relax. I wish I knew what he was thinking, Diary, but I don't have a clue.

232

Could he be falling for Jessica? It doesn't make sense . . . or does it? After all, he fell for me and she's my identical twin. And now that I think of it, she was the one he was attracted to in the first place. Remember? That was why he wanted to meet me—because he'd seen Eric Parker's talk-show interview! I mean, technically that was me, but I was impersonating Jessica—her voice, her style. So maybe the way Sam sees it, he ended up with the wrong twin and now he wants to start over . . . with my sister.

I hope that's not what he's after. All I know for sure is that Sam may be watching Jessica, but she still has no idea who he is, and it would be simplest for all involved if we just kept it that way!

Part 3

Dear Diary,

I don't know what to do about my sister. I just popped into her room to borrow her Jamie Peters's CD and I found her reading a dirt-bike magazine. My blood froze in my veins. She's been hanging out a lot lately with April Dawson, and April's gotten her interested in the sport. I'm just praying that Jessica's curiosity about dirt-bike racing fades fast. She seems mostly impressed by the clothes, which she's decided are even cooler than surfing gear. I pointed out that one of the key words in dirt-bike racing is dirt, and it's a messy, unglamorous activity, but she'd already

234

tuned me out, in typical fashion. What if April takes her to a rally? I just have a bad feeling about this.

Meanwhile, Todd and I had an argument today. Just when our relationship gets back on track, something always seems to come along to send us off balance again. Love is a roller coaster. This time it was a silly disagreement about, of all romantic things, plumbing. Todd drove me home from school, and when we headed to the kitchen for a snack, we discovered the sink was all clogged up. Todd fixed it—one of Jessica's barrettes had gone down the drain and lodged in the U-bend of the pipe. So, fine. Todd saved the day—I didn't have to call the plumber. I gave him a big kiss as a thank you—what more could a guy ask for?

But then he made this offhand, totally sexist comment, basically implying that I was a helpless, incompetent female who couldn't fix a clogged drain if my life depended on it. Needless to say, I pointed out that that was absolutely the worst kind of gender stereotyping. So he elaborated: "There are just some things guys do better than girls, and other things girls do better than guys." Can you believe it? And he considers himself enlightened!

Well, I don't take that kind of thing

sitting down, as you know. I challenged him to a contest: He'd give me a list of three things he does well and I'd give him a list of three things I do well. We each have to do the tasks on the list, and whoever successfully completes them first wins. Loser picks up the tab for dinner at a really nice restaurant. Todd's challenge to me is to change a car tire, build a shelf, and replace the washer on the dripping faucet in Jessica's and my bathroom. My challenge to him is to sew an apron, do his family's grocery shopping for a week, and cook me dinner. I'm fired up, Diary! I'll prove to him that women can be just as "handy" as men. Anything Todd can do, I can do better!

Saturday, 6:00 P.M.

This has been a long, long day. Jessica went to a dirt-bike rally today to watch April and Mike race, and she's still not home yet. I've been pacing back and forth in my room for hours and I've chewed my fingernails to stubs. I thought writing in my journal might calm me down a little, but I'm still frantic. I just don't know what's happening to me, Diary. When Jess told me she was going to the rally, something inside me snapped. . . .

236

"Come on, Liz," Steven urged. "Just a couple more inches."

I stopped pumping the handle of the car jack and wiped my perspiring face on my T-shirt sleeve. "This isn't good enough?" I panted.

Steven shook his head sternly. "You want to do it right, don't you?"

I stuck out my lower lip and exhaled, puffing air upward to lift the damp hair from my forehead. "Yeah," I grunted. "I do."

After what seemed an eternity, I had Steven's yellow VW jacked up high enough to satisfy my brother. "OK," he told me. "Now remove the hubcap."

"Ah," I said, peering at the tire. "The hubcap. Yes, of course."

It had seemed like good luck that Steven was home from college for the weekend and could "advise" me on the first of the tasks on my list from Todd. But now that I was actually kneeling on the rough pavement of the driveway with the morning sun beating on my back, I was starting to wish I'd put this particular challenge off until later. *I should've warmed up on the shelf or the washer,* I thought, prying at the hubcap. *Those are bound to be easier!*

When the hubcap popped loose, I gave a shout of triumph. Just then, someone behind me said, "What on *earth* are you doing, Liz?"

I turned around. My twin sister stood in the driveway with her hands on her hips and a baffled look on her face. I had to smile, thinking about the contrast we made. I was grubby and sweaty, while she looked fresh, cool, and immaculate in a pair of pink shorts and a sky-blue tank top. "What does it look like?" I replied. "I'm changing a tire."

"But *why?*"

"Because girls should know how to do this kind of stuff," Steven interjected. "Hang around and pick up a few tips, Jess."

"Yeah, right." She laughed.

She started to breeze past us, the keys to the Fiat dangling from her hand. "Where are you off to?" I asked.

"I'm meeting April," Jessica replied casually.

I stiffened, my fingers tightening on the rim of the hubcap. I didn't have to ask *where* she was meeting April. The previous day, I'd heard April telling Jessica about the dirt-bike rally in which she was entered. "Um, you know, Steven's right," I burst out. "You should help me with this, Jess. It's really important to know how to change a tire."

She laughed again. "Look, Liz, just because you were stupid enough to make a stupid bet with Todd doesn't mean I have to get my hands dirty too."

"But what if you were driving someplace in the Fiat and you broke down?" I demanded.

She shrugged. "Isn't that what tow trucks are for?"

I tried a different approach. "So, you're going to the rally, huh?"

"Yep."

I tilted my head, my gaze critical. "And that's what you're wearing?"

A flicker of uncertainty shadowed her eyes. I'd hit a nerve. She'd probably just spent an hour and a half deciding what to wear. "You don't think this shirt goes with these shorts?" she asked doubtfully.

I narrowed my eyes. "It goes, but I bet you won't see much pink at the rally."

"Well, I want to fit in and stand out at the same time," she said. "I mean, I don't want to be mistaken for a biker."

"Ahem," Steven said impatiently. "Are we changing a tire here or having a fashion consultation? I don't have all day, Liz."

"Just a sec, Steve," I said. Jessica was opening the driver's side door of the Fiat, which was parked next to Steven's VW. I put the hubcap down and ran over to her. "Are you sure you should go to the rally?" I asked, a note of desperation in my voice.

"You mean, because I risk total humiliation if I'm the only person wearing pink?" Jessica joked.

"No, because . . . because of the motorbike thing." I played my last card. "You know how Mom and Dad feel about that, ever since Todd's and my accident."

"I'm watching the race, not entering it," Jessica reminded me. She started the Fiat's engine. "Later, Liz!"

I stepped back as she pulled out of the driveway and roared off. My delaying tactics had failed utterly. Jessica was headed to the dirt-bike rally and I was powerless to stop her. *Sam will be there for sure,* I thought. I knew for a fact that he'd already noticed Jessica. The question was, would this be the day that *she* noticed *him?*

> *I did all but throw my body in front of the car, Diary, but it was no use. The rally was probably over hours ago. She must be having fun . . . a lot of fun. Too much fun! I'm going crazy wondering. Where is she? Who is she with?*
>
> *Hold on . . . yep! There's the car now. I'm about to find out!*

> Sunday, 11:00 A.M.

> *Fate can be so merciless. Just when I'm learning to forget Sam Woodruff, my sister has to fall for him.*
> *Yes, Diary. Jessica met Sam yesterday, and from the sound of it, sparks flew. When she got home last night, she couldn't wait to tell me every single excruciating detail. . . .*

"Dirt-bike racing is *the* coolest sport," Jessica declared with typical overstatement. She flung herself onto my bed. "I had the best time today!"

"Oh?" I perched myself on my desk chair,

240

tucking my feet up and wrapping my arms around my knees in a vain attempt to stop myself from shaking. "The rally was fun?"

"It was totally thrilling," Jessica confirmed. "The race course was incredibly hard—tons of bumps and sharp turns. You should've seen April fly, though! She's better than any of the guys. She raced with Artie Western instead of with Mike because Mike had to go visit his sick grandmother, but she still won. It was awesome."

"So, then what did you do?"

Jessica sat up, her lips curving into a smile that grew wider and wider. "Liz, I'm in love."

My heart stopped momentarily, then started up again with a weak hiccup. "In love?" I squeaked.

"His name is Sam," she continued breathlessly. "Liz, he's the most wonderful boy in the world!"

It could be a different Sam, I told myself, breathing deeply to slow my pulse. Sam Smith. Sam Jones. But an instant later, Jessica dashed my feeble hope. "Sam Woodruff," she went on. "Isn't that a great name?"

"Yeah," I whispered. "So." I cleared my throat. "You met um, Sam, at the rally?"

"I guess he was in the race," Jessica told me, "but with a helmet and chest protector on, he didn't stand out in the crowd. A bunch of people met at the Dairi Burger afterward, though."

I smiled weakly. "And he stood out then?"

Her eyes sparkled. "Boy, did he ever."

I decided to make light of my sister's new crush. *These things never last more than a day or two,* I consoled myself. "So, what makes Sam special?"

"First of all, he's cute," Jessica told me. "No, make that breathtaking. Tall and lean, with these wide shoulders and really muscular arms. And his *hair.*" I thought she was going to swoon. "It's blonder than mine and really thick and curly. And his *eyes.*" She fell back on the bed, her arms flung out limply to the sides. "They're light gray and they just burn right through you. But they're sweet too. Twinkly. Mischievous. And his *smile.*" She sighed blissfully. "He has the *best* sense of humor! He had me laughing the whole time."

I knew only too well how wonderful Sam's eyes were, what a great sense of humor he had, and how good it felt to be the object of his attention. Tears tickled the back of my throat. I clenched my jaw, struggling to remain composed. "He really sounds terrific," I managed.

"He is, Liz," Jessica gushed. "How am I supposed to survive until he calls me?"

"You gave him your phone number?" *Not that he needed to ask for it,* I added silently. *He already knows it . . . from calling me!*

"No, but he can get it from April, or look me up in the book. I know he'll call," she said with complete confidence. "You know how it is, when you meet someone and you just *click*."

"Yeah," I said with secret sadness. "I know how it is."

It shouldn't hurt so much, Diary, but it does. And I'm worried to, for my sister's sake. She's fallen for him hard, but does Sam genuinely like her or is he playing some sort of cruel game? He must know he's rubbing salt in my wounds. What can he be thinking?

I just have to hope Jessica loses interest in Sam after a day or two like she has with all her other "true loves."

Tuesday, late

Tomorrow is a school day so I should be in bed, but there's no point in turning out the light yet. I wouldn't be able to fall asleep. My heart is still hammering from my phone conversation with Sam earlier this evening.

He called Jess the other day and they went out on their first date to Guido's Pizza Palace. She's more smitten with him than ever, and it looks as if this time, for her at least, it's serious. I've never seen her so happy. She's dancing around the house, humming, singing, and doing nice things for everybody—like cooking dinner even

243

*though it was my night, and buying Mom a
big bouquet of fresh flowers, and giving
Prince Albert a perfume-scented doggy
bubble bath. I couldn't stand it, Diary—I
couldn't stand not knowing what Sam's
motives were. So I dialed the phone number I still know by heart. . . .*

Jessica was over at Cara's, so I knew I was
safe—there was no risk that she'd overhear me and
wonder why on earth I was telephoning her new
boyfriend. *Why* am *I doing this anyway?* I thought
as I listened to the phone ring on the other end.
Then someone picked up. "Hello?" said Sam's
deep, familiar voice.

I didn't have any time to get my story straight,
to rehearse my lines. "Uh . . . Sam?" I said, my own
voice a nervous squeak.

"Jessica?" he asked. There was a pause. Then
he said, with a note of disbelief, "Elizabeth?"

"Yes, it's Elizabeth," I said.

"Well . . . hi," he responded. "This is a surprise."

Sam's voice was cool and completely bereft of
emotion. He didn't sound pleased; he didn't sound
angry. I, meanwhile, felt a mix of about a thousand
conflicting emotions—I wasn't sure what I was
feeling, exactly, but I was feeling a lot, and none of
it was good. "I just want to know," I began, sum-
moning my nerve, "what you think you're doing
dating my twin sister."

I could sense that I'd shocked him. "What *I'd* like to know," he countered, after a moment of brief, charged silence, "is what business of yours that could possibly be."

"Oh, come on, Sam," I snapped. "Don't pretend it was a coincidence that you ended up at the same table at the Dairi Burger the other night. Did you get April to bring Jessica to the dirt-bike rally?"

"I'll admit I've had my eye on her," Sam told me. "She's a beautiful girl, just like you are. But there's no conspiracy here, Elizabeth. I didn't have anything to do with her coming to the rally. But was I psyched to see her there, and to finally get introduced to her? You bet."

Suddenly this conversation seemed absolutely otherworldly. Could I really be talking to Sam Woodruff, with whom I'd been madly in love just a few weeks ago, about how psyched he was to be going out with my twin sister? No. Something was wrong—very wrong. "You're using her to get back at me, aren't you?" I accused him. "I hurt you and now you're trying to hurt me."

This time, I hit a nerve. "I would never do something like that," he insisted.

"How can I be sure of that?" I demanded.

"Are you saying I have to prove myself to you?" Sam laughed mirthlessly. "Look, Elizabeth. I was never anything but honest with you. You're the one who lied and cheated. Frankly, I don't care what you think about Jessica and me, but for what it's worth, you have my word that I really care for her. In fact, I'm nuts about her. And do you want to know why?" He didn't wait for my answer. "Because maybe she looks just like you, but that's where the resemblance ends. I know she doesn't already have a boyfriend. I know I can trust her. She's as open and truthful as you are deceitful. Good-bye, Elizabeth."

Sam hung up. I sat for a long moment with the phone still pressed against my ear, his parting words echoing in my head. *"She's as open and truthful as you are deceitful. . . ."*

I replaced the receiver, my lip trembling. Sam hadn't given me a chance to defend myself, but I supposed it didn't really matter. Because I couldn't defend myself. I was guilty as charged.

I understand why Sam said that, Diary, but it still stings. I think of myself as an honest and loyal person. As for Jessica, of course I couldn't have said something so mean-spirited about her to Sam, but sneaking around to get what she wants is practically a way of life for her!

It just seems incredibly unfair. I know that lying to Sam and going behind Todd's back was a serious mistake. But how long do I have to keep paying for it?

246

Dear Diary,

Jessica went out with Sam again last night, and she can't stop talking about it. She's acting like this is "it," like she's ready to settle down for life. Don't you think it's too soon for her to feel that way? I don't want to see her hurt, I really don't, and no matter what Sam said the other night, I still can't help suspecting that he's using Jessica, that this doesn't mean as much to him as it does to her. So I decided it was my duty, as a sister, to warn Jessica that Sam isn't the boy she thinks he is. My duty to stop her before she gets in too deep. I knocked on her door, intending to tell her all about Sam and me. . . .

After dinner, I sat down at my desk to do my homework. It was hard to concentrate on my math and French, though, when in the distance, I could hear Jessica's animated voice. She was in her own room, chattering on the phone, and I had a hunch I knew with whom. Sam.

Half an hour passed. Then there was a brief silence, and then Jessica's stereo started to blast. Pushing back my desk chair, I cut through the bathroom and tapped on her door.

"Come in," she called cheerfully. "Oh, hi, Liz. Music too loud? I'll turn it down."

Since when did Jessica volunteer to turn down her stereo before I even asked her to do it? Her good mood made her eyes sparkle and her bronzed skin glow. I hated to ruin her spirits, but I reminded myself it was for her own benefit. "Jess, can we talk for a minute?" I asked.

"Sure." She plopped down on her unmade bed and patted the mattress beside her. "What's up?"

I sat down cross-legged, wondering where to start. Should I simply announce, "I used to be secretly involved with Sam Woodruff?" Or should I go back to the very beginning? "It's about . . ." I took a deep breath, deciding to burn my bridges. "It's about Sam. Sam and—"

Jessica cut me off before I could say, "Sam and me."

"Oh, Sam," she said rapturously. "Liz, I never thought I'd meet such a wonderful guy. I mean, where has he been all my life?" She held up a hand, motioning for me not to talk. "Wait, don't answer that. It's probably just as well I didn't meet him sooner, because you know how I've always felt about going steady. That's your style, not mine. But I think . . ." She grabbed one of my hands and squeezed it tight. Her smile was beautiful, so pure and hopeful. "I think this relationship is going to last. I *want* it to last."

Wordlessly, I squeezed her hand back.

She shook her head, her smile becoming rueful. "Sorry for babbling like that, Liz. You were going to say something about Sam. What was it?"

"I was going to say . . ." I gazed into Jessica's expectant eyes. I pictured how the joy reflected there would change to shock and dismay if I told her about my own relationship with Sam. *She'd never forgive me for ruining this for her,* I realized. And I realized something else too. If I destroyed my sister's happiness, I'd never forgive myself.

"I was just going to say that Sam sounds nice and I'm really glad for you," I finished. "You deserve to be happy, Jess."

As Jessica leaned over to give me a hug, I saw tears sparkling in her eyes. "Thanks, Liz," she whispered.

I don't regret my decision to remain silent, but if Sam does anything to hurt Jessica . . . I just have to hope he was telling me the truth about his feelings for her. But if he was, then he's as crazy about Jessica as she is about him, and that means they're about to become a serious couple. As in, Jessica will want to bring him home to meet the family, double date with Todd and me, and who knows what else. How am I going to stand it?

I wasn't lying to Jessica before, Diary. I am happy for her that she finally met a great guy . . . but why did it have to be this guy?

What a morning. I spent hours trying to put up a cookbook shelf in the kitchen, my second task from Todd's list. I'll never admit this to him in a million years, but I'm definitely not cut out to be a carpenter! Just buying the supplies at the hardware store was a nightmare. First, I took Enid with me, but we didn't even know what we were looking for. When the salesman asked, "Rawl plugs or toggle bolts?" (or something like that!), we ran out of the store without buying so much as a single nail. I went back later with Jessica, and by flirting her head off, she got this one stockboy to help us. We got the wood and stuff, but it was so humiliating!

As if that wasn't enough, while I was laboring over my shelf, Jessica was off playing tennis with Sam. And as if that wasn't enough, I had to deal with Mom's questions about Jessica's new beau. "Doesn't he sound nice? Doesn't he seem to be a good influence on Jessica? When will we meet him?" And on and on! What Mom doesn't know is that she may not meet Sam for a long while. Jessica's afraid to bring him home because she knows Mom and Dad will disapprove of him riding a motorbike. Jess will have to tell them one of these days, though. All I know is, I'm staying out of it.

Yesterday turned into a wild day. Artie Western had a bad spill from his dirt bike and ended up in the hospital.

Here's the story: Right after I wrote the previous entry in here, the phone rang. It was April Dawson, and she was in a total frenzy. She was looking for Jessica, but since Jess wasn't here, she told me what was going on. Her boyfriend, Mike, had challenged Artie to a dirt-bike race—just the two of them. The two guys used to be best friends and dirt-bike partners, but a while back Mike got hurt in a race and he blamed Artie for it and has never forgiven him. Ever since, they've been in this intense feud, and so naturally when April heard they were planning to race, she knew they'd both be reckless and she was really afraid someone would end up hurt.

Well, she was right. Enid and I hurried off to meet April, and the three of us sped over to Secca Lake where the guys were racing, but we didn't get there in time to stop them. We saw the whole thing, and it was terrifying. Mike and Artie were neck and neck coming down a steep hill on this twisty, narrow track and Mike must've swerved to hit a bump. Artie swerved too,

251

and ended up flying over the bars of his bike and somersaulting down the hill.

I'll never forget the sight for as long as I live—he looked like a rag doll. Miraculously, he wasn't seriously injured and will be able to come home from the hospital soon. He has a dislocated shoulder and a couple of cracked ribs. But it could've been a lot worse, and it made me realize all over again what a dangerous sport dirt-bike racing can be. Even though he's my sister's boyfriend and not mine, if anything ever happened to Sam . . . !

Speaking of Sam, he stopped me in the hospital parking lot this afternoon—Todd and I had just been to visit Artie, and Sam was on his way in to do the same thing. As hard as it is to accept, Diary, I'm finally realizing how much Sam does care for Jessica. . . .

We were halfway across the parking lot of Fowler Memorial Hospital when Todd remembered that he'd left his jacket in Artie's room. "I'll just run back in and get it," he told me, handing me his keys. "Meet you at the car."

I continued on, lost in thought. Artie was going to be OK, and that was a big relief, but it had still shaken me up to see his cuts, bruises, and bandages. It didn't take much imagination to picture Sam in a similar hospital bed, with similar—or

252

worse—injuries. *He doesn't race as seriously as April, Mike, and Artie,* I reminded myself. *He mostly rides for fun. Anyway, why do you care? What is Sam Woodruff to you?*

I raised my eyes from the pavement . . . and looked straight into the face of the boy I'd been thinking about. I stopped dead and so did Sam.

After an uncomfortable moment during which neither of us spoke, I ducked my head and started to scurry past him. "Elizabeth, wait," Sam called after me.

Reluctantly, I turned to face him again, my hands shoved into the pockets of my khakis to disguise my nervousness. He'd made it pretty clear the other night on the phone that he didn't think much of me. What did he want?

"I'm glad I ran into you," Sam began.

"You are?" I said, surprised.

"Yes." He ran a hand through his curly blond hair and gave me a hesitant half smile. "I wanted to apologize for what I said to you the other night. I was kind of harsh on you, and I shouldn't have been."

He doesn't hate me. In fact, maybe he still likes me a little! I thought, an unexpected hope blossoming in my heart. I glanced over my shoulder. Luckily, Todd was nowhere in sight. "It's OK," I assured him, somewhat breathlessly. "I think I understand."

"I was just upset," Sam explained, "because I'm not using Jessica and I wouldn't want you or her or anyone to think I'd ever do something like that. I like her. I like her so much, more than I've ever liked any girl, and that's the plain and simple truth."

I wasn't sure whether to laugh or cry. I felt incredibly stupid that for a split second I'd deluded myself into believing that Sam was about to confess that he still had feelings for me. Instead, he was standing here telling me how much he cared about my sister. *He likes Jessica more than any girl ever*, I thought, swallowing back the bitter tears. *More than any girl . . . including me.*

"Apology accepted," I said quietly.

"Good." Sam looked relieved. "So, Elizabeth, if you don't mind my asking . . . Jess hasn't invited me over yet. I mean, to meet the folks and all that. I was kind of wondering . . . I mean, it doesn't have anything to do with you, does it? You haven't told her about . . . ?"

"No, I haven't told her about"—I nearly choked on the words—"about us. I haven't, and I don't plan to."

"Me either," he concurred.

I could have let Sam go on wondering and worrying. I didn't *have* to be helpful. But the last thing I wanted to be was spiteful. He cared about Jessica, and so did I. I made myself focus on her happiness, rather than my own disappointment. "I'm pretty sure it's because of the dirt-bike thing," I told Sam. "Jess thinks that when Mom and Dad find out you ride one, they'll do something drastic, like forbid her to go out with you. But they're perfectly reasonable people and I happen to know that they already like you even though they haven't met you yet, because . . ." I got the words out with only a slight stammer. "Because of how happy Jessica's been·lately. So my advice is just to come by the house and introduce yourself. They're pretty nice people. You'll get along fine."

"Thanks, Elizabeth," Sam said.

I looked away, unable to meet his eyes. "No problem."

We were left with nothing to say to each other. Sam waved a hand at the hospital. "I'd better get inside and say hi to ol' Artie."

"Yeah. See you."

"See you."

I walked the rest of the way to Todd's BMW without looking back. Todd joined me just as I was unlocking the passenger-side door. "Hey, was that that Sam guy from Bridgewater, Jessica's new boyfriend?" he asked.

I nodded as I slid into the seat. "Yeah," I said, my voice carefully neutral. "That was Jessica's new boyfriend."

I wish I didn't feel this way. Haven't I wanted for ages to see Jessica happily paired up with some wonderful guy? I figured, when that day finally came, I'd be just as happy as she was. But of course I couldn't anticipate that she'd fall in love with some-one I'd once loved. And when I remember what I said to Sam the day I first broke up with him—"Try to forget about me. Some other girl will make you happier. . . ." It hurts, hearing Sam say how much he likes her. I can't deny it, it just plain hurts.

At least Sam and I had a civil conversation. I suppose I should be grateful for that. It's going to be tough, though, Diary. I can't hide from the fact: Like it or not, Sam Woodruff is going out with my sister.

Tuesday, 4:00 P.M.

Just an update on the April-Mike-Artie drama. It's hard to keep track of who's mad at who! Before, Mike was mad at Artie and at April too, because she'd become friends with Artie, and Mike took that as a betrayal. Now April's refusing to talk to Mike—she thinks he made Artie fall on purpose, because of their old feud. Meanwhile, Artie's back in school and seems to be feeling OK. I get the impression he's ready to patch up his friendship with Mike, but April may not let him! Stay tuned. . . .

Friday, midnight

Jessica just woke me up to tell me about her date with Sam. I had to listen to every single detail of the movie they saw, their Mexican dinner afterward, and of course, Sam's goodnight kiss. She's definitely fallen in love with him, and fallen hard. I tried to be supportive, Diary, I really did. I'm pretty sure I said all the right things anyway—she seemed satisfied. But I feel so cold inside. Why does Jessica always get everything she wants while I have to make all the sacrifices? I know I'm not being fair. I'm just crabby because while she was out being romanced by Sam, I spent the evening unsuccessfully attempting to fix a leaky faucet. Am I just the most selfish person in the world? Is that it? Even though I decided I didn't want Sam, I can't bear to see him so absorbed with my sister!

If I actually try to answer any of these questions, I'll be up all night!

Saturday, 10:30 A.M.

Guess who's in my front yard at this very minute? Sam Woodruff. He came over to introduce himself to Mom and Dad, just like I told him to when I bumped into him at the hospital the other day. Jess is out running errands, so he's showing them his dirt bike and explaining what safety precautions he takes when he rides, and I can tell (not that I'm sitting at my desk with my window open spying or anything!) that Mom and Dad are completely charmed and impressed by how responsible he is. Needless to say, I almost died when he rang the doorbell. Mom and I got to the door at the same time. After Sam shook her hand, he turned to me, and I said something like, "I think we've met," and then sprinted back upstairs so no one would see me cry.

Jessica just drove up. She looks pretty surprised to see Sam here. But he's smiling and Mom and Dad are smiling, so she's relaxing already. Now Sam's got his arm around her. Dad's pointing to the dirt bike and Sam's nodding. I can't hear everything Dad's saying, but I think it's something about it being OK for Sam to take Jessica on the bike as long as he has their permission. Now Jess is kissing Sam. Looks like everybody's happy.

Almost everybody.

Later on Saturday (10:30 P.M.)

Todd and I went to the rally this afternoon to watch Mike race. Dirt bikes don't usually do it for me, but this race turned out to be unusually exciting. At the last minute, April stood in for Roy, Mike's new

258

*racing partner, and she and Mike won! I'm
so glad April and Mike have made up, and
that Mike and Artie are friends again too.
After Artie's accident last weekend, Mike
realized that the time he fell was an accident too—it wasn't Artie's fault. Mike also
finally recognized that his overcompetitive-
ness was warping his perception of things.
He was all set to give up racing if it would
save his relationship with April and restore
his friendship with Artie. Not surprisingly,
when April heard Mike was willing to
make that big a sacrifice for her, she soft-
ened up. Anyway, it was good to see those
three together again, all best friends, the
way they should be.*

*Sam and Jessica were at the rally too,
of course. I have to admit, they make a
good-looking couple. But then, so did Sam
and I. . . .*

"Wasn't that the most exciting thing you've ever
seen in your entire life?" Jessica exclaimed, her
eyes shining. "When that rider came tearing
around the final curve way out in front of everybody else, and Mike figured out that it was April
on Roy's bike!"

"It was a great race," Sam agreed, wrapping
his arms around Jessica and resting his chin on
top of her head.

There were still a lot of people milling about, congratulating the winners, rehashing the race, discussing strategy, and checking out each other's dirt bikes and gear. But Jessica and Sam were acting as if they were the only two people on the planet. They couldn't keep their hands off of each other. It wouldn't have been so bad if I didn't have to stand there watching them, but I'd finally had to do what I'd been avoiding for all I was worth: introduce Todd and Sam. To my chagrin, they'd hit it off, so Todd wanted to hang around with Sam and Jessica. And every time Sam took my sister's hand or brushed her cheek with a kiss, I felt a sharp pain in my heart. Despite April and Mike's victory, it hadn't been a fun afternoon.

"Yep, April and Mike make a great team," Sam reflected, his arms still locked around Jessica.

She smiled up at him flirtatiously. "So do we, don't you think?"

Sam smiled back at her. "Do I ever."

Jessica slipped her arms around Sam's neck and pulled his face to hers for a kiss. *I've got to get out of here,* I thought desperately. I glanced around, looking for April, ready to bolt. I developed an instant enthusiastic interest in the kind of tires she had on her dirt bike, how much horsepower or whatever there was in the engine—anything was preferable to this!

Before I could take a step, though, someone came up behind me and wrapped strong, muscular arms around my waist. "How'd you do with the sink last night?" Todd murmured into my hair.

"OK," I replied.

We stood like that for a minute or two. As always, Todd's embrace felt cozy and comfortable— being in his arms was like coming home. But instead of feeling content, I found myself feeling confused and sad. *I don't begrudge Jessica her happiness*, I thought. *I really don't. That's not it at all. She deserves to be happy . . . but why does she have to be happy with Sam?* Watching them made all my own memories of Sam's and my time together—our talks, our walks—surge to the surface. When I was with Sam, it was always so romantic. We never talked about fixing sinks!

"Don't forget I'm making you dinner tonight," Todd said. "The last task on my list. It's going to be a culinary masterpiece. *And* it's going to be romantic," he promised. "Candles, music, the works."

I nodded bleakly, glad that he couldn't see my eyes. "Great," I said. I didn't tell him that candles and music might not be enough to create romance between us. That had to start in our hearts, and mine just wasn't up to it.

Todd cooked me dinner and I gave him an A for effort, but a C+ for taste. The rice was crunchy and undercooked, the salad was soggy, and he put peppermint extract instead of vanilla in the chocolate chip cookies, which made them peculiar to say the least! He tried, though. And it's not as if I did so well on all my tasks either. I did manage to change the washer on the sink, but now it drips more than ever! So Todd and I called it a tie—we'll go out to dinner next weekend and split the tab.

So, was it romantic, you want to know, the way Todd promised it would be? I guess it was. We laughed a lot anyway, because just as we were finishing the meal, the cookbook shelf that I'd mounted on the kitchen wall came crashing down. That's one thing Todd and I have going for us—we make each other laugh. He has a great sense of humor and he understands me. I can't complain, Diary. Quite the opposite. I should consider myself the luckiest girl in Sweet Valley. But I have a horrible feeling that I'll never be one hundred percent happy with Todd again, not as long as Jessica's dating Sam. Seeing them together is going to make it impossible for me to keep my secret, unfulfilled wishes locked away, the way they should be. I'm always going to wonder what might have been. I'm always going to want what I can't have.

Thursday afternoon

I haven't written in here for a few weeks—sorry, Diary. But there hasn't been a whole lot going on. I don't want to sound self-pitying, but I'm feeling kind of alone today. I hardly ever see Jessica anymore. She's really busy organizing Pi Beta's rush and on top of that, she and Sam are closer than ever. They're together constantly. Just last night, she snuck out to meet him even though she was supposed to stay home to study for a math test.

Meanwhile, Todd's totally absorbed with recruiting new pledges for Phi Epsilon. He never used to be that active in the fraternity because it's mostly dominated by Bruce Patman and Bruce's obnoxious country club friends, but recently Todd and Winston decided they should try to turn things around and make the frat fun again. Todd invited his basketball buddies Jim Daly and Tom Hackett to rush. When Bruce heard that, of course, he turned right around and invited snobby Ron Reese and Paul Sherwood to pledge. It's turned into a major war. Bruce is determined to keep Todd's friends out of the frat, and Todd's equally obsessed with keeping Bruce's friends out. I always thought fraternities were about camaraderie and brotherly love. Guess not! Personally, I don't really care if Jim, Tom, Paul, and Ron get into Phi Epsilon. I don't even care that

*much about the sorority rush. But I do
care about the fact that Todd never seems
to have time for me anymore. . . .*

I'd stayed late at *The Oracle* office, finishing up
an article about Sweet Valley High's plans to ex-
pand its athletic program. By the time I emerged
from the school building, the sun was low in the
cornflower blue sky. Basketball practice was long
since over, and the cheerleaders were gone too. In
fact, the Fiat was the last car left in the student
parking lot.

I drove home alone, thinking about my newspaper story. *I wouldn't mind asking Todd to take a
look at it,* I mused. *He knows more about sports at
S.V.H. than I do.* On an impulse, I signaled for a
right turn onto Country Club Drive. I'd stop by
Todd's house right then. If he had any suggestions,
I could revise the story at home that night and still
get it to the typesetter on time the next day.

As I pulled into the Wilkinses' driveway, I had
another inspiration. *I'll ask him over for dinner,* I
decided, parking the car. My parents were taking
one of my dad's clients out to dinner that evening,
and I knew that Jessica had plans with Sam. Todd
and I would have the house to ourselves for an
hour or two. *We can cook together,* I thought.
*Pasta, or maybe a big salad. Put on some music,
light a few candles. . . .*

I rang the doorbell, a smile of anticipation on

my face. When Todd answered, I stood on my tip-toes to give him a light kiss. "Hi. Doing anything?"

"Not at this very minute, but—"

"Good." I scooped my arm around his waist and pulled him onto the front step. "Hop into my chariot, sir. I'm cooking dinner for you tonight. We can stop at the farm stand on the way and pick out a bunch of fresh, yummy stuff, and then—"

"Whoa, hold on," he said, disentangling himself. "I can't, Liz."

"Why not?" I asked, disappointed.

"Fraternity meeting," he said briskly. "At my house."

I rolled my eyes. "Not another meeting!"

"We have to update our rule book and decide on the pledges' next tasks," Todd replied somewhat defensively.

"You mean, what they did today wasn't enough to prove they're good enough for Phi Epsilon?"

There had been some excitement at S.V.H. during lunch period that day. It was traditional during rush to assign the pledges tasks. Usually they were silly and not that difficult—for example, among other harmless pranks, this year's Pi Beta pledges had raided the boys' locker room. But Bruce and Todd weren't pulling any punches. Bruce had made Todd's two pledges move the hands on the Romanesque clock on the front wall of the school ahead one hour . . . without using a ladder. And Todd had made Bruce's pledges "borrow" a school bus and take it to Guido's Pizza Palace.

"We always assign three tasks," Todd reminded me. "The guys have to prove their mettle."

"But you and Bruce are deliberately trying to come up with things the pledges won't be able to do!" I accused. "You *want* them to fail. It's pretty mean, if you ask me."

"Well, no offense, Liz," Todd said mildly, "but I didn't ask you."

I stepped back, stung by his words. "Fine," I snapped. "Have fun at your meeting."

I stomped back to my car. "Hey," he called after me. "Don't be mad."

"Why not?" I retorted. "All you care about these days is one-upping Bruce."

"It's for a good cause," Todd insisted. "For Phi Epsilon."

"And that's more important to you than I am?"

I didn't hear his answer because by then I was behind the wheel of the Fiat, backing down the driveway. And when Todd called later, I let the answering machine pick up. He left a message apologizing for the "I didn't ask you" crack, and he really did sound sorry, but sometimes sorry isn't enough. The insult lingered. *Maybe I'll call him back later,* I thought, *and maybe I won't!*

I left in such a huff, I forgot that I meant to ask him to help me with my Oracle story. Oh, well. It's in pretty good shape—I don't have any qualms turning it in as is. I know I'm being a little bit childish, Diary. Todd's entitled to put some time and energy into the fraternity, and I suppose he's also entitled to dislike Bruce's pledges. Maybe it's just the contrast between where his and my relationship is at these days and the way things are between Jessica and Sam. Those two are so infatuated, it's sickening. Sam is spoiling Jess rotten: flowers, candy, sweet little thoughtful presents for no reason, the works. Jess and I have our own private phone line now, but I never get to use it because she and Sam are always yapping. And they already have a zillion secret, inside jokes that make them giggle all the time. Ugh!

When I broke up with Sam, I didn't expect him to remain celibate for the rest of his life. I just wish he hadn't decided to date someone who lived in my house!

Saturday, 4:00 P.M.

Jessica's stomping around her room so loudly, it feels like an earthquake. She's mad because Mom just grounded her for letting her math grade slide and for tearing up the warning slip that Ms. Taylor mailed to the house. Sometimes I can't believe the outrageous *things my sister expects to get away with. Did she really think Mom and Dad weren't going to find out that she's failed two math tests in a row?*

Anyway, Jess is as mad at me as she is at Mom. In classic fashion, the fact that she's failing math and got grounded is somehow all my fault. If Liz weren't such a good student, if Liz hadn't done this, if Liz hadn't said that, blah blah blah. She wants me to try to convince Mom and Dad not to punish her! Well, I'll tell you, I'm sorry she got in trouble, but I'm tired of always having to cover for her. This has been the pattern all our lives: She makes a mess and I clean it up. This time, I'm not getting involved. She's grounded and so she can't go out with Sam—now she has to deal with it. It's not my problem.

Tuesday, 7:00 P.M.

Jessica is the grumpiest person I've ever seen. Not only is she grounded—no mall, no beach, no dates—but Mom and Dad are also limiting her telephone time. A fate worse than death!

Rush is still the big news at school. Todd and Bruce made the Phi Epsilon pledges do two more practically impossible stunts: *Check one hundred books out of the S.V.H. library over the course of a single school day (without cutting class), and move the entire contents of the office of Mrs. Green, the guidance counselor, to the lawn outside the school building. The amazing thing is that Jim, Tom, Ron, and Paul pulled it off without getting into trouble. I have to give those guys credit. They're ready to walk through fire to get into Phi Epsilon, where they'll have the dubious pleasure of listening to Todd and Bruce bicker. I'm not sure it's worth it!*

The sorority rush is proceeding smoothly and peacefully in comparison. We have five pledges and they're all terrific: Lisa Walton, Rose Jameson, Stacie Cabot, Lynne Jacobs, and Aline Montgomery. Rose is new at S.V.H.—her family moved here from Massachusetts—and I really like her. I don't know why a sweet girl like her wants to be a Pi Beta, but since she does, I'm glad she's been able to pass muster with Jessica, Lila, and the rest of the sorority. If it were up to me, I'd admit the pledges without subjecting them to the third degree, but Jessica and Company feel it's essential for Pi Betas to have the right "background." Spare me, please. Not that Jessica's having much to do with the final phases of rush. She won't even

*be able to go to the induction party and
dance this weekend because she'll still be
grounded. She's already whining about how
unfair it is, but I just can't sympathize. I
told her she could use the time alone to reflect on her behavior. She has to learn that
the world does not revolve around Jessica
Wakefield, and that actions have consequences. You reap what you sow.*

Wednesday, 5:30 P.M.

*I can't believe what I just did, Diary.
I'm a bad person and a really bad sister.
Sam called to talk to Jessica . . . and I answered the phone and pretended to be her!
It wasn't premeditated or anything—I
would never plan to do anything that devious. It just somehow sort of happened, and
once I started, I couldn't stop. . . .*

The one exception Mom and Dad had made
about Jessica being grounded related to cheerleading practice. They knew she had a responsibility, as
co-captain of the squad, so they were letting her
stay after school two days a week. This afternoon,
we drove home together. After snacking on some
cold pizza, she stripped off her workout clothes
and jumped in the shower. I headed into my own
room to get a head start on my homework.

I was just opening my science textbook when the phone rang. I grabbed it, expecting Enid or Todd. "Hello," I sang.

"I know your folks don't want you talking on the phone, so I figured I'd call while they were still at work," a guy said. "What's up, Jess?"

It was Sam, and he'd mistaken me for my sister. My heart took off like a tumbleweed. *I'd better set him straight*, I thought, *before he says something mushy that will embarrass us both.*

But for some inexplicable reason, I hesitated for a split second, listening to the sound of the shower. When I did respond, the words that came out of my mouth weren't the ones I thought I was going to say. "Nothing much," I told Sam in my very best bored Jessica imitation. "You know how it is when you're grounded."

"I can't stand not being able to see you." His voice was husky with longing. "How much longer are they going to keep you locked up there?"

"Two weeks and three days," I replied. "It really *is* like being in prison. Except the food's not bad."

"Are you studying your math?" Sam asked in a paternal way.

From what I'd seen, Jessica was mostly spending her time behind bars thumbing through fashion magazines. "Of course," I said.

"I'm gonna quiz you," he warned playfully. "You don't want to fail any more tests or they'll never let you out again."

"Don't worry," I assured him. "I'll end up acing Ms. Taylor's class. You'll see."

"I know you can do it," he said. "You're the smartest girl I know."

"The smartest?" I couldn't help sounding skeptical. How could Jessica be the smartest girl Sam knew?

"Yeah. *And* the prettiest, and sexiest, and most fun."

Sam sounded so loving and sincere that all at once I felt sick to my stomach with guilt. What was I doing, pretending to be Jessica and stealing one of her precious private moments with Sam, snaking my way into a personal conversation where I didn't belong?

"Uh, Sam," I said quickly, "I hear my mom's car in the driveway. I'd better get downstairs and start dinner."

"I'll call you later," he promised.

Suddenly, it occurred to me that Jessica could find out about my trick, if Sam happened to mention this phone call when he next spoke with her. "Sure," I said. "But remember, I'm not supposed to be talking on the phone. In fact, let's pretend we didn't have this conversation, OK? I've been studying all afternoon without a single break."

"Right." Sam chuckled. "Love you, Jess."

I echoed his sentiment, though it left a bitter taste in my mouth. "Love you too."

I'm crossing my fingers that Jessica doesn't find out about this. How on earth would I explain myself to her? I really feel absolutely terrible. I intruded on her personal life in an unforgivable way. Maybe I did it because my own personal life is not so great lately. It's weird, though, Diary, because it made me realize something that should be obvious, but which I've been having trouble accepting. Pretending to be Jessica on the phone forced me to climb into her head and heart for a minute, and what I discovered there was a perfectly normal, happy relationship. The conversation with Sam was the kind of lighthearted chat any girl might have with her boyfriend, like I've had a million of with Todd. In other words, it was worlds apart from the secretive, hushed, tormented calls Sam and I used to have.

This is what I have to face, Diary: Sam is hers now, not mine. My sister is Sam's girlfriend, which I never was. He loves her—that's plain as day—and she loves him too. For the first time in her life, she's in a relationship that may last. As for me, the best thing I can do is stay out of it. I don't have to be ecstatic over her happiness—I'll never forget my own history with Sam—but I should support her instead of sabotaging her. So, from now on, I'm going to make a real effort not to be petty and selfish and resentful and jealous and secretly glad that Jess can't see Sam as often as usual because she's grounded. I'll probably need some help keeping these resolutions, Diary! But I do want to be a good sister. I want to be fair. Fair to everyone: Jessica, Sam, Todd . . . and to myself too.

Friday, 7:00 P.M.

Something astonishing happened at the Pi Beta pledge picnic at Secca Lake this afternoon. We found out that Rose Jameson has been lying about her family background, and even her name! I've mentioned Rose, haven't I? She made a splash when she moved to Sweet Valley recently. She's beautiful and poised and sweet and funny and everyone thinks she's wonderful—the guys are falling all over each other to ask her out, and the girls like her too and want to be friends with her. The Pi Betas were all totally psyched when she decided to pledge the sorority. At her rush interview, Rose had them swooning, describing how her ancestors came over on the Mayflower and were one of the oldest families in Boston, how she's distantly related to Queen Elizabeth, and on a recent trip to England sat in the royal box at Ascot with Prince

Charles, and on and on. Lila, Jessica, Caroline, Suzanne, and the rest of them were literally drooling. In fact, I remember Jess saying, "This girl is too good to be true!"

Turns out, Jess was right. While the Pi Betas were picnicking at the lake today, there was an accident nearby. A little girl fell down an old abandoned well shaft. We all rushed over to see if we could help, but we couldn't get to her—the well was dry, thankfully, but too deep. The worst part was, the little girl spoke Spanish, not English, and didn't understand the things we were saying to try to calm her and keep her from endangering herself while we waited for help.

It was touch-and-go for a minute, but then Rose started talking to the child in fluent Spanish. The Pi Betas were dumbstruck. After the fire truck came and the rescue workers got the little girl out (she was unhurt, thankfully), Rose made a confession. Her family is actually from Texas by way of Mexico, not Massachusetts, and her name is Rosa, not Rose. She didn't want the Pi Betas to know she was Hispanic because she was afraid they wouldn't want her in their sorority if she didn't come from the "right" background.

There was a long, tense moment when it looked as though Lila and the snobby Pi Betas might turn their backs on Rose, but the rest of us—Enid, Maria, Annie, Jean, Sandra, and me—stood up for Rosa and told her that of course we still wanted her to be a member. She saved that child's life— we're proud to have a hero in the sorority! And I think Rosa will fit in just fine. Her background doesn't matter. In fact, I think our sorority would be better if the members had more diverse backgrounds.

As for our male counterparts, the Phi Epsilons, I can't say they're being as fairminded. For their final task, Jim and Tom have to "acquire" some pom-poms from the El Carro High cheerleaders during tonight's basketball game, and Ron and Paul have to "borrow" racquet covers from the Palisades High School tennis team players during tomorrow morning's match. All four of the pledges are already in trouble with their coaches because of the pranks they've been pulling—they'll either fail the tasks and not get in the fraternity, or succeed and probably get kicked off their teams. I simply refuse to talk to Todd about any of this anymore. He doesn't listen to me when I try to point out that he's being as elitist and exclusionary as Bruce—he's totally stubborn and unreasonable. I guess by tomorrow night, we'll know the outcome. Maybe Todd will save Phi Epsilon . . . or maybe he'll help destroy it.

Sunday, 11:00 A.M.

Diary, I feel like a new woman. What a difference a few days can make! First of all, apparently Jessica never found out about my little impersonation on the telephone. She hasn't said anything anyway, and there's no way she'd keep mum if she suspected I'd pulled a stunt like that. And last night was the induction ceremony for the new Pi Beta pledges at Fowler Crest, and amazingly, I had a fantastic time! Jessica almost made me late, coming into my room before I left and complaining about the injustice of having to miss the party. I started to give her a lecture ("If you hadn't lied about your math grade and torn up that warning slip . . ."), but then I caught myself. Who am I to preach? Instead, I gave her a hug and said it wouldn't be the same without her there and I was sure everyone would miss her tons. That seemed to mollify her a teeny, weeny bit.

Back to the party. It was great. Pi Beta has four new members: Stacie, Aline,

Lynne, and Lisa. Four, not five, because at the very last moment, Rosa Jameson declined our invitation to join the sorority! It was very dramatic, Diary. Rosa was wearing this beautiful, hand-embroidered Mexican dress. When it was her turn to receive the Pi Beta pin, she stood up and very gracefully announced that although she hoped to remain our friend, she didn't want to be in the sorority after all. She realized that she doesn't have to be like everybody else in order to fit in—she's proud of who she is. It was a really moving speech, and it gave me a lot to think about. I definitely want to get to know Rosa better—I think she's extremely brave and interesting.

So much for the Pi Beta Alpha rush. The Phi Epsilons were at Lila's too, because they cosponsored the dance. And for me, the best part of the evening was making up with Todd. . . .

After the sorority inducted its new members, the Phi Epsilons started to arrive, and Lila went inside to put on some dance music. The scene was magical and lovely: Lila and her friends had decorated the poolside area behind Fowler Crest with garlands of fresh flowers, bouquets of pink and silver balloons, and dozens of flickering candles. All

278

the girls wore shimmering party dresses—mine was pale blue—while the boys were in jackets and ties. It looked like a fairyland.

"There's Todd." Enid gestured to the opposite side of the patio.

"I know," I said grimly, not budging from my position near the punch bowl.

I'd seen him arrive and my heart had given a brief flutter—he looked incredibly handsome in a navy blazer and khakis. But then I'd reminded myself that I was disgusted with the way he'd been behaving about Phi Epsilons' rush. I'd attended both the basketball game and the tennis match and had seen with my own eyes that Jim and Tom never went anywhere near the El Carro cheerleaders' pom-poms—ditto for Ron and Paul and the Palisades players' tennis racquet covers. While Pi Beta had been welcoming its new members that evening, the boys had been at Winston's, holding an induction ceremony for no one. Yes, Lila's backyard looked like a fairyland, but Todd was no Prince Charming.

"So, you're still mad at him?" Enid guessed.

"You bet," I replied. "You don't see Ron or Paul or Tom or Jim, do you? Bruce sank Todd's pledges and Todd sank Bruce's. I think that stinks."

"Wait a minute," said Enid. She pointed again, this time in a different direction. "Look who just got here!"

To my amazement, the four Phi Epsilon

pledges had just marched up. I gasped. Pinned to the lapel of each of their jackets was a shiny gold fraternity pin. "But, what—" I began.

Just then, Bruce and Todd stepped up to the cloth-draped podium where Lila had stood earlier to welcome the Pi Betas. Bruce waved a hand for attention. When the gathering remained noisy, Todd put two fingers in his mouth and emitted a piercing whistle.

Everybody turned to look and listen. "Go ahead," Todd said politely to Bruce.

"No, *you* go ahead," Bruce said with equally mild manners.

Enid and I glanced at each other. I raised my eyebrows, then looked back at Bruce and my boyfriend.

"Before the dance begins, we have a brief announcement," Todd said after clearing his throat and tugging on his necktie. "As you can see, tonight the Phi Epsilons are lucky enough to have four teriffic new members: Paul Sherwood, Ron Reese, Jim Daly, and Tom Hackett." I clapped heartily along with the others. "Bruce and I were letting our petty rivalry get in the way of what the fraternity is supposed to be all about, but these four guys got us back on the right track."

Just then, Winston trotted up, brandishing an armful of pom-poms and tennis racquet covers. The Pi Betas greeted his appearance with a buzz of laughter. Enid and I exchanged another bemused glance.

"As you can see, despite Wilkins's and my best efforts to make them fall flat on their faces, the pledges succeeded in their third and final tasks," Bruce explained. "And they did it by teamwork. Unbeknownst to the rest of us, they decided to help each other. Ron and Paul got a hold of the pom-poms for Jim and Tom, and Tom and Jim returned the favor this morning while Ron and Paul were competing at the tennis match."

"By the way, ladies, we'll return all this stuff to El Carro High and Palisades High on Monday," Winston piped in. "Scout's honor." There was more appreciative laughter.

"Anyway," concluded Todd, "I learned something about sportsmanship today. I think Phi Epsilon is going to be a better fraternity thanks to Paul, Jim, Tom, and Ron. Now, let's party!"

On cue, music began to pour from the poolside stereo speakers. Pi Betas and Phi Epsilons started to pair up for dancing. I made my way through the whirling crowd, heading straight as an arrow for Todd. He'd done the same, and we met halfway.

"Very eloquently said, Mr. Wilkins," I told him, my eyes shining.

Todd shrugged. "I'm just glad people bothered to listen," he said ruefully. "Patman and I have been acting like such jerks!"

"Can't argue with you on that point," I said with a smile.

Todd took my hands in his. "I'm really sorry,

Liz. I don't usually get this obsessed and competitive. I don't know what came over me."

"Testosterone?" I teased.

He grinned. "Maybe. Anyhow, when Patman and I found out what the pledges had done, we both felt incredibly stupid. We knew we had to make it up to the frat, but even more important, I knew I had to make it up to you. The only question is, how?"

"Well, you can start right now," I told him. He looked a little taken aback by my brisk tone. I let him sweat for a second or two, then I smiled. "By asking me to dance."

It turned out to be the dreamiest evening I've had in a long time, Diary. Todd and I danced to every single song. I really feel as if our relationship is finally back on track for good. And do you know why? Because Todd and I have proved to each other that we have more than just love, although of course that's the most important ingredient of any romantic partnership. We also have resiliency. We make mistakes and we learn from them. Sometimes we fight, but we also always forgive. We give each other room to grow.

Of course, I hope that Todd will never find out about my worst mistake—Sam—because if he did, I'm not sure he'd be able to forgive me. But I think it's enough that I've learned from that mistake and forgiven myself.

> *Sunday, a week later, 2:00 P.M.*

Dear Diary,

Todd and I are spending more time together than we ever have, and I'm loving every minute of it. Just for laughs, we joined the new Sweet Valley High bowling club, and I think it'll actually turn out to be a lot of fun. You gotta dig those crazy shirts and shoes! It's a totally different crowd than the one Todd and I usually hang out with, but everyone's friendly. We all had such a good time at the first practice, we stayed an extra two hours at the bowling alley! Todd and I both have a long way to go technique-wise, though. I'm not sure which of us threw the most gutter balls, but we were up there in the double digits. I expect we'll improve fast—the coach, Justin Silver, is a champion bowler and really good at explaining and demonstrating things. Plus he's extremely cute! Not that I noticed, I mean, really noticed. Todd's the one for me.

So, things are great with Todd, but I can't say the same about my relationship with my sister. I don't think Jessica's forgiven any of us for the fact that she was grounded. I understand that it was a tough three weeks for her, hearing about her friends doing fun things without her, and not being able to spend time with Sam and all that. But I assumed she'd get right back to her normal self once Mom and Dad let her off the hook. Instead, she's acting really weird. It didn't help that she and Sam had a fight the first day she wasn't grounded because she wanted to go shopping but he'd entered a dirt-bike race. She was pretty steamed at him, and she paid him back by turning down a couple of dates with him. Don't you think that's bizarre? Talk about cutting off your nose to spite your face! She's acting the same way with Lila and Cara and Amy—avoiding them, basically. Avoiding the beach, the mall, all the places she was dying to go while she was grounded.

My theory is that she's punishing us for having a good time when she couldn't. As if we should all have sat home twiddling our thumbs just to keep her company! I've been trying to be extra-nice to her, to make up for being kind of mean while she was grounded, but she hasn't been receptive at all. Just this morning, though, things got really weird. I was ready to call the tabloids and report that an alien had taken over my sister's body. . . .

I woke up on Sunday morning to the tantalizing aroma of something cooking in the kitchen. I glanced at the clock radio on my nightstand: 8:30 A.M. *Dad must've gotten up early to make pancakes and bacon,* I guessed, stretching. I bundled into a robe and slippers and shuffled downstairs, following my nose. Fresh-brewed coffee, sizzling bacon . . .

At the door to the kitchen I stopped, blinking in sleepy surprise. "Jessica?" I said.

My twin sister was standing at the stove, ladling pancake batter into a skillet. "Tall stack or short?" she asked briskly.

I flopped into a chair at the table, where my parents, also in their bathrobes, were sipping fresh-squeezed orange juice and reading the Sunday paper. "Um, short," I replied, smoothing back my sleep-rumpled hair.

I poured myself a glass of juice from the pitcher. "Does anyone else think this is a little strange?" I murmured to my parents. "A, Jessica's up before noon, and B, she's cooking breakfast. *Cooking* breakfast," I repeated with emphasis, "as opposed to tearing open a package of Pop-Tarts."

My mother arched her slender blond eyebrows and smiled. "Yes, it's a little strange, but why knock it?"

"You're right," I agreed as my sister carried a platter of fluffy pancakes and crisp bacon across the room and set it in the center of the table. "Wow, Jess. That looks great."

285

"I really hope you enjoy it," Jessica said.

My brain was still a little fuzzy. Jessica's tone befuddled me further. She actually sounded . . . *sweet*. I studied her blandly smiling face, my forehead crinkled. "I thought you were mad at us, Jess," I said.

"Mad?" She shook her head. "Why would I be?"

At that instant, I noticed something else odd about my sister this morning. "Jess!" I squealed, laughter bubbling up uncontrollably. "Where on earth did you get those *pants?*"

The grunge look is in with some kids these days, but Jessica's never gone for it and neither have I. The outfit she was currently wearing, though, was beyond grunge: It looked as if it had come off a thrift shop's clearance rack.

Jessica looked down at her shapeless trousers. "What's wrong with them?"

"First of all, they're *brown*," I pointed out.

"Maybe they're not fashionable, but they're clean," she said, bristling. "And practical."

Practical? I stared at her in disbelief. Had I just heard my vain, style-obsessed sister refer to an article of apparel as practical? "And that *shirt*," I went on, another giggle bursting from me. Even my dad had a hard time smothering a grin. "It makes Todd's and my bowling shirts look glamorous!"

Jessica frowned. "Do you really think that's important, Liz?"

"I suppose I don't, but I always thought *you* did," I answered.

"Well, you thought wrong," she snapped, pivoting on her heel and marching back to the stove. "Now, if you'll excuse me, I'm going to wash some dishes."

Mom and Dad and I didn't have much choice but to dig into our breakfasts. "It's just a mood," my mother speculated in a low voice.

"A phase," my father agreed.

"Maybe the drama club's doing a new play and she's trying out for a part that involves wearing tacky clothes and doing nice things for people," I joked, "and she's just trying to get into character."

"You know Jessica," Mom concluded. "It's always something."

I've seen lots of Jessica's "phases," Diary, but nothing quite like this. She brightened up after breakfast, though (although she didn't change her clothes!), and headed off to spend the day with Sam, so maybe whatever it was, she got it out of her system.

Time to meet Todd and the rest of the bowling team at the Fast Lanes!

Monday, 8:00 P.M.

Guess what, Diary? My bowling coach, Justin, just called and asked me out! Can you believe it? Of course I said no, but I'm so flattered. I can't deny it's fun to be noticed by a cute guy, although it has been getting a little embarrassing at bowling club practice. At first I didn't realize Justin was singling me out for special attention, but then everyone (including Todd) started to tease me about being the teacher's pet.

Anyway, I reminded Justin that I have a boyfriend, and he said he knew that, but he figured he'd just double-check. He was really very sweet about it. Do you think I should tell Todd about the phone call? Nah. Why worry him?

Thursday, 7:00 P.M.

Another family dinner where Jessica didn't show up at the table. Lately, she's been taking a plate upstairs to her desk so she can study while she eats. Yes, I'm talking about my twin sister, Jessica! And that's not all. She's keeping her room as neat as a pin. You can actually see the carpeting and the bedspread, which ordinarily are buried in clothes, magazines, and general junk. Speaking of clothes, she's still dressing like an old-fashioned librarian, and the other day I caught her reading a book called How to Be a Better You. And she hasn't been talking about Sam that much (although I have to admit that that's OK with me!). It's a total mystery, Diary. It's like she's on an antifun campaign . . . but why? What is she trying to prove?

At dinner, Dad told us about a new case he's working on. His firm is investigating this bogus charitable group called the Good Friends that's set up shop in Sweet Valley. The Good Friends collect money by telling people it's for charity, but most of it finds its way into the private bank account of the group's leader—at least, that's what Dad's trying to prove. I've seen some of the "Friends" hanging around the mall, with their long hair and grubby jeans and their collection cans. They look pretty young—around my age, I'd say. They have the spookiest expressions, these blank smiles and empty eyes. Dad says he'd bet anything they've been brainwashed. I hope he can get to the bottom of the whole thing soon and kick Adam Marvel—that's the head guy—out of town.

Friday evening

Justin was hitting on me again at bowling practice today. I thought I was pretty definite when I said no the other day, but maybe it didn't come across that way. So this time I made it crystal *clear that, as attractive as he is, I'm not interested. I already have a terrific boyfriend. . . .*

Todd dropped me off at the bowling alley after school, but he couldn't stay for practice because of a dentist appointment. When I strolled in alone, Justin pounced immediately, clearly psyched that for once Todd wasn't around to keep an eye on us. I kept ducking away from him, down to one of the far lanes, hoping he'd decide to coach some of the other kids for a change, but Justin just chased after me. As usual, I ended up with what amounted to a private lesson!

When practice was over, I prepared to sprint outside. Todd had promised to swing by the lanes after his dentist appointment and get me. But before I could make my escape, Justin placed a hand on my arm. "Liz, wait," he said, moving close to me. "I want to talk to you."

I turned to face him, clutching my bowling ball in its faux-leather carrying case—it made a good buffer zone. "What's up?" I asked.

"Don't get mad at me," Justin began, "but I just have to give it one last try. In case anything's changed between you and Wilkins. Will you go to a movie with me tonight, Liz?"

"Nothing's changed, Justin," I told him. "I'm sorry, but I can't go to a movie with you."

"How about tomorrow night?"

"Not tonight, not tomorrow night, not any night," I stated firmly.

Justin raked a hand through his shaggy blond hair and smiled ruefully. "I've been kind of pushy, huh?"

"Let's just say, I'll be relieved if you don't ask me out again, because then I won't have to quit the team."

"I don't want you to do that," he assured me. "You can't blame a guy for trying, though, can you?"

"I suppose not," I said.

"Still friends?"

"Still friends," I agreed.

We walked out of the bowling alley together. "Todd's a lucky fellow," Justin commented. "He appreciates you? Treats you well?"

"Yep," I said.

"'Cause if it ever gets stale, you know who to turn to," Justin persisted.

"Thanks, but I have a feeling Todd and I will be together for a long time," I told Justin. "We're really happy." And at the instant that I said that, I realized something wonderful: It was absolutely true. *Todd and I are happy,* I thought. We'd been through some tough times lately, some genuine relationship blues. My love for Todd had been severely tested by my feelings for Sam. But now things were better than ever. I wasn't even the tiniest bit tempted by Justin Silver, attractive though he might have been.

Just then, I spotted Todd's BMW pulling into the bowling alley parking lot. Todd waved at me and I waved back. "We're really happy," I repeated.

I said good-bye to Justin and ran over to Todd's car. I hopped into the passenger seat, and before he could even say hello, I planted a big kiss right on his lips. A feeling of perfect love and security wrapped around me like the warmest and fuzziest blanket imaginable.

I was back where I belonged.

Friday night, a week later

Something really disturbing happened this evening. While Todd and I were eating dinner at the Dairi Burger, Sam Woodruff rushed in. He was looking for Jessica, but couldn't find her anywhere and was hoping we'd be able to help. Sam's really worried about Jess, and after I heard what's been going on between the two of them lately, I am too. It turns out they've been fighting a lot, and Jessica's been lying to him and to all of us about where she's going. For example, yesterday she told Sam she had a sorority meeting at Amy's, but when he stopped by the Suttons' house hoping to catch up with her, the other girls told him that she'd never shown up. This kind of thing has been going on for more than a week, Sam says. Jessica refuses to make plans with him—she always has something else to do, like rushing off to a meeting, or going to the library, or meeting a friend. Tonight she said she was going over to Lila's for dinner, but Sam drove over to Fowler Crest and she wasn't there. I really feel badly for Sam. He wants to know what's come over Jessica, why she's acting so strangely, why she's pushing him away—but I don't have any answers for him.

I don't have answers, but now I have a suspicion, and it's not a good one. I decided to try to talk to Jessica about what's bothering her. I realized we hadn't really talked in weeks—she's been avoiding me the same way she's been avoiding Sam. So when she got home tonight, I knocked on her bedroom door. I didn't want to ask straight out why she's been lying to Sam. I thought we'd chat about some harmless, unrelated topic for a while first, so I randomly mentioned Dad's firm's case involving the Good Friends. You can imagine how surprised I was when Jessica leapt to their defense. She got really mad at me for calling them a "cult" and she claimed that they do a lot of good work and aren't breaking any laws. When I asked how she came to know so much about the group's activities, she announced she was going to bed and turned out her light. End of conversation.

I don't know what to think, Diary. Could Jessica be involved with the Good Friends? It might explain the strange way she's been acting, the shabby old clothes, her evasiveness. But why would she turn to an organization like that? Has she really been feeling that unhappy and isolated? I feel awful because the truth is, I've been pretty resentful of her lately, ever since she started seeing Sam. I wasn't nice at all to her when she was grounded—I rubbed it in her face instead of trying to make things easier for her. Now I wish she would confide in me, but she's treating me like a stranger and I can't entirely blame her. Why should she trust me when I've acted so coldly toward her?

Saturday, 5:00 P.M.

The plot thickens, Diary. Sam found out where Jessica's been going every day and it turns out my hunch was right—she's hanging out with the Good Friends. He rounded up Todd and me, and we all drove over there in his mom's station wagon to check things out. You're probably thinking: "What a cozy threesome!" You're right. It was beyond awkward, at least for me. Sam was pretty much preoccupied with his *concern for Jessica, and Todd was oblivious to any undercurrent of tension, but my nerves were jangling as if I'd just drunk ten cups of cappuccino. Riding in the car with Sam and Todd, it dawned on me. Jessica's not the only one who's been playing a dangerous game. . . .*

It was early afternoon. Todd and I had just finished lunch at my house and were on our way out the door to head to the bowling alley when a car pulled into the driveway, tires squealing. Sam jumped out, and even before he spoke I knew something was terribly wrong. His gray eyes were frantic, and his jaw was set in a hard, worried line. "Jessica?" I asked.

He nodded grimly. "I found out where she's spending all her time. I followed her this morning. She said there was a cheerleading jamboree at Big Mesa, but take my word for it, she didn't go to Big Mesa."

I already knew that. I'd felt slimy checking up on my own sister, but after Jessica supposedly left for the jamboree, I'd called Sandra Bacon, one of her fellow cheerleaders. Just as I'd suspected, there was no such event taking place.

Before I could ask Sam about the Good Friends, he hustled Todd and me over to his car. "Come on," he exclaimed, his tone urgent. "We've got to get over there."

On the way, Sam told us what he'd seen half an hour earlier. Jessica had parked her car in front of an old house at the outskirts of town and then disappeared inside. He'd considered ringing the doorbell, but then decided against it. "The way she's been acting, I knew she'd just get furious," Sam said. "She'd refuse to talk to me. We're on the verge of breaking up as it is."

Todd was in the passenger seat and I was sitting in the backseat. As Sam said this, he glanced in the rearview mirror and caught my eye. There was a tortured expression on his face and I felt my own face flood with color. "I just can't bear to lose her," he went on, a catch in his voice, "not after . . ."

He didn't finish the sentence, but I knew how it would have ended if he and I had been alone in the car. ". . . *not after what happened with you, Elizabeth.*"

I clasped my hands tightly together in my lap, praying that Sam wouldn't let anything slip in front of Todd. I hadn't hesitated to jump into Sam's car along with Todd—my concern for my sister overshadowed everything else. But now I had a chance to reflect on my own situation. I was sitting in a car with my boyfriend . . . and with another boy with whom I'd been romantically involved behind my boyfriend's back. Sam and I hadn't parted on particularly good terms. There might as well have been a ticking time bomb resting on the car seat next to me. *One word is all it would take*, I thought. Sam could destroy me.

I almost fainted with relief when, a minute later, Sam braked in front of a ramshackle, unpainted house on Cedar Street. It was a run-down neighborhood, the kind with broken-down cars parked on the overgrown lawns. "Are you sure this is it?" Todd asked dubiously.

But there was the Fiat, parked right out front. Then I saw the small sign hanging from the house's eaves. "The Good Friends!" I cried. "I knew it!"

"Knew what?" Sam demanded. "Who are the Good Friends?"

I filled him in on what I'd learned from my father about the shady organization that might be a cult. Sam's face went white. "We've got to get her out of there!" he said, his voice filled with urgency.

Before Todd and I could stop him, Sam had sprung from the car and was striding toward the house. He began beating on the door with his fist, the sound echoing along the quiet street.

We waited for a few minutes, but no one came to the door. "There was a van here when I drove by before," Sam said, "and now it's gone. Where do you suppose they went?"

"To the mall to beg for donations," Todd guessed.

I bit my lip, picturing Jessica, dressed in one of her drab librarianesque getups, smiling that blank Good Friends smile while she solicited money from strangers. "What are we going to do?" I wondered.

"Stick around until she gets back," Sam said, folding his arms across his chest.

"Let's go back to Liz's and tell her parents," Todd proposed. "Mr. Wakefield's a lawyer—he'll know how to handle this."

"No, wait." I held up a hand. "That won't work, you guys. If we tell Mom and Dad, she'll think we're ganging up on her and trying to get her into trouble. It'll just make her trust us less and need the Good Friends more. And we still don't know for sure that the Good Friends are doing anything wrong."

Sam turned to me, his shoulders slumping. "You're right. This is hopeless!"

Without thinking, I put a consoling hand on his arm. "It's not hopeless, but we have to be careful. I'll talk to her when she gets in later. I'll get her perspective on this and then we can figure out what do do next."

Sam looked down at my hand. I drew it back quickly and another blush heated my face. "In the meantime, let's get out of here," I suggested, already scurrying back to Sam's car, "before the Good Friends get back!"

Was I ever relieved to see Sam drive off when we got home to Calico Drive. I couldn't get out of that car fast enough! If I'd had to be alone with the two of them for a minute longer, I think I would've had a nervous breakdown. Thank goodness Todd didn't notice me blushing and trembling and stuttering, and thank goodness Sam is such a kindhearted person. I used to wonder about his motives for dating Jessica, but it's plain as day now that he doesn't hold a grudge against me. But that doesn't mean that I'm in a hurry for the three of us to hang out alone again!

Now I'm sitting in my room, wondering when Jessica will get home . . . and wondering what I'll say to her when she does. I want to talk some sense into her, without scaring her away, but she's been so prickly and defensive lately. Wish me luck.

Sunday, 8:00 A.M.

I confronted Jessica about the Good Friends last night. It was a horrible conversation, Diary, if you can even call it a conversation. She didn't bat an eyelash about being caught lying about the cheerleading jamboree and stuff like that—she screamed at me like I was the one who'd been sneaky and dishonest. And then she went through this really scary instant personality change. With this glazed look in her eye, she told me all about how wonderful the Good Friends are. She's in real trouble, Diary. . . .

"I can't believe you followed me," Jessica shouted, her complexion marred by angry red splotches. "What kind of sister are you?" When I tried to explain myself, she jabbed an index finger at the door. "Just leave me alone. Leave me *alone!*"

My sister and I have gotten in plenty of arguments over the years, but she'd never spoken to me in such an accusing, hysterical tone before. I didn't know how to respond, but one thing was certain. I couldn't just walk away. I had to get to the bottom of this.

Instead of leaving, I sat down on Jessica's bed. "Look, Jess," I began, trying to make my own voice as soothing and unthreatening as possible, "I'm not your enemy. I'm not necessarily opposed to the Good Friends. I just want to understand what's going on with you. I want you to open up to me instead of shutting me out. Tell me about the group. How did you meet them? What kinds of things do you do together?"

For a long moment, Jessica stared at me, her breath coming quickly, her eyes wild. Then she inhaled slowly. Gradually, the white-hot fury faded from her eyes and an angelic smile spread across her face. When she spoke again, her voice was cool and smooth. "I'm sorry I yelled at you, Liz. I just can't bear to hear anyone say bad things about the group, because they've really changed my life. I'm such a better person than I used to be!"

I didn't agree, but I didn't want to say anything

to antagonize her. "You certainly have changed," I conceded. "How did it all come about?"

"Well, I was at the mall a few weeks ago," Jessica remembered enthusiastically. "It was a Saturday, the first day I wasn't grounded. I wanted Sam to go shopping with me, but he went to a dirt-bike rally instead. So I was in a pretty crummy mood, and all of a sudden, right in the middle of the mall, I burst into tears. I was sitting on this bench crying and feeling sorry for myself when this incredibly nice boy, Ted, came over and started talking to me. He told me about Adam Marvel and the Good Friends and invited me over to the house to meet them. . . ."

Jessica talked for half an hour without stopping. She described Adam Marvel and the young people who lived in the Good Friends residence. She told me how they all pitched in to do the chores after spending the day going door to door collecting donations. I cringed at the image of my sister, dressed in her librarian outfit, ringing doorbells and giving earnest speeches about the Good Friends' saintly deeds. "Adam and the others are the best friends I've ever had," she concluded, her eyes starry. "They have real depth. They're caring and spiritual and unselfish, not catty and shallow like my old friends from Sweet Valley High . . . or how I used to be."

"They sound . . . nice," I lied. "But Jessica, you don't need to change. You were wonderful the way you were, before the Good Friends. That was the *real* Jessica."

"You're wrong," she said, a flicker of anger returning to her eyes. "You weren't even listening, were you? You made up your mind already. You don't care about the truth!"

"I *do* care about the truth, and that's why I think you should stay away from them," I insisted. "Dad says the Good Friends are—"

She covered her ears with her hands. "I don't want to hear any more lies!" she exclaimed. "You don't know them and you don't know me. How would you like it if I tried to tear *your* best friends to pieces?"

"You just met them—they can't be your best friends," I reasoned. "What about Lila and Amy and Cara? What about Sam? What about *me?*"

There was a long, pregnant pause. Then Jessica said quietly, "The Good Friends were there for me when no one else was."

She turned her face away. There was nothing I could say, so I just stared at her stony profile. *She's right*, I thought, stricken with guilt. *She wouldn't have needed a group like the Good Friends if the rest of us hadn't let her down. This is my fault as much as anyone's.*

I was right back where I'd started.

I almost let Jessica have the last word on the subject, but then I decided to try one more approach. I assured her that I was willing to give the Good Friends the benefit of the doubt, and I'd even keep her involvement with them a secret from Mom and Dad. But in exchange, I wanted her to promise that she'd drop them if it turns out Dad's right and Adam Marvel's up to something illegal. Luckily, she calmed down and agreed to my proposal. We're not out of the woods yet, though, Diary. The Good Friends have sunk their claws in deep. I can almost feel Jessica slipping away from me. . . .

Thursday, 5:00 P.M.

Guess what I did last night, Diary? I impersonated Jessica. No, I didn't go on a date with Sam, pretending to be my twin. I've outgrown any desire to do that, thank heavens. This time, I did it for her own good. I wanted to see for myself what Adam Marvel and Company are up to, so I infiltrated the Good Friends. And let me tell you, it was pretty spooky. Jess is definitely in over her head—way over.

It took some scheming, needless to say. Wednesdays are "discussion night" at the Good Friends' house and Jessica didn't want to miss out. But I made her go to a movie with Sam, hinting that I'd tell Mom and Dad about the Good Friends if she didn't. Once she was out of the way, Todd and I drove over to Cedar Street. My knees were knocking when I walked into that house. I had no idea what I was going to find. I just knew it would be something weird . . . and boy, was I ever right about that!

About a dozen teenagers were sitting in a circle while this Adam Marvel guy, who's in his thirties and looks more like a movie star than a cult leader, led a so-called "discussion" about life goals. You should have seen the way these kids looked at him—like they totally worshiped him. They all agreed with everything he said completely. No one had a single independent thought, or made a remark that might generate even the teeniest bit of controversy. I think Dad's right—I think Adam Marvel brainwashes them. And the scariest part of it was that everyone welcomed me, "Jessica," as if I were one of the family. Clearly, she's been fitting right in.

I thought I did a pretty good job impersonating Jessica, considering that I had no idea how she acts around these people. Except for Adam Marvel, I didn't even know their names. I picked up the names quickly, though, and basically just did my best to look and sound like the rest of the members: plastic smile, adoring gaze, all peace and harmony and agreement. When I first joined the circle, Adam M. looked straight at me with this stare that seemed to penetrate right into my soul and for a split second I was absolutely terrified that he could tell I wasn't Jess. But after a while, I realized that that's just how he looks at everybody. His gaze envelops you, possesses you. And he's charismatic, I can't deny it. I can understand, sort of, how lonely kids might turn to him for affection and guidance. They wouldn't even realize that instead of helping them, Adam Marvel is only making them dependent on him so he can use them for his own purposes.

The discussion evening ended abruptly. A bunch of Good Friends came back to the house in the middle of it and reported that one of the group, a boy named Brian, had "disappeared" while they were collecting money at the mall. For a millisecond, I think I saw the real Adam Marvel and he was not Mr. Peace, Love, and Understanding. He got downright mad—he ordered the kids to make tracks back to the mall and find Brian or else. I mean, he didn't say "or else," but that was definitely the implication.

Anyway, I took that as my cue to

*leave—believe me, I was ready. On my
way out, something else strange happened.
This girl named Susan walked me to the
car (Todd was waiting down the road
where no one would see him) and whispered a warning. "Get out of here, before
it's too late, and don't come back!" Before I
could ask what she meant, Adam appeared—he seems to be the all-seeing and
all-knowing type. It shook me up, though.
Susan doesn't seem like as much of a robot
as the others—I got the impression that,
like Jess, she's relatively new to the group.
Has she found out something about Adam
Marvel? What does she know that the rest
of the group, including my sister, doesn't?*

*I might have been really scared while I
was in the house, but the whole time, I
knew Todd was outside waiting for me and
would come to my rescue if I needed help.
He told me afterward that he'd hidden in
the shrubs next to the porch and peeked in
the window once or twice to make sure I
was OK. Good old Todd. He's always there
for me. I'm so glad we're still together!*

*So, what do you think I should do,
Diary? I don't like the fact that this Adam
Marvel character has my sister under his
sway, but I know if I say anything bad about
him, she'll just get defensive and turn away*

*from me. Maybe I'm overreacting. After all,
we still have zero proof that Adam Marvel's a
crook. I wish Dad would hurry up and crack
that case! And Jess does seem happy . . . but
it's an unnatural kind of happy. I miss my
bubbly, vivacious, fun-loving twin sister.
How am I going to get her back?*

Friday, 10:00 P.M.

*Dad had big news at dinner tonight.
Remember how, when I was impersonating
Jessica the other night, the Good Friends
were all in a tizzy about a member named
Brian who'd disappeared? Well, Dad has the
inside scoop. It turns out Brian had run
away from home to live with Adam Marvel
and the others. His parents had tried and
tried to get him to come home, to no avail.
They were afraid he'd been brainwashed—
his personality had gone through a radical
change. It sounded just like what's going on
with Jessica! Anyhow, according to Dad,
Brian's parents kidnapped their own son
and took him back home. Dad says that as
soon as Brian's recovered, he'll testify against
Adam Marvel in court. "We've got enough
evidence now to put that charlatan behind
bars"—those were Dad's very words.*

Jessica was at the dinner table and

heard it all, and I could tell it really upset her. When she excused herself and ran upstairs, I went after her. At first, she was still in a total state of denial. She was convinced that Dad had the whole thing wrong—"Adam's not like that," blah blah blah. But then I confessed about pretending to be her at the Wednesday night discussion. She was pretty indignant, but after a while my arguments finally seemed to sink in. I said I'd tell Mom and Dad if she didn't promise to stay away from the Good Friends and she agreed, "until it's proven that they haven't done anything wrong." Since it's pretty obvious (to me anyway!) that it's just a matter of time before Adam Marvel gets arrested, I feel pretty confident that my sister is out of harm's way. Hearing Brian's story gave me chills, though. Jess had a pretty close call!

Sunday afternoon

Dear Diary,

Jessica tried to run away from us last night. Thank goodness she's safe, and Adam Marvel is in police custody. But if Sam and I had arrived at Cedar Street a few minutes later, the Good Friends might

*have whisked Jessica off in their van. I
might never have seen my sister again. . . .*

All day Saturday, Jessica was somewhat quiet
and subdued. She kept to her room and I didn't
bother her—I figured she was a little bit sad about
leaving the Good Friends and I didn't want to get
in the way while she worked through her feelings
about the whole situation. I felt as if I'd been en-
gaged in a tug-of-war. For now, I'd succeeded in
pulling Jessica back into our family, but if we made
the slightest wrong move, I'd lose my advantage.

At about seven o'clock, Jessica left to drive over
to Sam's. I was relieved to see her going on a date.
*Sam's got the best chance of any of us of convincing
Jessica that she doesn't need the Good Friends,* I
mused as I changed into a pair of retro seventies
pants and a close-fitting zippered top to go bowling
with Todd. *If she'll just open her eyes and see how
much he loves her.*

At that moment, the phone on my nightstand
rang. I picked it up. "Hello?" I answered cheerfully.

"Elizabeth?"

"Yes." It was weird hearing the voice of the person I'd just been thinking about. "Sam?"

"Hi. How are you?"

"Fine," I said, surprised that for some reason, I
didn't feel funny about talking to him. It didn't
seem awkward any longer. *Maybe the past is finally
past,* I thought. "What's up?"

"Well, I know Jess isn't feeling well," Sam began. "Maybe she already went to bed. But if she's still up, I thought I'd come over and keep her company for a while. It's boring to be sick, you know?"

"What?" I said, puzzled.

"She told me she didn't want to see me in case it's catching, but I really don't care," Sam elaborated. "Do you mind just checking on her for me?"

I clutched the phone with fingers that had suddenly gone cold and rigid with dread. "Sam, Jessica's not here. She left for your house about fifteen minutes ago."

"But she called this afternoon to cancel our date because she has the flu," Sam said, sounding as confused as I'd been a moment earlier. "You don't think she . . ."

"The Good Friends," I choked out. "Sam, we've got to get over there. Fast!"

"I'm on my way," he declared hoarsely. "I'll pick you up in ten minutes."

It seemed to take forever for Sam to get to my house. Waiting was pure agony. With every minute that ticked past on the clock, I pictured another horrible fate befalling my sister. Waiting for Sam also gave me a chance to remember something. Just before Jessica had said good-bye to me half an hour or so earlier, I'd noticed her purple duffle bag tucked under the hall table next to the stairs. I hadn't given it any thought at the time, assuming it was just cheerleading gear.

But now I saw that the bag was gone.

She's run away to live with them! I deduced, panic flowering in my stomach. I recalled a remark of my father's at dinner the other night. "We've got to sew this case up fast, before Marvel quits town. That's the pattern. The Good Friends wear out their welcome after a few months, and then, just a step or two ahead of the law, they're off to exploit some other gullible community."

Jessica's not just leaving home, I realized, ten times more worried than before. She might be leaving Sweet Valley too!

Soon, Sam and I were speeding through town, tires squealing at every turn. "My parents were out, so I called Todd. He's meeting us at the Good Friends' house," I told Sam, "*and* he's bringing the police."

"I just hope we're not too late," Sam muttered.

"I hope so too," I whispered.

Cedar Street was nearly deserted. As we approached the Good Friends' house, I could see the van parked out front, its tail lights bright red in the shadowy dusk. "The van's still here, and there's the Fiat!" I cried, pointing. "She's here, Sam. They haven't taken her away!"

"And they're not going to," he insisted with grim determination.

Yanking the steering wheel, Sam braked abruptly. The instant he shifted into park, we were both out of the car and running toward the van. Two people were sitting inside it, and two others were in the process of climbing in—Adam Marvel and Jessica!

"Jess!" I screamed. "Stop!"

She turned and looked back, her eyes wide with surprise. Adam Marvel's arm was around her shoulder. Glaring at Sam and me, he tried to propel Jessica into the van. "Come on, Jessica," he urged. "It's time to go."

"Oh, no, you don't," Sam declared. "You're not taking her anywhere."

"She's her own girl," Adam insisted. "Aren't you, Jessica? Are you going to let them make up your mind for you?"

Jessica had been leaning away from him, as if she were ready to run to Sam and me. Adam Marvel's words had a powerful effect on her, however. She shrank against him, her eyes clouding with fear and uncertainty. "No," she murmured. "They can't tell me what to do. I'm a free person."

"But, Jessica, they're going to hurt you," I cried. "They're breaking the law!"

"Don't listen to her," Adam Marvel commanded.

"I'm doing what's best for me, Liz," Jessica said weakly. "Say good-bye to Mom and Dad for me."

"It's not what's best at all," I protested. "Stay here, Jess. Stay with the people who love you."

"The Good Friends love me more than you do," she retorted, tears sparkling in her eyes.

Sam stepped forward. "No, they don't." His voice was vibrating with love and urgency. "They can't love you as much as we do, as I do. Listen to me, Jessica. If the Good Friends had nothing to hide, they wouldn't have to sneak out of town in the dark of night like this. There wouldn't be lies and secrecy."

Jessica bit her lip. "But—but—"

Adam Marvel gripped her arm. "Into the van," he instructed roughly.

"You don't need to run away to find love, Jessica," Sam persisted. He took a few more steps. He was almost close enough to touch her. "Stay with us. Stay with me. Let me prove to you how important you are to me. I promise you'll never feel alone and unloved again."

Jessica stared at Sam, the tears shining on her pale cheeks. I held my breath. "Sam, I—" she began hesitantly.

Suddenly, about ten things happened simultaneously: Adam Marvel tried to push Jessica into the van. Jessica twisted free from his grasp. Sam leapt toward her, pulling her to him. Behind us, a siren broke the night's silence with a powerful blare. And Todd's BMW careened around the corner, screeching to a stop fifty feet away. Two police cars, lights flashing, were right behind him.

In no time at all, police officers had surrounded Adam Marvel and the van. Sam cradled a sobbing Jessica in his arms, stroking her hair and murmuring soothing words. And I was in Todd's arms, hugging him with all my might. "She's going to be OK," I whispered tearfully. "We're all going to be OK."

It was a wild night, Diary. Adam Marvel turned out to be even more of a crook than anyone suspected. When the police searched the Good Friends' house, they found Susan unconscious on a bed upstairs, bound and gagged. Adam Marvel was going to leave her there to die!

Back at our house later, Susan told us the whole story. It turns out she's a reporter, and she'd infiltrated the group to write a story exposing Adam Marvel. Susan thinks Adam started to suspect something was fishy because she just couldn't quite imitate the docile, worshipful behavior of the others'—her reporter's skepticism always came through. Maybe he searched through her things after overhearing her the night she tried to warn me. Whatever—he's been booked for attempted murder as well as fraud. Good riddance!

Jessica bounced back pretty quickly from her ordeal. While Susan was telling her story, Jess sat on the couch holding Sam's hand as if she'd never let it go. It's the funniest thing, Diary. I was so glad to see those two together. The jealousy I once felt over Sam is completely gone. When he was

*trying to persuade her not to run off with
the Good Friends, there was such love in
his eyes, such devotion in his voice. He
would've done anything to save her at that
moment, and I think she knows it. I'm so
glad my sister has a boyfriend like Sam
Woodruff! And I'm so glad I have one like
Todd Wilkins.*

*By the time Mom and Dad got back and
we'd filled them in on what had happened,
it was pretty late. As everyone headed
home, I took Sam aside for a moment and
asked him to meet me at our old spot on
the beach first thing the next morning. He
looked confused, but he agreed to come just
for a few minutes. . . .*

It was still early when I arrived at the beach.
The morning sun, low in the bright blue sky, cast
long slanting shadows across the sand. As usual,
the beach was nearly deserted. Sam stood facing
the water, watching a few surfers, his arms folded
across his chest. I paused for a moment, my
throat tightening as I remembered the other
times I'd hurried here, driven by a fierce longing,
and found him standing in the same position,
wearing the same leather jacket. We would rush
into each other's arms. . . .

I walked briskly toward him. When he
turned to greet me, I flashed him a warm smile.

315

"Sorry to get you up at the crack of dawn."

The soft morning breeze ruffled his hair. "No problem." He returned my smile, but there was a question in his eyes. "I woke up in a pretty good mood, just knowing Jess is all right."

"She's sleeping in," I reported. "Back to normal!"

"Glad to hear it." Sam stuck his hands in the pockets of his jacket. "So," he said.

"So," I echoed, feeling awkward all of a sudden. I didn't want to launch into a huge speech that might have embarrassed us both, but at the same time, I knew it was important to express what was on my mind. I held out the sweater I was carrying. Sam's sweater. "I've had this in the back of my closet for months," I told him. "I'm sorry I didn't give it back to you sooner."

Sam raised his eyebrows. "Is that why you wanted to see me?"

"Yes," I said, nodding. Then I shook my head, smiling ruefully. "No. I mean, partly. I mean, I suppose I could have mailed it back to you! But I kind of needed to do it in person. Because . . ." I turned pink as I made the confession. "Because I've been holding on to more than the sweater."

Sam didn't ask me to explain myself. His serious gray eyes told me that he understood. "For a while, I didn't want to let go either," he admitted softly. "Then I met Jessica."

He still hadn't taken the sweater. "Here," I said, offering it again.

Sam shook his head. "No, you keep it. As a token of our friendship. You know that, if you ever need me, like last night, you can count on me."

My eyes sparkled with grateful tears. "Thanks, Sam," I whispered.

"We had something special, didn't we?" His own voice was thick with emotion.

I nodded. "We did."

"But now we both have more solid relationships. The kind that will last."

"Jessica makes you happy."

"She really, really does," said Sam, smiling. "And you?"

"I'm happy too," I told him.

"Todd's a terrific guy."

"He is," I agreed wholeheartedly.

By unspoken agreement, we started to stroll back to the parking lot. The sun was higher, but the morning air was still cool and I was only wearing a short-sleeved shirt. Sam must have seen me shiver, because he stopped with me by the Fiat and, taking his sweater in his hands, wrapped it around my shoulders. "Take care, Elizabeth," he said, his eyes holding mine for a long, meaningful moment.

At that instant, I remembered my long-ago dream, in which Sam and I parted, and he walked off to join Jessica, and I gave them my blessing. It had come true after all.

"See you around." I smiled.

He grinned. "You can count on that."

When I got home from the beach,
Jessica was up, having breakfast outside by
the pool. I can't tell you how wonderful it
was to see her smiling again. It was like the
sun breaking through the clouds after a
storm. We had a really good talk and now I
feel as if all my relationships are back on
track. . . .

Jessica had changed into a swimsuit and an
oversized T-shirt. She sat on a lounge chair on the
patio, a glass of orange juice and a plate of pastries
within easy reach. When I pushed open the sliding
glass door to peek outside, she beckoned to me to
join her. "The sun feels great," she called.

I pulled up a chair next to hers. "Did you sleep
well?"

"Like a log. And I had the *best* dreams." She
smiled, her dimple flashing. "About Sam, of course!"

"Of course," I said, smiling back.

"Liz," she began. She pushed her sunglasses up
onto her loose, blond hair and fixed me with
somber eyes. Her face was her own again—she
didn't look like a Good Friends clone—but there
was still a trace of uncharacteristic fragility and vul-
nerability in her expression. "Do you think I'm a
total idiot for falling for a fake like Adam Marvel?"

I shook my head. "It's not a crime to trust people.
And you weren't the only innocent kid who thought
the Good Friends had the answers. Ted, Annie,

Daryl, Sky—they all made the same mistake."

"I just can't believe I came this close"—she held up one hand with her thumb and index finger nearly touching—"to running away with them. To leaving Sweet Valley. Leaving you and Mom and Dad and Steven."

"And your CD collection and your wardrobe and your Jamie Peters posters and seventeen different shades of lipstick and your curling iron and—"

She grinned. "I'd packed the curling iron, actually."

We both laughed. "Seriously, though, Jess," I said. "I hope we both learned something from this. You have to promise you'll always come to me if something's bothering you, and I promise I'll listen more carefully."

"OK," she agreed.

We sat for a few minutes in relaxed, reflective silence. Then Jessica said, "Sam was wonderful last night, wasn't he? Standing up to Adam Marvel like that."

"He's crazy about you."

"I know, and I'm crazy about him. I can't believe I almost threw it all away! I guess I was just insecure. I mean, ordinarily when I meet a new guy, it's a breeze. I'm just in it to have fun. But with Sam . . ." She sighed deeply. "I really, really want it to work. To last."

"I have a hunch he feels the same way," I told her.

Jessica gave me a wistful smile. "But falling in

love is scary! I kind of wish we were at the stage you're at with Todd. You know, an established couple, ready to get married, buy a house, have kids."

I laughed. "Don't be in too much of a hurry," I advised, thinking about the first blush of love with all its excitement, unpredictability, and promise. "You have a lot to look forward to, the two of you, but you'll never get these early days back. Enjoy them to the fullest."

My talk with Sam on the beach this morning was really a sweet final scene to the drama of our relationship. I'm incredibly glad he and I are friends. For so long, I felt guilty and torn up about this secret, but now I'm at peace with it. If I could go back in time, maybe I'd choose not to get involved with Sam behind Todd's back. I know it wasn't the right thing to do. But in the end, I think I'm a better person for knowing Sam. Being with Sam allowed me to discover a part of myself I'd only dreamed of, and that part of me doesn't have to die just because Sam and I are through. What I learned with him will enrich all my relationships—even my enduring love for Todd.

Epilogue

Closing my journal, I reached for the box of tissues next to my bed. Reading my diary had made me smile, but it had also made me cry. The memories it brought back were bittersweet, because now Sam was gone forever, killed in a car crash. Jessica had found her true love only to lose him, and I'd never been able to tell her how much I shared her pain and grief. She'd never known that I'd loved Sam too.

I blotted my damp eyes and looked toward the open window. A gentle breeze fluttered the curtain, bringing the fragrance of garden flowers into my room. A feeling of peace settled over me—I hardly even remembered why I'd been upset.

I should read my journal more often, I mused, stroking the cloth-bound volume. Its pages told me so much about myself! Some were smudged with tears—on others, I'd doodled smiley faces and sunbursts in the margins. My handwriting varied from fast and loopy to neat and careful, depending on the mood of the moment. I'd never used a computer for journal keeping and never planned to. Writing by hand is part of the satisfaction of expressing myself. Typed words leave out the heart—they don't tell the whole story.

And there were so many lessons to be learned. I thought of Robin Wilson's battle with anorexia, about the times I subbed for Jessica on the talk show and during the beauty pageant. I remembered Rosa Jameson's decision to embrace her Mexican heritage, Artie and Mike patching up their feud, Scott Trost vowing to become a better person because he'd fallen in love with Jean West, Tom McKay's identity crisis, Jessica's narrow escape from the clutches of a cult. *Life in Sweet Valley is never dull*, I concluded. *Especially not my life!*

Though it wasn't that late, my sister was home from Lila's party. Through my window, I could hear her and Seth laughing in the driveway. "Let's put on suits and go for a swim in the pool," Jessica suggested to Seth.

"We could skip the suits," Seth replied, making Jessica giggle.

I smiled to myself. I wasn't mad at her anymore for forgetting to give me Todd's message. She hadn't done it on purpose. *She's just flaky sometimes*, I thought tolerantly, *and besides, she was busy looking forward to her date with Seth*. Who could blame her for that?

Jessica had experienced tragedy in losing Sam. It had taken her a while to recover—it had taken us *all* a while—but eventually she'd resumed living her life with her trademark zest and enthusiasm. Now, for a moment, I found myself envying my sister what she was experiencing tonight: the excitement of getting to know someone new. There's nothing like it in the whole world.

Still holding my diary, I sighed deeply. Then the sound of the doorbell startled me. "Jess must've locked herself out," I guessed as I put my journal aside and hurried downstairs.

When I opened the front door, however, I didn't see Jessica and Seth, who apparently had walked around the side of the house to the backyard. Instead, my boyfriend stood on the step, his hands clasped behind his back, an apologetic look on his face. "Todd!" I exclaimed, surprised. "What are *you* doing here?"

"Sorry to come over so late," he said. "I mean, I wish it could've been earlier—I wish we could have spent the evening together. What I'm trying to say is . . . here."

He extended a hand and I saw that he'd been holding a small, gift-wrapped box. I took the box with a puzzled smile. "What is it?" I asked.

Todd grinned. "Why don't you open it and find out?"

Carefully, I slipped off the satin ribbon and removed the wrapping paper. Inside the little cardboard box was another box made of velvet: a jewel box. Holding my breath in anticipation, I snapped it open, then gasped when I saw what lay inside. "Oh, Todd," I cried, "it's *beautiful!*"

The gold locket was shaped like a heart and engraved with a garden of infinitely delicate birds and flowers. When I opened the locket, I found myself looking down at a tiny picture of Todd and me. It was the most romantic gift I'd ever received. "It's beautiful," I said again, my voice thick with tears.

"Read it," Todd urged. "Read the back."

I turned the locket over in my hand. A sentiment had been engraved on the back: "Liz, I'll love you forever, Todd."

I couldn't speak. Gently, Todd took the locket from me and fastened the chain around my neck. "I had to drive a couple of hours up the coast to pick it up," he explained. "I suppose I could have found something almost as nice at a local place, but someone had told me this store had really special one-of-a-kind things, and I thought, 'That's for me, because Liz is one of a kind.' Anyhow, I was really worried I wouldn't make it back on time."

"In time for what?" I asked, still confused.

"Maybe you don't remember, but I'll never forget this date for as long as I live," Todd said. "Tonight is the anniversary of the first time you told me you loved me."

I don't know precisely when Todd put his arms around me, but we were holding each other close. I gazed up at him. His eyes were a little misty.

"That's the sweetest thing anyone's ever done for me," I told him, sincerely moved.

"Then you forgive me for canceling our date? Or rather, for postponing it a few hours?" he said hopefully.

At that moment, we both heard a loud splash. *Seth and Jessica jumping into the pool*, I thought.

Earlier, I'd been envying my sister. Now, I knew I wouldn't trade places with her for anything. If reading my diary had reminded me of just one important thing, it was that all the excitement in the world couldn't replace a moment like this one.

I smiled up at Todd, my eyes shining with happy tears. "Of course I forgive you. And I'll love you forever too," I said, and meant it.

If you've enjoyed reading *Elizabeth's* secret diary, why not take a peek at her twin sister's too?

SWEET VALLEY HIGH™

JESSICA'S SECRET DIARY
Volume III

Dear Diary,

You'll never *believe* what's happened to me!!! I got noticed by a big movie producer, Charles Sampson, for my star turn on my fave soap opera. *The Young and Beautiful*. I've been discovered! I'm going to be a *gigantic* celebrity! Diary, I'm so excited, I'm having trouble breathing. Inhale. Exhale. *Relax*.

Charles says I can't tell anyone yet. He wants to choose exactly the right moment to launch my career. That's cool, since Sam, my perfect boyfriend, might be a little jealous of Charles's attentions. But that's silly – Charles just sees me as a hot property. He's not *interested* in me. Right?

Read all about Jessica's chance at stardom in this special edition featuring classic moments from Sweet Valley High™ books 83 to 94. The third volume of Jessica's captivating secret diaries.

ISBN: 0-553-50670-6

Look out for these super collections of Sweet Valley High titles!

Francine Pascal's

SWEET VALLEY HIGH™

Romance Collection

THE BOYFRIEND WAR
Jessica Wakefield and her best friend, Lila Fowler, are at Club Paradise, a fabulous island resort owned by Lila's uncle – and they're at war with each other!

ALMOST MARRIED
Elizabeth Wakefield unearths an amazing secret from the past – that her mother was once married to Bruce Patman's father! Could history repeat itself? For now Bruce and Elizabeth are feeling an attraction too – to each other!

OPERATION LOVE MATCH
Jessica Wakefield's horoscope says that everything in her life is about to go wrong! But Bruce Patman's parents will get divorced – unless *she* can make them fall madly in love again! What chance have Jessica's plans if all the planets are lined up against her?

A sizzling trilogy of titles – Sweet Valley has never been so hot!

0 553 811991

Francine Pascal's

SWEET VALLEY HIGH ™

Winners and Losers Collection

JESSICA QUITS THE SQUAD
It's cheerleading madness when glamorous, popular Heather Mallone moves to Sweet Valley – and Jessica Wakefield starts the biggest feud in cheerleading history!

THE POM-POM WARS
Determined to outdo Heather Mallone, the new captain of the official team, Jessica Wakefield forms her *own* cheerleading squad – and prepares to show up her old team in the greatest cheer-off ever!

'V' FOR VICTORY
The Sweet Valley cheerleaders are going to the nationals! And Sweet Valley's biggest rivals are Heather's old squad. . .

A fabulous trilogy of titles – will the Sweet Valley cheerleaders make it to the top?

0 553 81200 9

All Bantam titles are available by post from:
Bookservice by Post
PO Box 29
Douglas
Isle of Man
IM99 1BQ

Credit Cards accepted.
Please telephone 01624 675137 or fax 01624 670923
or Internet http://www.bookpost.co.uk
or e-mail: bookshop@enterprise.net for details.

Free postage and packing in the UK.
Overseas customers allow £1 per book (paperbacks)
and £3 per book (hardbacks)